PRAISE FOR

T0282907

"*Culprits* slams the bull's eye f ....t. From the heart-stopping robbery that opens the book to each of the linked short stories that follow, you'll find the nine murderously good noir authors of this smart collection deliver a plate brimming with suspense, thrills, and violence. Sit down and savor. What a ride."

Gayle Lynds, New York Times bestselling author of The Assassins

"*Culprits* has a consistently strong lineup of writers and a great hook! Brewer and Phillips have done a fantastic job putting together this multi-layered story and I couldn't read it fast enough!"

Steve Hamilton, Edgar Award-Winning Author of Exit Strategy

"A well executed heist, like fine wine, pleasures the palate and can age well. In *Culprits*, liken the aftermath of the criminals from a heist to craft beer and a bumpy ride. Prepare to stay up all night!"

Cara Black, New York Times bestselling author of the Aimée Leduc *series*

"*Culprits* is quite a lot of fun... If you are looking for a smart, entertaining book then this is it."

Unlawful Acts

"*Culprits* lights off where other heist books end, neck deep in the bloody aftermath. Brewer and Phillips do their gritty best in this linked anthology that ties together the work of some of the hottest writers out there. Rife with lust, betrayal, and bullets, this one flies."

Gregg Hurwitz, NYT Bestselling author of the Orphan X *series*

"Move over *Heat*, *Inside Man*, and *The Bank Job*. Make room for *Culprits*, a unique spin on the big heist."

Reed Farrel Coleman, New York Times Bestselling author of Blind to Midnight

"The questions behind *Culprits* are so good I wish I'd thought of them myself: What happens after a successful heist? Do we really expect a gang of now-rich criminals to just live happily ever after? And when you put the fate of each gang member into the hands of a different top-notch crime writer, what do you get? You get this book. *Culprits* is a tour-de-force of imagination and style, taking off from where a heist story usually ends. Each individual story is terrific; their combined effect is simply a knockout. Read it; you'll feel like you've gotten away with something."

SJ Rozan, best-selling author of The Mayors of New York

Edited by Richard Brewer and Gary Phillips

CULPRITS

DATURA

DATURA BOOKS
An imprint of Watkins Media Ltd

Unit 11, Shepperton House
89-93 Shepperton Road
London N1 3DF
UK

daturabooks.com
The score is worth the sacrifice

A Datura Books paperback, 2024
Copyright © 2018, 2024 Richard Brewer and Gary Phillips
The Heist © 2018, 2024 by Gary Phillips and Richard Brewer
Aftermath © 2018, 2024 by Gary Phillips
Last Dance © 2018, 2024 by Jessica Kaye
The Wife © 2018, 2024 by Zoe Sharp
The Financier © 2018, 2024 by David Corbett
Snake Farm © 2018, 2024 by Manuel Ramos
Eel Estevez © 2018, 2024 by Joe Clifford
I Got You © 2018, 2024 by Brett Battles
Racklin © 2018, 2024 by Gar Anthony Haywood
Showdown 2018, 2024 © by Gary Phillips
Hector © 2018, 2024 by Richard Brewer
All Debts Paid © 2018, 2024 by Richard Brewer and Gary Phillips

Cover and jacket design by Francesca Corsini
Set in Meridien

This novel is entirely a work of fiction. Names, characters, places, and incidents are
the products of the author's imagination or are used fictitiously. Any resemblance to
actual events, locales, organizations or persons, living or dead, is entirely coincidental.

Datura Books and the Datura Books icon are registered trademarks of Watkins Media
Ltd.

ISBN 978 1 91552 362 4
Ebook ISBN 978 1 91552 363 1

Printed and bound in the United Kingdom by CPI
9 8 7 6 5 4 3 2 1

Contents

FOREWORD

The "Heist." A classic branch of the crime fiction tree. The very word itself, "heist", conjures up images of intricate planning, split second timing and heart pounding escapes all in the pursuit of a big payoff.

The set-up itself is well known. A group of criminals, sometimes a rag tag group of amateurs with big hopes and sometimes a slick group of professionals with big expectations are pulled together to pull off the theft of... something big. Each member of the crew brings to the crime their own unique set of skills and the target can be a bank, a casino, a cruise ship, a train or Fort Knox, for that matter. Whatever the target, this collection of criminals must work together as a team in order to pull off the big score.

These stories, give or take some complications along the way, can end in several ways, but in general fall into two categories: disaster or triumph. Either the culprits fail, losing their objective, or they come out on top, eluding the authorities, splitting up the ill-gotten goods and going their separate ways. But what happens after the heist? It was that question that led to the creation of this book. We wanted to know what happened to the crew once the big job was over and done. Where did they go? What did they do? Who did they do it with… or to? How did they spend their cut of the loot? In other words;

What happened next?

So we sat down and wrote out a heist. We tossed a glitch or two into the storyline to spice things up and pulled together a crew, giving each of them their respective roles in the gang (financier, safe-cracker, wheelman, muscle… etc.) Then we contacted seven authors and fanned out the characters in front of them like a magician fans out a deck cards. We told them to pick a character, any character and then tell us the story of what happened to that character after the heist.

Tell us what happened next.

There was no hesitation from any of the authors we reached out to. Each one snatched up a character and proceeded to give us seven diverse, entertaining and exciting stories. Each story is complete and individual in and of itself, but they also fit together as part of a whole. We could not be happier with the stories our group of writing culprits have come up with, and we hope you will feel the same after you've read them.

So come on, turn the page and get started. Come and see what happened next.

Richard Brewer and Gary Phillips
February, 2018

CHAPTER 1
The Heist
by Gary Phillips and Richard Brewer

O'Conner crossed his arms before his face as the blast from the shotgun knocked him down.

Less than two weeks before, he'd gotten a cup of coffee from the ink-laden barista with the pierced lip and boxer's biceps. At the setup on the side where various types of sugar and dairy were located, he poured some half and half in his cup. As he stirred his unsweetened coffee, he scanned the people in the national chain coffee emporium. He didn't used to frequent such places, coffee was coffee, for Christ's sake, and he didn't see any reason to spend five dollars for his caffeine fix. But as of late, he'd found himself in them more often given Gwen Gardner's addiction to her premium lattes.

He almost smiled at the notion of how domesticated he'd become. Or rather, how he presented the illusion of domestication. Though it was true he was less inclined to take on jobs these days. His lady Gwen had inherited several Fix & Go auto body shops in Southern California from her deceased father. An enterprising type, Papa Gardner had opened the first one in Gardena in So Cal's South Bay in the mid '80s. O'Conner, something of an enterprising type himself, had amassed a decent amount of money from his various scores over the years. Cash he'd squirreled away in numerous locales; buried under a couple of snow birds' vacation homes in Lake Tahoe, a storage locker in Palmdale, and a long non-working oil field of rusting automated pumpers in El Segundo among his hidey holes.

He'd gathered a percentage of these funds, laundered them through the Financier, and invested the clean monies in Gwen's shops. Coordinating with her, he helped oversee the operations, with a closer attention to detail than she had before the two lived together. The result of their collaboration was a significant increase in the quarterly bottom line. That, along with his infusion of money, allowed the company to open a new outlet in Culver City with another one coming to the West Adams area of Los Angeles early the next year.

As the auto body shops were not the only legit and underground businesses he'd invested in, O'Conner had income and comfort and a good woman to share it with. What he didn't have was the rush. He didn't have the heightened edge to his senses that planning and pulling off a heist brought. And he missed it.

"Better than sex?" Gardner had teased him yesterday, her hand and head tenderly on his chest as they lay in bed.

"A close second," he'd breathed. Then they made love again. "A distant second," he amended hoarsely, losing himself in their ardor.

O'Conner allowed a brief smile to alter his placid face at that tactile memory. He sat at a small table toward the rear of the shop, sipping his coffee. Nearby were two women in their twenties laughing and muttering as they both looked at something on a smartphone screen. Cats, he considered, it's always cat videos.

The man he was here to meet came through the front door. He nodded at O'Conner and walked to the cold case next to the order counter. The Financier extracted a plastic square bottle of a viscous green liquid and paid for his choice. He came over to O'Conner.

"It's been a while," the newcomer said, sitting opposite. He wore a sport coat and pressed slacks in contrast to O'Conner's dark windbreaker, grey t-shirt underneath, and washed black jeans.

"You reached out."

"And you answered," said the man. "I wasn't sure you'd be interested."

"Yes, you were."

Though semi-retired, or whatever the term for his current self-imposed status, O'Conner still used the old methods when someone wanted to contact him. In an era where smart TVs could spy on you, the physical drop was as reliable now as when first developed by the Culper Ring during the Revolutionary War, he reasoned.

O'Conner maintained a mailbox under a false name in a shipping store twelve miles from Hemet, California where he and Gardner lived in a suburban housing complex. He varied his route to the box, but once a week would make the trip to see if there was mail. Few knew of its address and he'd been curious when he'd read the terse message from the man sitting across from him. Then, once read, and as was his practice, he burned the sheet with the five sentences on it along with the envelope. He then flushed the ashes down the toilet and made a call from one of his SMS encrypted phones at an appointed time to the number of a similar device that was answered by the other man. The phones were designed not to record messages which could be retrieved by law enforcement. O'Conner and only a few others knew the actual name of this man. To most of the criminal world in which he operated he was only known as the Financier.

Toned and fit, the Financier, with his short, sandy-colored hair and angular face, was in his mid-fifties, maybe eight years older than O'Conner. He showed even white teeth as he undid the plastic strip securing the cap of his concoction, a kale and acacia berry smoothie, the label indicated. He shook the bottle briefly. "I figured there was only so much of civilian life you could stand. Thought it might be time for a break in the routine, as it were."

"In Texas," O'Conner said.

"An eighteen-thousand-acre cattle ranch outside of Fort Worth called the Crystal Q." He drank some of his smoothie, dabbing at the corner of his mouth with a finger when he set the bottle down.

"Clovis Harrington is the owner of the ranch. More importantly, he is the head of the North Texas Citizens Improvement League."

"And they would be?"

"The League is a major fixture all across the Lone Star State. Several of its members, if not exactly in the inner circle of Bush, that is W, were in the immediate outer orbit. Truth be told, a few of them were hoping for a different outcome to the presidential election, but whichever way things went, red or blue, capitalism is capitalism and they knew they would have a seat at the big kid's table."

"Still, I would think it's a bigger one now given who's in office."

The Financier regarded his health product, as if debating whether he'd done enough penance for today and would have an order of french fries for lunch. "That is true, and their good ol' boy ex-governor is a cabinet secretary, but our mercurial president and the ones who have his ear whisper dire things about the League, and not without good reason."

"They have ties to the teabaggers," O'Conner gleaned.

The Financier nodded. "Or whatever they are calling themselves these days. But that gets me to this: Harrington's group knows that no matter how much they prop up the bogeyman of voter fraud to justify their questionable ID laws and help configure districts to ensure the white vote, the brown factor looms just over the horizon – despite the current immigration policies. To combat the dark flood takes an excrement load of ready cash."

O'Conner had more of his coffee and declared, "They've got a slush fund."

"And they've beefed it up with an eye toward the midterms and the future. They've always bribed judges, water commissioners, and the like. But if the Latino tide is coming, odds are that no matter how committed to La Causa any future school board, city council member, or mayor might be, one does have to pay for those damn braces the kids need."

"Or have boats to buy," O'Conner observed dryly.

"Or sex scandals to quiet." The Financier finished his health drink. "For every three or four torch bearers, there will always be the greedy ones with a hand out and an eye to turn."

In their arena, notions like altruism were alien concepts. O'Conner noted that the two women had left and a trendy type with a beard, hair knot, and skinny jeans had sat down in their place. He got busy on his laptop after he'd slipped on his noise cancelling headphones. O'Conner imagined he was listening to the best inspirational hits of that tall, big-toothed Tony Robbins, or something on how to start your own artisan cheese and toast shop.

"So, what are we looking at?" said O'Conner.

"The League members have recently levied a tax internally, and my estimate is there's some seven million in untraceable money being housed in a vault in the wine cellar at the Harrington spread."

"How do you know this?"

The Financer looked back at him with the slightest of smiles.

"You have a source," said O'Conner. He'd already come to this conclusion, he only wanted confirmation. "Close?"

"Close as silk sheets."

Momentarily, O'Conner's eyes focused elsewhere as he examined various parameters of the potential job. "How much does your inside man want of this bounty?"

"Inside man and woman. He wanted two million but I told him as the crew would be handling the heavy lifting, he would have to settle for six hundred grand... for the both of them."

Crossing his arms, O'Conner sat back. "And what's the complication?"

The Financier managed a wry smile. "Seems there always is one, doesn't it?"

O'Conner didn't respond, waiting.

The Financier added, "The info comes from the wife's side piece. But he doesn't really have much of anything to do with this, it's really she who is the source."

"What's the boy toy's name?"

"Zach Culhane."

"He solid?"

The Financier's chair was at an angle to the table and he crossed one leg over the other. "If by that do you mean is he a cocaine fiend or prone to maudlin drinking and spilling his guts to strippers, the answer is no. At least he wasn't when I dealt with him in the past."

"What do you know about her?"

Expressionless, he said, "The former Miss Range Rider Beer. She's the third wife, about twenty-two years Harrington's junior. Her name is Gracella Murieta-Harrington, originally from Corpus Christi."

"And she's willing to go along with the takedown for that amount?"

"Apparently. From what Culhane told me, they both came upon this idea during some pillow talk about a month ago. Her husband is bored with her and she with him, but she pretends otherwise, at least externally. She knows about Culhane's past and he's the one who reached out to me through an old crime partner from back when. He used to boost cars for an outfit I bankrolled once."

"What I mean is," O'Conner said, "if this thing goes down, he and the wife won't be able to sit tight until the heat dies down. I'll bet the number of people who know about this slush fund and where it's kept could be counted on one hand. Maybe the wife isn't supposed to know, but how long will the husband believe that? She and the this guy could be sitting right in the crosshairs."

"I hear what you're saying," the Financier said. "Harrington will suspect this is an inside job and may put the screws to his wife as the logical suspect. Which would lead him to the kid and maybe to my involvement."

"Does the go-between, the one Culhane reached out to, does he know how to find you?"

"Where I lay my head?"

"Um-hmm."

"No."

O'Conner assessed this. It wasn't his concern if the Financier was found out. Everyone took a risk in this kind of thing. It was more about making sure he remained as untraceable as was possible. The wife and boyfriend were both sources of vital information and the weakest links. There was going to be no foolproof way for them to effectively mask their own involvement should one or both of them fall under suspicion, get pressured, and crack. What that would mean was that the crew would have to move quickly and effectively. In, out, and be in the wind before anyone could get a bead on them. Judging from what the Financier said, O'Conner was sure the League had a certain reputation in the Fort Worth area, so there was that. Maybe there was a way to throw suspicion elsewhere, minimize their exposure.

"Is there any way I can scope out the layout of the ranch beforehand?" O'Conner asked. "Maybe the wife wants to get some redecorating done."

The Financier huffed. "This might be very un-PC of me, but you do realize you might be a little implausible as an interior decorator."

"Be that as it may."

"I think that might be too chancy." He paused for a moment. "But the wife should be able to get some shots done on her cell. She can send them to the address of a techie cutout I know who can retrieve them and I can then get them to you."

"Is there a timeframe?" O'Conner said.

"Three weeks."

"What happens then?"

"There's a shindig planned at the ranch. Congress people, lobbyists and what have you, are coming out for a big ol' Remember the Alamo bar-b-que and political soiree. In all that hoo-rah, the job could go down."

O'Conner had pulled off heists during functions in the past, pretending to be the hired-on waitstaff or even the magician clown once. But he said, "I don't know. A bunch of strapped, Second Amendment loving Lone Star State lovers pumping beer and Jack through their veins and feeling all sovereign and shit. No, there's too much to control. Too much to go wrong. It only takes one asshole thinking he's Goddamned Wyatt Earp to pull his piece and piss on our parade."

O'Conner paused, then, "But a bash like that takes a lot of prepping. That means strangers being seen at the house before the event. That wouldn't be so odd. They could be helping plan things, or be extra help getting the place ready."

"I can see that," the Financier nodding in agreement.

O'Conner recalled watching one of those tours of celebrity homes with Gardner one night on TV. "Is there an on-site chef?"

"There is," the Financier affirmed.

"Know what he drives?"

The Financier pulled out a smartphone and swiped at the screen. "Yes, he has a van. He uses it for errands and such, sometimes he transports a side of beef from one part of the spread to the house. Fresh slaughtered meat being a perk of a cattle ranch."

O'Conner said, "I would imagine overseeing the upcoming celebration means he's got a lot to handle, making several runs throughout the day, dealing with the various vendors." O'Conner wasn't talking so much to the Financier as working out details, thinking aloud as he did so.

"You thinking of having the wife send him off on a specific mission? That might be too much of a giveaway," said the Financer.

"Possibly," said O'Conner. He continued, "Have the boyfriend get word to the wife. Have him tell her I need the chef's cell number and a few pics of the van so I can match the make. Make sure he gives her a burner phone to use, and that she destroys it afterward. Have her throw the thing in a river or smash it up and bury the pieces in a pile of cow shit."

He paused for a beat. "You're sure she's up for this?"

"From what I gather, she's game. She really hates her husband. She'll come through."

O'Conner considered that and several other variables. "Nothing out of the ordinary. If she can, have her do up a diagram from what she remembers as far as the layout of the place and anything else she can give us that will help when we get there. But only what she remembers. I don't what anyone wondering about why she's prowling around. Does Harrington have an airstrip on his ranch?"

"He does," said the Financier. "No self-respecting cattle baron wouldn't. Several other ranches around there have them too."

"That's good," O'Conner mused.

He wondered if there was a way to spook Harington, give him a reason to want to move the money and do the snatch with the goods in transit. Keeping that possibility to himself, he added, "We can probably assume the safe where they keep the cash is an electronic make and not manual."

"That's my guess," the Financier said. "But I really don't know. Could be anything."

"Well, the man I have in mind is up for the challenge," O'Conner said.

"The Mexican gentlemen?"

O'Conner said, "He's A-Number One, reliable and up for whatever is thrown at him. He'll get the job done."

The two talked over several other particulars, including where O'Conner would retrieve the Financier's cash investment he'd use to put together the equipment needed for the takedown. The two then left the coffee shop and said their goodbyes. He drove away in his recent model Cadillac CTS with the Carbon Black package, having been turned on to Cadillacs by the old box man Gonzales back when. O'Conner began to put the pieces together for how the job could go down. First, he was going to do his research.

At a local library, he used one of the computers to look up articles on the North Texas Citizens Improvement League. From left wing sources like The Nation and Mother Jones, he scanned reports that talked about its influence in conservative politics. He also found a profile of Clovis Harrington. A native Texan, he had a lean face, a trim mustache, and in the picture he committed to memory, wore designer glasses. There was a granite cast to those eyes behind the lenses. The shallow smile on his face told you he was polite to a degree but those eyes said he was a motherfucker when it came to his business. Or you messing with it.

As was expected, he was an avid hunter, gun rights enthusiast, and vocal supporter of all things freedom as defined by right of center politics. There was also speculation in more than one piece he scanned about Harrington's below the table dealings, naming names of certain associates. There had been a Securities and Exchange Commission investigation of the League about five years ago but as far as he could tell, nothing came of it. Still, that gave him an idea.

In the parking lot of the library, O'Conner opened his trunk and from a lockbox hidden in a compartment he'd installed under the spare tire, he extracted one of his encrypted sat phones. From memory he called a number and the line connected after the signal bounced around through several satellites so as not to pinpoint the location of the person he was calling. At least not in the short amount of time he'd be on the phone.

"This is O'Conner," he announced. He didn't have to tell the one he was talking to the line was secure. Given that person's technical expertise, their equipment told them it was.

"Well, well," a voice said. It was electronically modified.

"How long does the SEC keep files? This would be an inactive case but less than six years old." He related the specifics.

"There should be a trail in their database as it might be a case they would re-open at some point," came the reply.

"How much to see if it's there and to get a copy?"

"Ten thousand," the hacker on the other end said without hesitation. Or rather hacktivist, as she and her colleagues would say, and O'Conner was pretty certain the person was a she though they'd never met. The target being a group she was ideologically opposed to was added incentive.

"Deal."

"Very well. My procedures have changed since last we did business but I'll communicate the details to you."

"I still use the drop," he said.

"Under the name Donald Lassen?"

"Yes."

"You do know this is the twenty-first century?" said the hacker.

"So I've been told."

A chuckle. "Okay, we're cool. I'll get everything to you."

"Right." O'Conner severed the call and returned the sat phone to its compartment. In his car again, heading onto the freeway, he felt like a pro athlete who'd been sidelined for most of the season but now was back on the field. There was a familiarity, but there were always new plays and players coming at you. If you let your old moves make you complacent, you'd be blindsided for sure. For missteps in this kind of endeavor were fatal.

A half smile shadowed his face as he drove on.

Four days later, O'Conner sat in a Cessna Skyhawk, banking over the land near the Crystal Q ranch. A number of small planes were common in this part of the landscape, several spreads had their own airstrips as the Financier had said. O'Conner and the two other men in the plane with him weren't concerned about raising unwanted notice from their target.

"That tributary flows behind that maintenance building," Hector Gonzales pointed out. The building was a modified corrugated metal barn. A man wearing a straw cowboy hat was working on a tractor near the structure.

Gonzales was well into his sixties, but his eyes were still sharp and he was one of the best cracksmen O'Conner had ever worked with. He was an expert on anything that had a combination, an electrical code, or just needed to go boom. Whatever kind of safe held the money, Gonzales could open it.

"I noticed that," O'Conner said as the pilot brought the

plane back around in a circle. "About three miles to the southwest, past that tree line, was that lake we saw. If we slipped in there and scuba'd back here, we could plant the charges to ignite that building." On his lap were a pair of military grade binoculars and a hand-drawn map on which he'd been making notations. "Assuming we overcome any sensors and the like."

"Draw them away from us," Gonzales finished, nodding his head slightly. "I'll put together something lovely."

The pilot, a pleasant-faced thirty-plus man named Ellison with pale eyes and thin lips, stared straight ahead. Neither O'Conner nor Gonzales had worked with him before. Howard Racklin, their wheelman, had brought the pilot on, vouching for him. O'Conner liked the fact that the pilot didn't feel the need to chitchat or try to ingratiate himself with him or Gonzales.

"One more pass around," O'Conner said to Ellison.

"Okay." He pulled back on the controls and the small craft's engine revved.

O'Conner turned some in his seat to address Gonzales, who sat behind the two. "After we land, let's map out how we get into and out of that lake area. We're not in fishing season but that doesn't mean there won't be campers to contend with. Plus, I'm thinking there might be someplace we can plant a couple of ATVs for the getaway."

"Right," Gonzales said, looking out the side window as the Cessna veered back over the Crystal Q ranch.

"You sure you're up to this?" O'Conner asked. It had been a while since he'd last worked with Gonzales, and it seemed to him that for the first time since he'd known him, the old crook was showing his age.

"Don't worry about me," Gonzales said. "I'm good to go."

"I'm just saying we can't be bringing a walker along with us on this trip."

"Wait, did I say don't worry about me or fuck you? Damn, you get to be my age and... You know what? Just assume I said both."

O'Conner grinned and turned back around.

Below, the work day of the modern mega ranch of thousands of heads of livestock took place, with pickup trucks equipped with automatic feed dispensers, ranch hands astride horses, and ATVs going about their duties. Various buildings and covered pens dotted the land. The fact that the ranch was of some size figured into O'Conner's calculations. The main house was some distance from all this and did not have a contingent of guards rotating about. From what they'd seen of other such homes, this one was modest by comparison. It was a three-story, nine-thousand-square-foot structure done in the southwest style. There was a large blue-green pool and built-in hot tub at the back of the house, all of it done up in stone, quartz, and jade. Leading up from this, atop what looked to have been a levee long ago, was a copse of old oak trees. Very old, O'Conner noted, judging from the size of their trunks and many branches.

From the Financier by way of the wife, they knew there were three housekeepers, the on-site chef and quarters for the wife's driver. There was also a woman named Susan Treacher who served as Murieta-Harrington's scheduler and all-around factotum. That the slush fund was located there wasn't known to many, and in this part of the country, who would dare rip off the North Texas Citizens Improvement League?

Done with their reconnoitering, the Cessna headed back

toward the single engine airport in Grand Prairie. They flew over a part of Fort Worth that was, as the term went, trending. What with its Thai-Oaxacan fusion eateries and art galleries springing up in empty spaces where once the likes of auto parts stores and pet suppliers existed.

In a rented house in a residential section not far from this nouveau-hip area, Gracella Murieta-Harrington and Zach Culhane were romping on the rug in the front room. Culhane had his hand inside the woman's lacy panties, his finger rubbing her clit. He sat on the floor, naked, behind her, and she snuggled against him, sitting inside the V of his legs, her back pressed to him.

"Mmm," she murmured as he pleasured her. She turned her head up and they kissed as he plunged his wet finger inside her. On the sound system, one of those set-ups that included wireless speakers, Toni Braxton sang "Breathe Again." Culhane kneaded one of Murieta-Harrington's luscious breasts as her chest rose and fell in a syncopated rhythm.

"Oh shit, Zach," she shuddered. "I want you inside me."

"Yes, ma'am."

Murieta-Harrington stood momentarily, sliding her panties off as her nipples dangled before Culhane's face. He suckled on them then he lay back on the rug. He was fully erect and she took him in her mouth and purposely made loud sounds as she gave him a teaser blowjob. She didn't want him climaxing just yet.

"Whoowee," he chortled.

Murieta-Harrington stopped what she was doing and got on top of him, guiding him into her. They went at it with the fury of battling ninjas and soon both were panting and spent. She reached over and plucked the glass of wine that was on the nearby coffee table. She took a gulp and handed the wine to him. He also drank some.

Murieta-Harrington asked, "Have you met this man the Financier brought in to do the job?"

"No."

"Aren't you curious?'

"Sure. But it was pointed out to me that it's better if I don't know who he is. You're the one who has to be at the house."

"Then I should meet him."

He stood, eyes moving about the living room in search of his knit boxers. "That's not going to happen. Other than when he's there doing the job." He retrieved his shorts from under an end table. The home had come furnished in the linear Scandinavian style that was all the rage at the moment, a collection of warm woods and chrome trim.

"Then how do we know we can trust him? We don't even know when the robbery's going down." Sans clothes, she sat in a grey and walnut finished lounge chair, crossing her muscular legs, an annoyed look on her face. It was as if she were the director of a nudist colony judging a new applicant who didn't meet her standards. She had not let her figure go after marrying Harrington.

He put on his shorts. "It's the Financier we're getting our payoff from. That's good by me."

"And you trust him?"

He spread his arms wide. "What choice do we have, babe?"

"They're thieves, cowboy," she snorted.

"So are we, darlin.' Anyway, the Financier doesn't cheat people."

"You mean to tell me he has a code or some lame shit like

that?" She crossed her arms, the trapped air in the room circulating between them. "It's not like you know him that well."

Now he was putting on his pants. "It's a little late to be worrying on this, ain't it? "

"I don't like us being so out of it. Having to depend on people we don't really know." She stood and walked toward her jeans thrown across the coffee table. She began to put them on with no underwear.

"This was your idea. Now we gotta see it through."

"Yeah, well, the only fuckin' I want is from you, honey chil'," she said, a Texas raised Mexican-American who could slip in and out of a thick Southern accent since her teenage years. She clipped her bra back on.

He came up behind her, putting his arms around her taut waist. "Oh, we'll be doing plenty of that, and in style."

She got a lopsided grin on her face as she placed her hand on his forearms. She looked at the wall where a near-empty bookshelf was save for some dog-eared issues of Flex magazine that Culhane had piled there, a screwdriver, and a pair of headphones. He wasn't much on book learnin', he'd said. She liked that about him. Just keep him pussy dazzled, she reminded herself, and everything would work out.

The three in the plane were dressed in casual but stylish attire, a trio out looking at Texas real estate their clothes said. O'Conner even wore loafers. Once on the ground, after the plane was checked in, they walked to the two vehicles they'd driven. O'Conner had outfitted any in the crew who had to interact with the public with fake IDs.

"You set?" O'Conner said to Ellison.

"Roger that," he affirmed. They'd previously gone over his part of the heist.

"See you then."

With that, Ellison got in a late model Jeep and the other two headed toward an Acura. When the Chrysler's engine fired up, O'Conner heard a voice on the radio as the driver's window was a quarter way down. Some wingnut yahoo who identified himself as McLeary was going on about how a cadre of Hillary Clinton's followers were not only funding Black Lives Matter, but using witchcraft and tantric sex magic to hypnotize the leaders to do their bidding. Getting behind the wheel of the Acura, O'Conner maintained his poker face while Gonzales in the passenger seat gave him a sideways glance.

"He seems okay," Gonzales said as they watched the Jeep drive off.

"Knows his way around a stick." O'Conner drove off too. "That was a smooth ride. And Racklin says he's cool."

"And how do they know each other?"

"Pulled a couple of jobs together, it seems," O'Conner said. "That haul from the cosmetic heir's compound in the Hamptons."

Gonzales nodded. "Yeah, I heard about that one. Flew the crew away in a seaplane."

"Given Harrington and the ranches around him have planes, the ground seems safer for a getaway. But he'll be useful."

Gonzales was quiet, staring out the windshield.

"What worries you?"

"Oh, I guess I'm getting old. I don't like working with newbies. If we need a pilot, why not use Billingsly or Lombino?"

"Billingsly is doing a five-year jolt in Merced," said O'Conner. "And Lombino is dead."

"No shit," said Gonzales. "What happened?"

"What do you think? Plane crash," said O'Conner. "I heard he was working some smuggling thing and tried to take off on a short runway with too heavy a load. He wasn't able to clear some telephone wires or some such. Flipped the plane and bam that was it."

"Damn," Gonzales said. "That's…"

"Yeah," said O'Conner. "Yeah, it is. So we get Ellison."

"Who else is in?"

"Racklin, Dollarhyde…"

"Dollarhyde's good." He added, "She's… something else."

"Easy, son," said O'Conner. "She'd chew you up."

"Yeah, but if you gotta go…" Gonzales said. "Anyone else?"

"Eel and Benny Parker."

"Okay. That's a good crew. I feel better."

"Glad you approve."

"Just watching our back," Gonzales said. He decided he'd bring a few items for extra protection the day of the job. It never hurt to be prepared.

At seven minutes past two a.m. on Friday, the day of the robbery, a pale half-moon in the night sky, O'Conner and Gonzales followed the tributary that descended from Lake Washaw, the body of water they'd spotted from the plane. Each man was dressed in black clothing and had an equipment bag strapped to their backs. Gonzales had a pair of night vision binoculars on a strap around his neck. They did not carry any scuba gear. O'Conner had studied a map of the area obtained from a wildlife center, and had determined the tributary was too shallow in this part to swim in. Instead, a small inflatable skiff had allowed them to work their way quickly and silently to the outer perimeter of the Crystal Q ranch.

Night vision binoculars to his eyes, Gonzales swept the landscape before them as they neared where Harrington's property line began. "I see some heads sticking up."

There was no fencing here but there were sensors buried about the ground. The intention was to know if a cow was wandering away and not so much to catch an errant hiker. The two didn't think there was someone monitoring the seismic devices around the clock, but no doubt any recorded movement up this way would be noted.

Taking a knee, the box man unlimbered his equipment bag. From inside it he extracted a device about the size of a shoebox. He placed this on the ground, pulling up an antenna connected perpendicularly to the main section. Gonzales powered up the battery-operated gadget. He studied its screen as he slowly turned first one dial then the next, O'Conner looking on. The thing emitted a low hum.

"I think that's it," Gonzales announced as the hum subsided.

"You're not sure?"

For an answer, Gonzales got up and, holding the device, stepped toward then past one of the sensors. This was a rounded black plastic head the diameter of a coffee cup lid. Beneath the ground was buried the rest of the sensor that sent a signal if movement disturbed its wave net. These rudimentary sensors couldn't tell a cow from a man, but as the two would not be meandering around, it could be concluded later that their deliberate movements were those of an intruder or intruders.

The machine Gonzales built was designed to cycle the

sensor's signal back on itself, thereby not noting their presence. That was the theory at least.

"Well?" he said, turning back to O'Conner. "You coming? We'll know soon enough if it's working or not."

The other man, standing over six feet, had remained stationary, his large hands down by his sides. It was as if he'd been formed from the rock and wood, inanimate until such time as he needed to expend energy. With cautious, controlled movements O'Conner followed the exact steps Gonzales had made and the two worked their way down to the maintenance building.

"Shhh," O'Conner hissed as they got close to the building.

Both men went stone. A sound hovered near the building before them. Though in dark clothes, both were exposed on open ground. Somebody was singing terribly offkey.

"Been around a loooong time, Marie," crooned the voice happily.

With nowhere to hide, both men rushed forward and went flat against the front of the maintenance building. From around the far corner walked an individual who was obviously drunk. He had a beard and was middle-aged. His dress shirt was unbuttoned, a pot belly expanding the athletic tee underneath. He wore slacks and cowboy boots. He also carried what remained of a bottle of Jim Beam. Whoever this man was, he wasn't so drunk that he wouldn't see the two interlopers.

"We can't kill him," Gonzales growled.

O'Conner was already heading toward the newcomer.

"Who the fuck?" the bearded man began, but before he could get anything else out O'Conner was on him. For his first blow, he sunk a fist in the man's stomach, doubling him over. He vomited, which smelled liked bubble gum and sour cabbage.

"Ah, gawd," he grumbled, bent over and staggering, the pain and booze making his head woozy. A swift foot against his ankle and a push to his shoulder sent him down on all fours.

"You done come for my gold, I knew this was going to happen," he sputtered. "The uprising has begun. McLeary was right."

O'Conner brought his fist down on the man's temple, dropping him onto his side where he lay, unmoving. Tim McLeary was a Texas-based right-wing talk show gabber who went on about this or that conspiracy, to the self-fulfilling delight of his loyal listeners. Among his theories was that Barack Obama was a secret ISIS insurgent imam and that a special ops unit of the government had been infusing our drinking water with chemicals to turn the red-blooded gay. Gold hustlers and wipes for men's taints were among his biggest advertisers.

"Now what?" Gonzales said, looking down at the bearded man who had begun snoring. "There's no hiding we were here now."

"So we don't hide it. We finish what he came to do but we make it look like something else."

Afterward, Gonzales understood what O'Conner was talking about.

Lottie Amaya wasn't much older than that Gracella, she noted for what had lately become something of an obsession with her. And really, to be honest, her ass was just as luscious as that woman's, though she had to grudgingly admit Gracella's rack was better, but damn. She knew homegirl was from the barrio like she was, yet here she was, the chick who used to pimp beer in a skimpy bikini raised to queen of the Crystal Q spread, while Amaya, who graduated with a B+ in algebra, was cleaning the toilets and unclogging the indoor Jacuzzi in this pinche ranch house. Not that a woman should get a break because of her body, she admonished herself, but still, damn. That goddamn B+ and two and a half years of community college hadn't exactly opened wide the doors of opportunity.

Dusting a salvaged wood cabinet in the upstairs hallway, she looked at her reflection in the 1940s era Églomisé mirror above it. She still had it going on, she surmised. Maybe rather than be all quiet-like as was advised when she got this job, she should try chatting the lady of the house up. Be all interested in whatever the fuck the latest thing was these rich bitches got into to occupy their time when they weren't shopping. What was it lately? Developing a line of coloring books based on famous football players from Texas? This somehow to benefit homeless shelters.

There were worse pastimes she could pretend to find fascinating, she reflected. The doorbell rang. As she was close to the stairs, she descended and opened the door. A striking-looking black woman stood there under the portico, morning light slanting across her tight form. Shit, was she some kind of personal trainer for Gracella, Amaya wondered. She was rocking Michelle Obama-worthy toned arms.

"Good morning," the black woman said pleasantly.

"Yes?' Amaya said. The woman was dressed in denim capris, a loose sleeveless number, and a sash around her waist. Nesting under one of her buffed triceps was a rolled-up yoga mat.

"I'm here for Mrs. Murieta-Harrington's ten thirty."

"I'm sorry?"

"Her krav maga session," she said matter-of-factly.

The hell is that? Amaya almost blurted. Well, she didn't know anything about no session, but then she wasn't in charge of the lady's schedule. That was for Susan to say.

"Hold on a second and let me get her scheduler."

"No problem."

And where the hell was Gracella? Amaya hadn't seen her since her coffee and two eggs and lox, and that was more than an hour ago. She must be in her bedroom because she wasn't out at the pool. Spacious was an understatement when describing that bedroom that was damn near larger than Amaya's apartment. The housekeeper turned and there was a man standing in front of her with a black hockey-style mask on, only his eyes showing. He pointed a handgun at her face. She gasped and was about to yell but he clamped a gloved hand over her mouth and put his wolf eyes close to her flushed face.

"Where is the lady of the house and the one called Susan?" said O'Conner from under the mask in a voice that was so calm and cool he might as well have been asking for directions to the local Walmart. "Are they together?" He relaxed the hand over her mouth.

Behind her, Amaya saw the woman slip by, a pistol grip shotgun retrieved from inside the rolled-up mat. She too now had on a mask, a curious contrast to the rest of what she wore. Amaya wished she'd paid more attention to what the woman had looked like, but who paid attention to the ones who constantly came and went, being paid to satisfy whatever the hell latest whim had gripped Gracella?

"I think she's in the library. Susan, I mean," Amaya answered, stammering some but then getting it together.

"I think Miss Gracella's in her bedroom." Despite the guns and forced entry, there was a calming quality to this man that soothed her. She could feel her heart rate slowing to normal. How crazy was that?

"Get Susan in here, please."

"I, ah…"

The man, wide in the shoulders with sizeable hands like her ex who worked construction, pointed at the wall intercom. "On that."

"Yes, sir."

"Nothing funny," O'Conner advised.

"Yes, sir."

He accompanied her to the intercom. The other woman had partially closed some of the drapes. Not all the way as they might look odd, but just enough, as if to block some of the harsh early light and also to better obscure their presence from any ranch hand walking by.

"Susan," Amaya said, pressing the button for the library, "you're needed in the front room."

"What is it?" came the reply, clear on the state-of-the-art equipment.

The home invader was holding a half sheet of plain paper with block lettered words on it. She read them. "One of the caterers is here," she read, verbatim. "Ferenzini, he says. There's a problem with the check they were given." How did he know about the upcoming party and who one of the caterers was? Who the hell are these people, she wondered.

There was a pause as Susan ran through her responses, but then said, "Very well. I'll be right there."

"Have a seat," her captor ordered. He was no kid, she could hear the years in his voice, but Amaya could tell he kept in shape. Each of his movements were efficient, measured. She sat on the couch.

"I'm going to tie you up and gag you," the man was saying to her, again in a reassuring manner, like a car salesman telling her he added the all-weather undercoating free of charge. She caught herself wanting to flirt and ask him was he going to spank her too. What was wrong with her? This was some serious shit going down.

Using zip ties, he began to truss Amaya up. She noticed there were two more men inside the house now, dressed similarly to the first one. Not in burglar's clothes like what you saw on old movies, but slacks, expensive casual shoes, and dress shirts. They looked like the vendors that had been coming and going all week getting things ready for the upcoming function the mister was throwing. The housekeeper tried to figure out what these robbers wanted – the original art on the walls? Gracella's jewelry? The missus had a few diamonds, pearls, a platinum band on a watch, but unlike what Amaya had seen on shows like the Real Housewives of Atlanta and whatnot, homegirl didn't go in for a lot of bling. No, she had a notion these thieves were after something else, something bigger.

The ties cinched, a bandana like you could buy in a liquor store in the 'hood was placed around her mouth. Maybe the robbery was going to be on the news, given that Clovis Harrington was well known. Maybe one of those entertainment sites would interview her about her harrowing ordeal. This could be the break she'd been waiting for, and damned if she wasn't going to take advantage. In her head she began practicing how distraught she'd be for the news cameras. Not too much, didn't want to overdo it. But give them just enough to let your audience fill in the blanks, that too sincere drama teacher had said, back when she played Mrs. Gibbs in her high school's production of *Our Town*.

O'Conner finished securing the housekeeper. Vivian Dollarhyde, the buffed woman from the doorway, held the Mossberg shotgun at the ready. She'd gone deeper into the house where a second set of stairs led to the next floor library. He and Gonzales started for the side hallway that led downstairs to the wine cellar. Benny Parker, who had come in behind her, was to remain up here on watch and lend Dollarhyde a hand just in case. The other two in the string were in position elsewhere, waiting for their cue.

Distantly, O'Conner heard the boom as the charges he and Gonzales had planted in the maintenance building went off. After planting the explosives, they'd ransacked several tractors, ATVs, and generators in the building, smashing diesel injectors, ripping out wiring, and so on.

Using Rustolium spray paint they'd found in the building, they'd graffitied the interior and exterior walls with slogans like "Meat is Murder," "Animals Have Rights," and "No hormones, No GMOs." The dodge being to make their attack look like an animal rights action so that when the drunk man was sober, him going on about the two whose faces he couldn't recall would be in keeping with those hippie activists types. Given this was a busy ranch with two other maintenance buildings on the acreage, the assaulted building was closed up pending repair. Now, after the explosions, there would be little left to fix.

O'Conner and Gonzales exchanged a look as they heard muffled cries from outside as vehicles sped toward the fire. Time was tight. The plan was to be in and out in under ten minutes, eleven tops.

* * *

Susan Treacher stepped out of the library, turning and pulling the double doors closed behind her. The annoyed look on her face was replaced with one of surprise as the masked woman appeared in front of her, a shotgun barrel pointed at her midsection.

"I need you to remain calm," the masked woman told her.

"Okay," she said. Years ago, when she'd managed a clothing store in a mall, she'd been robbed. She knew then, like now, that the best course of action was to do exactly what you were told. Still, the sense of being violated came flooding back to her. Like waving a gun around automatically gave you the right to take what wasn't yours.

"Where are the two other housekeepers?" Dollarhyde said. They'd been scoping out the house since early this morning and knew the chef – whose phone they'd cloned and tapped – had left on errands in preparation for the Remember the Alamo soiree. They'd planted a tracker on his van. That's why they knew to have Treacher come see about a matter he'd ordinarily attended to.

"You made Lottie call me."

"If you would answer my question."

"Cessie's in the east wing and Flora's in the wine cellar."

"Shit," Dollarhyde growled. "Why is she down there?'

Eyebrow raised as if that were an impertinent question, Treacher sniffed, "I told her the bottles needed dusting and the floor mopped. It wouldn't do to have guests down there and dirt and what have you in the air making people sneeze."

"Jesus, what, the rich have special noses?" the masked woman said. "Move." She jerked the shotgun toward the stairs.

Treacher complied. As they descended, Dollarhyde had to hold the shotgun with its shortened barrel in one hand while texting with the other.

"What?" Treacher said as the sound of the exploding equipment building startled her.

"Never you mind." Dollarhyde was putting the hand holding her encrypted cell under the gun's barrel and intended to give her prisoner a light jab. To her consternation, the civilian had stopped when the distant boom thundered.

The explosion riled Treacher. She'd heard about the animal rights business and figured this woman with the shotgun was part of that. A bunch of tree hugging Croc wearers. She would be damned if she was going to be part of any of that shit, made to pose with a cow carcass or painted with its blood. She pretended to stumble as they came off the steps and as she did so, came around and up with the house keys she wore on a plastic wristlet. One of the keys stuck out of her fist like a spike and she aimed this at the other woman's eyes like she'd been taught in her self-defense classes.

"Stupid," Dollarhyde said. She meant herself for getting distracted and letting the square get the jump on her. She blocked the keys but had to rear back. Treacher lunged at her and now had both her hands on the shotgun. They violently contended to possess the weapon. Treacher tried to use her foot to upend Dollarhyde but she was too quick and, turning sideways, putting her hip into the other woman, torqued her upper body while both still held the shotgun. Treacher found herself momentarily airborne then slammed down onto the hardwood of the back hallway. The Mossberg was wrenched from her sweaty hands.

"Now quit fooling around," Dollarhyde said, standing over Treacher, the gun barrel pointed dead zero at her head.

The whole thing had taken less than a minute. Treacher half expected to be struck with the weapon, but if she were knocked out, that would probably be too much of an inconvenience. She noticed the veggie militant wasn't even out of breath. She would be wary now for anything else Treacher might try. With a groan, she slowly got up.

"Let's go fetch Cessie, shall we?"

"Yes, ma'am," Treacher said edgily.

Then from upstairs, a door could be heard opening and Gracella Murieta-Harrington called out, "What was that? Susan? You there?"

The smell of cleaning fluids in the musty air reached O'Conner's nose as the text came in from Dollarhyde. He held up his hand and he and Gonzales paused on the stone steps. Holding the phone over his shoulder, he showed the safe cracker the message. The soles of their shoes were a rubber composition and by habit, they'd been careful coming down to the wine cellar even though they supposed no one was there. The two heard muffled music from around a near corner, a female rapper over the boisterous track.

"Been livin' long and tough like you was rough. But my game is strong an' you won't be around long."

Flora Tafani had her back to the two men who crept up behind her. She was bopping her head to the too-loud rap tune on her wireless headphones, bent over as she used her microfiber mop to clean the polished cement floor. She went stiff as a hand clamped on her shoulder and she reflexively bolted upright. Turning in the direction the hand indicated, she glared open-mouthed at two masked men, one of them with a finger to the mouth slit of his mask in a shushing fashion.

Before she could fully assemble what was going on, the headphones were removed and shut off. Gun to her temple, she sat on the floor, back to the wall where the taller of the two men indicated, right near a rack of Malbec and Merlot she'd recently dusted. Zip-tied and gagged, she watched as the men hunched down and reached in between the bottles, feeling around. She heard a grunt from one of the men, followed by a click, and damn if the rack didn't swing out smoothly over the stone floor.

Exposed was a formidable-looking safe door set into the stone wall that Tafani had no idea was there. One of the men tapped his gloved index finger on the electronic lock on the safe while the other one unlimbered a messenger bag and set it on the floor. From inside this he took out what looked to her like one of those pirate cable boxes her brother used to make. Various coated wires dangled from this thing as the man powered it on. A low hum came from the device.

The man who had tapped the lock let out a sigh of appreciation. "Well," he said. "Aren't you a beauty."

"Be cool," Dollarhyde said as she came further into the hacienda-style bedroom that had its own loft, taking up the second and third floors. Treacher was in front of her, the end of the Mossberg's barrel on her spine. There was a high ceiling with maple wood beams forming a hatch pattern above their heads and floor-to-ceiling windows overlooking the ranch's cattle and land. The heavy drapes were open but diaphanous inner curtains covered the windows, the light coming through bathing the three in warm, comforting hues. In addition to the massive four-poster bed, lounging couches and plush chairs resided over the herringbone pattern oak floor and the en suite bathroom included a full-size Jacuzzi that Dollarhyde glimpsed through the open bathroom door. There was a seventy-two-inch flat screen TV on one wall competing with over-sized art such as a print of Warhol's multi-image, multi-colored Marilyn Monroe.

Murieta-Harrington narrowed her eyes at Monroe's repeated face. It was as if those nine sly, sexy grins were a knowing wink that only she understood. The lady of the house had been having phone sex with Culhane on her burner when the explosion went off. She figured that it was a sign the robbery was going down, something that was confirmed when Treacher was brought in by the gun-toting woman in a mask. Now it was up to her to play the part of surprised victim.

In character, Murieta-Harrington back-peddled, raising her arms as she did so.

"Put them down," Dollarhyde advised. She didn't think anyone could see them up here through the curtains but no sense getting sloppy again. "Both of you sit on that love seat, if you'd be so kind."

Treacher sneered, "Like we have a choice."

Dollarhyde said to the back of her head, "Really, though?" She bumped the weapon against her back. "You do. Choices you have are easy, hard, or unconscious with possible concussion. Take your pick."

As the women sat down, a disguised Benny Parker appeared in the doorway.

"We good?" he said.

"Yeah, we're okay," said Dollarhyde. "Watch 'em while I get them settled.

Dollarhyde produced two zip ties from her back pocket and proceeded to bind the two women together. A buzzer sounded dully through the open bedroom door.

"What's that?" she said harshly.

The others exchanged a look. Murieta-Harrington answered, "The side door. The hands use it when they need something."

Dollarhyde gagged the two women.

Cassie Warner was taking another toke on her joint when she heard the side door buzzer. She was in the toilet off the kitchen enjoying her unofficial smoke break. The spacious room contained only a toilet and a sink but was large enough for a shower. There was a louvered window and she'd discovered that by putting a towel down at the base crack of the door and blowing her fumes out the window, she could consume unmolested and undetected. To mask the aroma of weed clinging to her clothes, she employed the Lysol she carried in with her. She'd spray some on, covering the tell-tale smell with the nostril-stinging antiseptic.

The buzzer sounded again, followed by a knock. Reluctantly, she extinguished her joint and fanned her hands in front of her face. Hurrying, she didn't use her cover-all technique, but stepping out of the room, was glad nobody was around. She answered the door. One of the foremen, Raynor, she recalled, was standing there.

"Everything okay in here?" he said in his mild Texas drawl, face tanned from years of being outdoors.

"Yes, sure, why?"

"The boom," he said.

"Huh?" So that had been real and not an imagining due to her Fantastic Paradise fade. "What happened?"

"We're checking it out now. Looks like them damn animal lovers left us a goodbye gift. Anyway, figured I just better check in on y'all."

"Everything's fine," she said. Then there was a thud, followed by a grunt, and both looked toward the kitchen's swinging door leading into the rest of the ground floor.

"Well, since I'm here," he said, coming inside.

"Yeah," Warner said. "Come on."

The two went off toward the sound.

Gonzales studied the screen of his homemade electronic device. The safe's lock required a combination punched in correctly on its keypad. But he wasn't trying to hack the sequence. What he wanted was to short-circuit the alarm feature. He knew these modern safes were often linked to a smartphone app that would send out an alarm to the owner should someone try to tamper with them.

"Three and a half minutes," O'Conner announced, no worry in his voice, merely stating the fact. Using a chuck key, he tightened the carbide tipped titanium drill bit in place on the battery-powered drill.

"Copy that, jefe."

Gonzales carefully turned two black knobs on his box and could tell from the reading he was honing in on the override frequency, digital numbers flashing by on a smaller square screen in a corner of his box. Both men were aware that time was ticking by while the machine searched the airwaves for the correct contact.

"Ah, por fin," he announced triumphantly when the machine finally made the connection. He pulled one of the knobs out, locking the frequency in place.

"Phase two," he said, holding out his hand.

O'Conner handed the drill to the old man, being careful not to kick the humming box that Gonzales had set on the floor. With precision, he got to work drilling into the side of the case steel lock. O'Conner was at his side, occasionally spraying some WD 40 on the bit and the deepening hole as it bore, slowly but steadily, inward, metal shavings falling to the floor like robot tears.

Momentarily, both paused at a thump of something hitting the floor above them. Glancing at each other, they silently agreed to continue on. The others in the crew either dealt with whatever it was or they didn't. They were too close now.

Upstairs, the housekeeper and the ranch hand came into the front room and gaped at the sight of Amaya lying on her side on the rug. She'd managed to twist her body off the couch, despite one of her ankles being bound to one of the stubby legs. But she landed more off balance than she'd intended and was now tearful from the excruciating pain radiating through her lower leg. She realized she had at least dislocated that ankle if not broken it.

"The hell?" Raynor said as the two went over to the woman. He had a buck knife in a scabbard on his belt and got it out and was about to cut her zip tie loose.

"That'll be enough of that," Benny Parker said. He aimed a Glock 19 with a custom-made suppressor at them.

The others were crouched down to the injured Amaya and Raynor sought to hide the knife between his body and hers.

"On the floor, shit-kicker," Parker said.

Raynor tensed and Warner touched his arm. "It sure as shit isn't worth it."

He looked from her to the pleading eyes of Amaya. He dropped the knife on the floor as Parker stepped closer and kicked it away.

"Good thing we have plenty of these," said Dollarhyde, holding up more zip ties.

Back downstairs, Hector Gonzales inserted what looked like a shortened straw in the hole he and O'Conner had made. Two wires, red and black, led from one end of it. The robbers stood and stepped away from the safe. Gonzales set off the charge by touching the two bare ends of the wires together. A low yield of Semtex handily blew the lock off. They'd used a higher yield of the stuff for their timed explosives in the equipment building.

Tafani jerked her body as the destroyed mechanism clattered across the metal floor to land next to her. Then the two thieves opened the safe's door to reveal stacks and stacks of cash. The two men pulled out four nylon duffle bags from under their shirts and began loading the money into them.

"We're a minute behind," O'Conner said, zipping closed his second bag as they quickly loaded the swag. "We gotta go. Our ride is here and waiting."

Gonzales was already heading for the stairs. Due to the time constraint and the weight of the bags, they left the drill and their other instruments behind, even the custom-made box whose signal was still broadcasting to whoever was monitoring the safe that it was still whole and secure. It wouldn't matter when it was found: the parts used to make it were available from any electronic outfit and the shell was a hollowed-out switcher box Gonzales had rescued from the trash. Same for the drill and bits. There was nothing identifying about them that could tie them back to anyone. Gonzales did make sure to take away any leftover explosive material.

Up top in the front room, O'Conner and Gonzales joined the rest the crew. On the couch sat Murieta-Harrington, tied to Treacher and Warner. Dollarhyde had cut Amaya free from the couch leg and she sat in a chair, her leg elevated on a stool, holding ice in a towel on it. Parker stood near Raynor, who sat on the floor, his hands zip tied behind his back and his ankles zip tied too. He glared at the robbers. There was a bruise the color of eggplant on the side of his jaw where Dollarhyde had struck with the stock of the Mossberg when he'd tried to yell out.

"Y'all gonna be in a world of trouble," he said. "Don't matter one goldarn you got your faces covered and all that. Mr. Harrington will see you pay. You jus' wait."

Outside, the duplicate of the chef's van idled.

Parker gagged the man who mad-dogged him like whatever they were absconding with was his personally. Warner too was gagged and, with everyone secured and silenced, as one, the four along with the stuffed duffels of cash left through the side door and got in the van.

"GPS tracker indicates the real chef is heading back this way," Howard Racklin said behind the wheel. "Damn near at the front gate." He was a square-shouldered individual with a bulldog's homely face and the temperament of a German shepherd. Loyal to a fault but a terror if crossed.

"Then drive, baby," O'Conner said.

"You don't have to tell me twice." Racklin descended the slope behind the house then went left along a road that they knew from their aerial scouting would take them toward the main entrance. A ranch this size, the four who'd invaded the house had hiked in on foot before sunrise but knew they would need wheels to hasten their exit.

"Shit," Racklin swore, eyes on the rearview.

"What?" said O'Conner. He, along with the others, looked out the rear windows in the rear double doors. A battered pickup was coming up fast behind them, a billowing plume of dust and dirt in its wake. A man stood in the bed, firing at them with a rifle.

"How'd they tumble?" Racklin wondered aloud.

"There," O'Conner said, pointing. In the receding distance, the real chef's van was parked near the house.

Several gunshots cracked and instinctively, the van's passengers ducked. Bullets pinged around them but none entered the interior. Dollarhyde and Parker were closest to the back and they pushed out the windows, designed specifically for that purpose in case they needed to shoot. Raising their weapons, they returned fire. The pickup veered off and Racklin took the van onto the rougher terrain, the after factory heavy duty hydraulics being able to handle the off road transition. He drove deliberately into a bunch of grazing cattle that were seemingly oblivious to the gunfire.

"What the fuck, Rack?" Dollarhyde yelled.

"Hold on," the getaway man said as he expertly maneuvered the van amid the cows that trudged out of the way but didn't scatter in a panic. Indeed, they were languid about the whole matter.

"You'd think they'd be livelier," Parker muttered.

"If you knew your fate was to wind up as meatloaf or ribeye, would you?" O'Conner observed.

"Deep," Dollarhyde said, patting her shotgun for reassurance.

"We got help on the way?" Gonzales asked.

"Yeah," O'Conner replied.

Racklin was blocked by some cows bunched together and began backing up, the flanks of the animals bumping and thumping heavily against the side of the vehicle. He was using the rearview mirror for guidance as his hands steered the wheel, occasionally turning his head to the side. His face was fixed in place, calm and determined as he expertly maneuvered the vehicle backward at speed. The ones in the pickup were at the edge of the cows and shooting again as they came forward. A cow's head exploded and red gore coated the passenger side window. A car came up, a ranch hand shooting from that too.

"Here he comes," Racklin said, the sound of a single engine plane vibrating through the metal roof of the van.

"Jesus," they heard the one with the rifle yell as the pilot veered over them at such a low level it made their pursuers duck their heads. Then a petrol bomb was dropped on the car, the flaming gasoline dripping inside the open windows. The occupants ran from the vehicle. The bombs had been previously put together by Gonzales and they began to explode all around them. One of the ranch men, his arm and upper torso on fire, went into a tuck and roll in the dirt while several of his buddies rushed to help extinguish him. Eel Estevez was in the plane with Ellison, dropping the petrol bombs.

Divots of earth, grass, and cow shit mushroomed into the air as two other bombs exploded. A man on horseback who'd come galloping up was thrown as the horse reared. This explosion proved to be the catalyst that caused the cattle to finally show some urgency as the driver of the pursuing Jeep tried to avoid being firebombed from the air. As the cattle panicked, two of the beasts collided with the pickup, or maybe it was the other way around; the bottom line was that the driver was thrown forward, his head cracking the windshield and the vehicle coming to a hard stop.

The van reached a tree line of twisted willows to the west side of the ranch, their branches like the petrified fingers of witches reaching up from the grave. Further in, Racklin killed the engine and they left the van amid the brambles and trunks. The quintet gathered their bags and weapons and headed off on foot. The vacated van held a timed device, again thanks to Gonzales, that in twenty minutes would set off an incendiary explosive that would destroy the vehicle and any trace DNA. Through the woods they went, doubling back to the trail that led to the lake, conspicuously making sure to leave noticeable footprints. Then they broke off and up a knoll, then another rise, then down to an overgrown fire trail O'Conner and Gonzales had come upon that day on foot after they'd cased the ranch from the air. In an area of sage and acanthus the group retrieved two two-person ATVs left hidden amid the foliage. Each had a roll bar cage, so with two seated in the vehicles and Benny Parker hanging on the back, they drove off.

Not too long later they abandoned the ATVs on the side of the highway, where they would hopefully be stolen. They got to the safe house in an SUV they'd hidden at the same spot under a camouflage of branches and brush. The "safe house" was actually a rent per day office in a rundown building east of I-35 in Fort Worth. An area not yet a gleam in gentrifiers' eyes. As far as the building's owners knew, the space was being rented for a two-day seminar on annuities and dividends by a small actuary firm.

The door to the second-floor office burst open and the crew, loaded with guns and bags of cash, piled into the front room. Even though it was after regular business hours, they had opted to take the stairs up from the ground floor to lessen the chance of being seen by any of the other tenants should anyone be working late.

"Holy shit," said Benny.

"You can say that again," Dollarhyde added. She lifted the duffel bag of cash she was carrying, the muscles in her arm flexing under her coppery skin, and placed it on the office conference table.

"Oh, I'm going to be saying that for some time," said Benny.

O'Conner looked over to Gonzales, who had a portable police scanner in his hands and an earbud in. The older man shook his head in the negative and disconnected from the device.

"Nothing?" said O'Conner.

"Knife fight at a bar downtown and some asshole threatening to jump off a building. That's it."

"After the ruckus we just caused?" Estevez said.

"The League is keeping the lid on," O'Conner observed. They were thieves who'd stolen unreported money. There was no going to the law about this.

"Well, that doesn't mean we should be standing around any longer than we need to," Ellison said. "Let's close this show and get outta here."

O'Conner and Gonzales picked up the four duffel bags of cash. They proceeded to pull the bundles of money out of them and stack them on a table. O'Conner divvyed up the proceeds. A sense of exuberance pervaded the room as they stared at the stacks of money.

"Holy shit," said Benny, shaking his head.

"Before we call it a day..." said Gonzales, holding up a bottle of tequila.

"Now that's a good way to cap off a job," Dollarhyde said. Gonzales handed her a sleeve of plastic cups and she handed them out to crew. One by one, Gonzales gave each of them a healthy dose.

Inwardly, O'Conner was pleased. It had been a good haul. Even with the insiders' cut, the Financier's overhead and share, everyone was walking away with plenty. He raised his cup.

"Good work," he said. "And good luck to us all."

"Sláinte," Gonzales said, the distinctly Irish toast getting questioning looks from the others.

"What?" he said. "I can't be multi-cultural?"

Benny said, "Dude, the kind of money we got today? You be whatever you want." With a chuckle, he and the others downed their shots.

Ellison motioned to the larger stacks of cash O'Conner was putting away. "Lot of green there."

"It is," O'Conner said flatly.

"You're gonna make sure all that gets delivered to all the right people?" Ellison said, not bothering to hide his skepticism.

O'Conner looked at him blandly, a spark like flint rocks striking behind his eyes. Stillness enveloped the room. A large dog barked beyond the walls.

"We just trust you. Right?"

O'Conner's voice was like cut glass. "You're saying?"

"Nothing." Racklin hit the pilot's shoulder with a stack

of bills. "He don't mean nothing. We're all good. Right?"

Ellison looked from Racklin to O'Conner. "Yeah," he said. "we're all good."

"Okay then," said Racklin. He quickly finished putting the rest of his money into his bag and lifted it. "Let's go. I want out of town and out of Texas, and I want it now."

As Gonzales and Dollarhyde wiped the place down, the others finished packing up their money and gear. Thereafter they left the office and once again took the stairs to the ground floor and exited the building. Outside on the dirt lot that served as the parking area, everyone began to head toward their cars. O'Conner came out last, buttoning up a windbreaker.

"What the hell?" Racklin exclaimed.

"What's up?" said Benny.

"Someone slashed my tires."

"Mine too," Dollarhyde said.

Ellison produced a pistol and slammed it across Racklin's head, sending him to the ground. At the same time a motorcycle roared from around a near corner, the rider left-handedly spraying bullets at the crew from a Tec-9 with an extended magazine. Everyone ran for cover, rounds burrowing into the dirt, pinging off the cars and the concrete of the office building. Ellison, firing the pistol, threw his duffle of cash into the hatchback of his Jeep, the only vehicle with its tires still intact. He then scooped up two fallen bags of loot and tossed them in to join his.

O'Conner went prone behind a bonded Monte Carlo, a gun in his fist.

The motorcycle rider continued to spray the area with bullets, keeping everyone down. He reached the periphery of the lot and, screeching back around, he continued shooting.

Steeling himself, a grim O'Conner partly rose from his hiding place, a round striking close to him. He took aim and fired three shots at the rider. The second one penetrated the rider's helmet and the man fell backward off the motorcycle.

O'Conner looked around for Ellison.

"Bastard," he heard Dollarhyde snarl. Ellison was pushing her ahead of him. He had her cut down Mossberg pointed at the woman's head.

"Keep your ass on the ground," he demanded as Racklin began to pick himself up.

"Go fuck yourself," Racklin said as he continued up.

The pilot stepped close and struck him again with the butt of the weapon.

"Hey," O'Conner said, stepping away from the Monte Carlo. "This is bullshit. People are looking down here from their windows. Cops will be here in a heartbeat."

"Motherfucker," Ellison said, his voice breaking with emotion. Pushing Dollarhyde to the side, he brought the shotgun up and fired. O'Conner raised his arms to cover his face but took most of the blast to his torso and went down hard. The money he was carrying dropped down too.

O'Conner grunted as he thudded onto the dry earth. The pilot ran over to get the dual equipment bags with the money, O'Conner laying on his side, his back to him, the bags on the other side of his body. Bending and reaching for them, O'Conner turned around and, sitting up, drove a knife into the pilot's thigh. He quickly pulled it free of Ellison's leg as he intended to plunge the blade into the man's chest. The pilot yelped, moving backward and avoiding blade. O'Conner got to his feet. The sleeves of his windbreaker shredded. Blood leaked from his wounded forearms beneath.

O'Conner had gotten a familiar feeling in the back of his

neck when Ellison groused about the split. Before coming
outside, he'd put on one of the special jackets Gonzales had
brought along – the old man being overly cautious these
days. The clothing was based on a design from a famous tailor
in South America who outfitted heads of state, including
U.S. presidents it was rumored, in suits and everyday wear
woven with his proprietary blends of polyester and nylon.
The bullet resistant windbreaker had protected him from
the majority of the shotgun's small gauge load. Apparently,
though, the knock-off garment was lacking protection in
the sleeves.

Rushing to the pilot, the two men grappled and grunted
for control of the shotgun, Ellison kneeing O'Conner and
breaking free. But now O'Conner had the weapon and was
readying to blast Ellison away when the pilot produced a
compact stun grenade and threw it at him. O'Conner wryly
noted the damn grenade had been among those made by
Gonzales. He dove away as the thing went off. Ellison then
lit and threw a remaining petrol bomb at the Monte Carlo,
setting the car's roof on fire. He'd put sugar in this one
O'Conner concluded, noting how the fuel didn't run down
the sides of the car. In that way, the stuff would stick and
burn. Nasty.

Ellison turned and ran, putting distance between him
and the crew he'd sought to double cross. The Monte
Carlo's fuel tank, having been punctured by bullets, had
leaked gasoline all around itself and proceeded to ignite in a
deafening blast that sent sections of sharp metal flying in all
directions. During this, the pilot managed to get to his dead
cohort's still idling motorcycle. With parts of the destroyed
car charred and smoldering, Ellison was a block away in a
matter of moments, leaving the battered thieves behind.

"We gotta get out of here," Gonzales said, gripping O'Conner's arm.

"He's got to be dealt with," O'Conner vowed, staring after the receding pilot.

"He will be," the older man said, knowing enough about the mindset of the man beside him. "But right now we have to get away."

The sound of sirens in the distance seemed to bring O'Conner back to the present.

"Right," he said. He looked over at Racklin who was looking at the pilot's abandoned Jeep. "That good to run?"

"Yeah, looks okay," he said. "Keys are in it. He was prepared to get the hell out."

"Yeah," said Gonzales. "With our money. The little shit."

"Okay," O'Conner said. "Everyone crowd in. Racklin, you good to drive?"

"Yes," he said.

"We'll drop each of you off one at a time. From there you're all on your own with your share."

"And you two get the car?" said Estevez.

O'Conner rasped, "You want to argue about it, Eel?"

He held up his hands. "Not me. I'm good, ese."

In the car, O'Conner said to Racklin, "You'll be the last to get out, we're gonna have words first."

"I know," a contrite wheelman said.

Within the next hour, the empty car had been wiped clean and left on the street. The crew had scattered to the winds, Racklin as well, but he was short a hefty part of his cut, due to his having been the one who vouched for the traitor Ellison. The Crystal Q job was now officially behind them and whatever came next, O'Conner reflected, he'd be ready.

CHAPTER 2
Aftermath
by Gary Phillips

O'Conner had several problems to deal with after letting off the crew and dumping the Jeep. His forearms were bloody, his sleeves were in tatters, and he was hefting three million plus dollars in cash in two equipment bags. But it was now dark and he'd managed to put more than a mile from what was a fresh crime scene as far as the Fort Worth Police Department was concerned. He had to ditch the bags for now as he knew soon the patrol cars would be making circuits away from that dirt parking lot where the motorcycle driver lay dead. First, though, the cops would determine what went down there, door knocking and badgering folks who, for many of them, the police meant harassment, not solace. O'Conner had picked this area for a reason. But this also meant here was where on the regular the denizens got jacked up by the law and he was nothing if not conspicuous.

He neared a storefront, its bright lights within bathing the cracked sidewalk. From inside came a voice in Spanish and English over a crackly PA system.

"God has a way for you," said the man's voice, his ragged breathing audible as he must have the mic right on his lips, O'Conner determined.

"Come to the light and up out of the darkness," the voice pleaded.

O'Conner paused at the edge of the storefront. There were people inside, mostly Latino but some whites too, he saw. Several men and women wore cowboy hats or were fanning themselves with them. The gathered sat on metal folding chairs and some had their hands raised and shouted their amens.

The walls were plain white and the worn carpeting industrial. It had been some sort of light color once but had faded to what was best described as aged oatmeal. Up front was a modest panel wood podium with the cross on it. A lay preacher in rolled up shirt sleeves and dark slacks extoled the gathered. Like James Brown in his heyday, he energetically moved back and forth behind the podium, bobbing and weaving as he ducked invisible blows from the Devil. He held a plastic encased mic that you had to press a button on to be heard. This was on a long-coiled cord attached to a portable speaker that had to be at least twenty years out of date. The fuzzy speaker sat on the floor, a few feet from the podium.

"There is only one way," the man said, the mic nearly pressed on his lips, the words virtually incomprehensible. But that didn't matter. What did was the good feelings as more who-zaas and exaltations bubbled forth.

For a moment, O'Conner considered walking in there and taking a seat, putting on the holy roller act. Rocking his upper body back and forth like Ray Charles on the piano. Then afterward, offering a donation to the La Luz de Jesus evangelicals if only they'd safeguard his belongings for a night or so. He smiled wanly and moved on. On the next block was an all-night laundromat. He went inside where there were two women of an older age busy with their wash and a young couple. They didn't seem to pay him any attention and he walked toward the back of the place like he belonged there.

In the tiny passageway, off to one side, was a locked door, and before him a doorway with a security screen on it. Past the security screen was a back area that contained what O'Conner concluded were the husks of junked appliances. He could hide the money in one of those rusted out wonders he weighed, but that meant his cash was too exposed for his tastes. He set the bags down, glancing out into the main room and noting again no one was keying in on him. From his back pocket he took out a folding knife and it didn't take much effort to overcome the cheap lock on the door.

Revealed was a small room with a mop and bucket in it, a tool box, goose neck lamp and a few parts on a shelf, as well as a toilet, apparently not for use by the customers, only the caretaker. It all smelled of mildew. O'Conner looked up, understanding he had little choice. The more he walked on with the bags, the more his chance of getting stopped by the law or some asshole trying to mug him. He closed the door on the room, turning on the gooseneck lamp. A weak warm light glowed, providing adequate illumination. He aimed the light upward. The toilet didn't have a lid, but putting the seat up, as it would slide around, he stood with his feet on the edge of the porcelain bowl. He pushed up the acoustic tiles and put his money inside the false ceiling, straddling the bags across the thin metal framework held in place by wire suspended from the true plaster ceiling. He reserved some bills for tonight. The door locked behind him and he walked out carrying the tool box. The idea being the people in here might have absently noted he'd been carrying something so better to reinforce that idea than be empty handed and possibly fuel curiosity. He ditched the tool box a door front later.

As Ellison's shotgun blast had concentrated on his torso, only a few of the pellets had blistered his forearms. Before entering the laundromat, he'd pushed up what remained of the material of his windbreaker, exposing his bloody trails so as to make the tatters less noticeable. The bloody wounds were mostly dried and as he walked purposefully, the customers hadn't paid him much mind. Could be if a cop showed up and pressed the people in the laundromat for a description, one of them might be forthcoming. But again, he judged the odds to be in his favor. He stopped at a liquor store and bought a plastic pint bottle of off brand vodka and some chips. He left with his black plastic bag of items, eating the chips along the way. At a 7-Eleven, he bought rubbing alcohol, mercurochrome, a USA Today newspaper, a disposable lighter, some cotton balls, and two pre-packaged burritos he microwaved there.

Walking along, he ate one of the burritos and on the advice of the clerk who he'd asked, found the nearby roadside motel. It was called the Cicero Pines. He checked in and, sitting at the tiny round table in the room, had a belt of his vodka. He spread out the newspaper below him on the floor. Then he heated the end of his knife and proceeded to dig the pellets out of his forearms, grimacing and gnashing his teeth but silent as he did so. He would wipe the knife clean with alcohol then repeat heating the blade. Only two pellets were in deep. Each time he took out a shot, he poured some of the rubbing alcohol on the area and dabbled it with mercurochrome to prevent infection. Done, he swept the bloody pellets off the table to join any that had fallen to the newspaper. O'Conner took this into the bathroom and, shaking out the newspaper, flushed the pellets down and away. He then burned the newspaper to ashes in the combo tub and shower so as not to leave any trace of his blood.

Back at the table, using more newspaper, he gathered up the stained cotton balls and crunched that all down into a ball. This he would take with him and not merely dump in the trash here at the motel. The second burrito was cold but edible. He ate that and had more vodka. There was no twenty-four-hour thrift store so he'd have to wait until morning for a change of clothes. He turned on the television but found no news report about the incident. He turned it off and, sitting at the table, sipping the vodka, outlined his next moves.

Taking care of Ellison was a priority, but getting out whole from Fort Worth was primary. Harrington's wife and Culhane were loose ends but he knew that going in. He'd already calculated one or both of them wouldn't be able to extricate themselves from the husband's grasp. But that was their lookout. He'd get the money to the Financier and they'd get their end. Assuming they were still around to collect. What happened afterward, well, thieving was not for the risk adverse as there were no guarantees of winding up in a rocking chair on your front porch. Though he had to admit he wanted to get back to Gwen and their subdivision home.

Before dropping him off, O'Conner having extracted his penalty on Racklin, he'd also gotten from him what he could as to who Ellison might pal or bed with – which wasn't much, though it wasn't his impression the wheelman was holding back. And on the subject of wheels, he ruminated as the cheap vodka burned its way down, he needed some transportation. The car he was going to use was back at the parking lot. It was cold so he wasn't worried about the cops towing it off. But who knew when they might clear out. Plus, if they found the office they'd used, they might leave a patrol car on post just in case one or more brigand wandered back.

He moved the drapes over the window slightly aside and scanned the lot. There were a couple of possibilities out there. He could lie in wait and strongarm whoever showed to drive off in that family van he liked. Probably an errant horny husband who could ill afford to summon the cops, he imagined. But that could be more of a complication than he needed at this time. He regarded what was left of the vodka and screwed the cap back on and set the bottle on the table. He had a slight buzz from the booze but this only heightened the edge O'Conner desired.

Because he assumed to be in and out of Fort Worth, he hadn't done any more advance work than securing the location. The crew had taken care of getting their own cars there. The locale had been obtained through an intermediary, someone who'd come recommended. Ellison had also been recommended, so O'Conner wasn't exactly in a trusting state of mind, but he had to start somewhere. He checked the time and called the go-between on his encrypted phone.

"Understand there was a shit storm," said the woman on the other end after he'd spoken. She had a raspy voice that nonetheless gave her an alluring quality. He only knew her as Kawolski.

"Nobody was caught," O'Conner said, "and it isn't on the news."

"Not yet."

"I don't rat."

"Okay," came her reply after a beat. He'd been vouched for previously. "You want wheels."

"Yes. Now."

"It's going to cost you."

"I'm in no position to complain."

"This is true."

Three hours later he was at the Fam-Ram salvage yard. He'd taken a bus and walked to get there. There were several such establishments in this area. The yard was cast in darkness but there were lights on in a wood and corrugated metal standalone office. Two men were there. One was in jeans, the other in overalls. There was a pit bull on a chain too. The dog sat on its haunches, eyeing the newcomer.

"Hear you need a ride, man," the one in overalls said.

"That's right," O'Conner answered. "Kawolski gave you my name."

"Yeah, so what?" the other one snorted. "That haughty bitch don't run us."

"How about we just do our business, okay?"

"How about you ain't calling the tune, man," overalls said, thumbs hooked in his pockets.

O'Conner kept his anger in check. "The agreed price was twenty thousand for a Hyundai Entourage minivan." An eleven-year-old vehicle, he didn't add. They were robbing him but the plates were solid, he'd been told.

"We're of the mind you got some real money," the other one stared, moving to O'Conner's side. "If you can afford twenty, thirty shouldn't be a problem for a high stepper like yourself." He grinned broadly at his buddy.

"That wasn't the deal."

"Fuck that," the one in jeans said. His bad breath was

laced with marijuana. He pulled a pistol and jabbed it in O'Conner's side.

"Uh-huh," O'Conner said. He whipped around with his knife and slashed the man's arm. Then he grabbed the wrist of the pistol hand and twisted it violently. At the same time, his foot swept behind the other's heel and, leveraging, he had him down on the ground flat, the gun now in his hand.

"You let that dog loose, I'll shoot it first then you," he said to overalls, who held the dog's chain. The dog reared up in its hind legs, barking and snarling at O'Conner.

"Show this motherfucker we is real, Boyd," the one on the ground demanded.

O'Conner stomped him in the face, never letting his eyes off of Boyd and the dog. "Harness that beast," he demanded.

The chain attached to the dog's collar was secured this time, O'Conner making sure overalls padlocked the links in place. He said, "Give me the keys."

"Give me the money."

O'Conner shot him in the foot. "The next one is in your heart." He'd had his fill of backstabbers today. He drove away in the van. Back at the laundromat, he retrieved his goods. He took a nap in the vehicle and not long after dawn, was on the road heading out of Fort Worth.

CHAPTER 3
Last Dance
by Jessica Kaye

Maybe Zach Culhane had seen Urban Cowboy a few times too many. He had heard it called a chick flick but John Travolta's smooth combination of cowboy dancer and lover reminded Zach an awful lot of himself, or, at least, who he wanted to be… who he intended to be. He'd been dancing all his life, growing up in Fort Worth where he and all his friends loved music. Didn't everyone? As they got to middle school and then high school, their ability to keep pace with each other's moves to hip hop or alternative or even classic rock became an integral part of their entertainment.

After high school, he worked a job here, a job there. He didn't have what folks called a career. He had been a dishwasher, worked on an oil rig, clerked in an office and at the local Walmart. There weren't too many jobs he hadn't tried, he figured.

He got by. He didn't get rich and he didn't put much aside for a rainy day but he paid rent and drank all the beer he wanted and still went dancing. A fun and good-looking boy could find ways to pick up a few extra dollars, and he fit the bill.

Along the way, there had been petty larceny, an occasional

burglary. He never resorted to violence, never attempted armed robbery or assault. No one groomed him, no one readied him for a higher level of crime and its higher level of payday, but this was a wealthy town and sometimes good fortune found its way to him. Good fortune was how he found his steady gig.

He was between jobs at the time, spending days at home in front of the computer, binge watching Netflix, or out at the local Starbucks for the air conditioning and an occasional iced coffee. Nights were spent with friends, at each other's homes to watch whatever sport was in season or out for beers. He was broke, not destitute, and a man had to stay social, didn't he?

It was another hot day and he was waiting to order at Starbucks. "Grande iced coffee, room for cream," the man ahead of him said. Zach smiled and said, "Same thing I order." The customer glanced at him, turned back to the clerk, and said, "Make it two." He returned his gaze to Zach and said, "This one's on me."

Zach protested an appropriate number of times before thanking the stranger for his generosity. When the order was ready, it made sense that they would share a table. That was how Zach left the ranks of the unemployed.

Zach started working part time, driving his new boss around when the man didn't want to drive himself and then waiting while the man had his meetings. In time, he learned a few things about business, moving up from lackey to junior apprentice, learning to boost cars for the company chop shop.

He still loved to go dancing. Now that he had a little money, he could go out as often as he pleased. He dressed better, drank better booze. The ladies loved him and he had no trouble finding someone who would gladly take him home or to a hotel room.

The evening he met Gracella at a honky tonk gave him confidence that he was about to score on a par with the best criminal masterminds' greatest exploits. Spending that first night with her was fun, but becoming co-conspirators was even more orgasmic. They became an item, in as clandestine a fashion as was possible given each other's penchant for going out dancing and drinking. They weren't in love but they had a good thing going and they each appreciated it, for some of the same reasons.

It was Gracella who broached the idea first. Zach's surprise was genuine. He had assumed he would have to plant an idea in order to glean the information they needed. What she told him turned his smile into a grin. The payday he had been anticipating was looking like small potatoes compared to the haul Gracella described.

Seven million dollars in unclean money. How serendipitous that her wealthy rancher husband was also the bagman for an illegal slush fund. Even better, these folks used cash, and cash was king, thought Zach, a saying he had heard numerous times on a TV ad for a paycheck cashing service. Even after dividing the spoils among all the participants, that left a pretty good amount of mad money for him. Maybe more than he'd ever expected to see.

Zach kept his eyes on the prize and his mind on the details, but that didn't foreclose daydreams about having big money of his own and the dual scenarios of being offered partnership with his boss or starting his own company, an upscale gray market consulting service. Self-employment had great appeal: no one to report to, having complete control over saying yes or no to new clients, vacations whenever he pleased.

That would be after the gig. For this escapade, he contacted a man who went by the nickname "the Financier." Zach had stolen cars for the Financier's chop shop a few times when his own boss had loaned him out. It was just like the old movie studio system, Zach thought. He knew then that he was a star. From those occasional crossed paths, he also knew the Financier had the contacts to corral a posse with the skills they needed: safecracker, pilot, strongmen. Zach's part was to continue to be Gracella's lover and find out everything he could about the house, the cache, the guards, the works. It was no hardship to be with Gracella. She was easy on the eyes, fun in bed, generous, and a tad unpredictable. That added up to a good time as well as a good payday.

The date was set, everyone had their assignments. Zach didn't even have to be there. His work was done – all but the spending.

He didn't have many possessions. A little furniture, some clothes. Not much else. Sentimentality wasn't his strong suit. He had already given his furniture to St. Vincent de Paul. They'd taken it away in a truck. Who needed that secondhand crap? Traveling light made more sense. He was out the door and away.

That evening after the heist, the plan was for the team to meet at a prearranged location and the money was divvied up. The Financier delivered his share as promised. He told Zach that some of the gang had tried to cut the others out in a burst of unexpected ugliness but O'Conner took care of that bit of bad business, leaving an even larger share for the rest of them. It couldn't be a total surprise when thieves tried to steal from their fellow thieves. The Financier reminded Zach to be careful. This was big money and they had to be smart about their next moves.

Zach had already packed up his belongings and was ready to get the heck out of town. He didn't expect that his involvement in the caper would be traceable either by cops or the victims but he hoped he had found a way to protect himself in case the what-ifs became what-is.

Too bad about the girl. He would have liked the company but he couldn't imagine Gracella going unnoticed. She was too beautiful and too vibrant to escape attention. He hadn't been to very many places but he had heard people say that travel was much better when it is shared with a friend. He thought about calling her one last time to extend the invitation but he had worked on the dark side long enough to know better. Make the move, get the grift, and get gone.

Usually, the get gone part just meant laying low for a while, but this was too big a score. Zach had been a Boy Scout in elementary school. The Boy Scout motto was Be Prepared. He had never forgotten that.

There was no time for even a celebratory drink with his cohorts. They all knew to scatter too. He was going to head north in the car he had bought from his boss. Zach had purchased a few vehicles from him from time to time, when one or another caught his eye. Sometimes cars were more useful unchopped. Sometimes his boss had acquired cars legally. Those were the ones Zach opted for, as long as they met his aesthetic sensibility.

Traffic was light on the road north from Fort Worth. Zach had planned to make his way to Canada. Mexico was closer but it was also a place where he could be found more easily. Too many Texans knew too many Mexicans for him to avoid being spotted, no matter how low a profile he was keeping. The same went for flying. There were names on tickets, passengers had to show ID, and the potential of TSA agents who may have known Harrington added up to the logical conclusion that Zach should leave town by automobile.

He had his passport in the car. He would drive to Detroit because it was close to Toronto. He had figured he could be there in two days if he didn't sleep very much. From there, he would decide whether to cross the border legally, showing his passport, or to finesse his way into Canada. He wondered if the dancing was as much fun there as in Texas.

The big puzzle was how to get that much cash across the border. He needed an accomplice to help and the Financier had made an introduction. He could leave the cash behind in the States in the hands of a recommended aide, who would take a cut in exchange for depositing it in an offshore bank. There wasn't time to do anything else with that much money. He would meet up with his contact in Michigan.

He drove, stopping a few hours later in a barely populated rest area along the highway. He stepped out of the car to use the bathroom. As he walked back to the car, humming to himself, a knock on the back of his head took him down. He looked up, head throbbing and eyes swimming, into the eyes of his boss, who stood alongside a large man Zach didn't recognize.

"Wha..." was all he managed to say before losing consciousness.

The boss motioned to the other man standing nearby. "Let's get him to the ranch," he said. The other man slung Zach over his shoulders and took him to a spotless American four-door sedan with tinted windows. He got into the backseat with Zach, cuffed him behind his back, and then tenderly drew the seatbelt over him.

"That's kind of you," said the boss. "It's the last nice thing

anyone will do for him. He's part of Harrington's herd now."
He looked sympathetically at Zach. "It's too bad," he said. "I
like the kid."

They got the cash out of Zach's car, placing it in their own
sedan. They left Zach's car unlocked and with the keys in
the ignition, all but guaranteeing it would be stolen shortly.
The boss didn't bother to remove the location tracker he
had placed on the underbody of the car. It could be fun now
and again to see where the car's travels took it.

The boss placed a call. "We have him. I'll call you when
we get close."

They drove directly to the Crystal Q and carried the
groaning lad into the hacienda. Harrington had gotten
the second call announcing their impending arrival and
he welcomed them, motioning the team to carry Zach to
the wine cellar. He had them place the young man on a
stool in a corner far from the wine, so as to minimize the
risk to valuable bottles of notable vintages. Zach teetered
precariously from one side to the other, barely conscious.

"Hmmph," Harrington grunted. "I can see why my wife
liked him. He's a nice-looking boy. Maybe a little cleaner
than most of her entertainment. Maybe a little younger
too." He stared at Zach for another long moment. Then he
turned to the other two men. "Where's the cash?"

Neither missed a beat. Zach's boss said, "It wasn't in the
car, sir. We searched it. He must have left it with someone
he trusted before leaving town." The strongman nodded,
backing up the story.

Harrington gave each man another hard look. "You can't
expect me to believe that."

The two didn't change expression. "The money wasn't
there."

Harrington left this issue for another day. He would handle one thing at a time. Let them do his dirty work tonight and let someone else do it to them tomorrow. He nodded at the branding irons stacked in the corner and then gave his orders.

"Fun's over. I've got a party to get dressed for. I'll be back later, but leave him here when you've done your work. You can go back to my chop shop as soon as you're finished here."

"Yes, boss," said Zach's boss, and his henchman reached for the irons, already hot, as Clovis Harrington left the cellar without a backward glance.

CHAPTER 4
The Wife
by Zoë Sharp

Twenty-four Hours Earlier

Gracella arched away from the blade slicing down toward her back. The bite of it jerked at her wrists, then her arms flopped free. She tossed the remains of a severed zip tie and yanked the gag from her mouth. It came away in a ball of spit that she wiped inelegantly with the back of her hand.

"You okay, ma'am?"

A sheriff's deputy crouched in front of her. Although her robe was gaping open his eyes were on her face, a fact which was unusual enough for Gracella to register. The badge on his uniform breast pocket read Martinez, and she realized she knew about him. Married, with twin daughters in first grade, she recalled. Off duty, his tastes ran to the boys in the local biker gangs, and slim-hipped bull riders when the circuit was in town.

She pulled the edges of the robe closer, even so. "Yes... gracias, José."

He smiled, quickly releasing the two other women Gracella had been tied to. Susan Treacher first, then Cassie Warner, as if he recognized the hierarchy.

Gracella rubbed absently at her wrists, inspecting the damage. Clovis would know immediately if it didn't look

70

like she'd been a genuine hostage. But the skin was raw where the plastic ties had bitten in deep. It might even be enough to convince him.

She got shakily to her feet, legs barely able to support her, and went to Lottie Amaya. The maid was still on the chair where the robbers had put her after she'd struggled from the couch. She was clutching her injured leg, her face sheened with the sweat of genuine pain, although Gracella wouldn't put it past her to ham things up a little.

"You were brave to try, Lottie," she said, lifting the melting bag of ice from the woman's ankle. It was swollen and already starting to bruise. She clucked. "But foolish. Look what you did to yourself."

"I'm sorry, Ms. Gracella," Lottie moaned. "It's just, I-I thought maybe they were here to kidnap you, and I couldn't help myself."

Like hell you couldn't.

Gracella straightened, steadier now, put a hand on the woman's shoulder, and managed to murmur, "Thank you, Lottie," with a straight face. She glanced across to where Martinez and one of the other deputies were releasing Traynor. "We heard gunfire, and explosions. Is anybody else hurt?"

After a moment's hesitation, it was Martinez who answered, "'Fraid so, ma'am. They were dropping Molotovs from an airplane, from what we can gather. One of the guys is out cold, and a couple of the others are burned pretty bad."

"Them sons o' bitches," Traynor swore, then flushed. "Beggin' your pardon, ma'am."

Gracella waved a distracted hand in his direction. Her heart rate stepped up. Nobody was supposed to get hurt

– except Clovis, of course. A kick in the bank balance, where it would sting the old bastard the hardest.

"Where's Flora?" Susan Treacher demanded suddenly.

"She was down in the cellar," Lottie piped up. "They seemed real upset about that."

Susan headed for the door, only for one of the deputies to put his hand on her arm. "Best leave it to us, ma'am. Whoever these people are, seems they like to leave little surprises behind. Wouldn't want you finding none."

Susan paled, nodded, and stepped back.

Two of the deputies went out. A tense silence followed their departure and Gracella realized she didn't need to smother her apprehension, even if it was for a very different reason to the others.

If the men her lover contracted had failed to blow the safe, or hadn't gotten away with all the contents, then the whole plan was going to go to shit. And her along with it.

After only a minute or so, the sound of Flora's loud and indignant wailing floated upward, getting louder as the sheriff's men led the maid from the cellar. She entered being supported by deputies on either side, sobbing into the apron she held to her face.

Gracella let Cassie Warner take care of Flora with soothing words and pats and sympathy. There were limits to how familiar she wanted to get with the staff. She'd tried it when she first arrived, unused to servants and more than a little intimidated by the opulent ranch house where she found herself alone most days. Her attempts at friendship made all concerned uncomfortable. And once they'd gotten past that, they started trying to take advantage.

Despite the sleek dark hair, the 40DDs and the sultry black eyes, Gracella had never been anybody's wetback fool.

Martinez touched her arm, his face tight. "Ma'am, there's something I think you should take a look at down there. Will you come with me, please?"

What does he know?

Alarm flashed through her system, manifesting as sudden gooseflesh that broke out along her bare forearms. As she made to follow him, Susan Treacher hustled in. "I'm Ms. Gracella's personal assistant. I should–"

"With respect, ma'am," Martinez cut her off, "this concerns Mrs. Harrington."

"It's Mrs. *Murieta*-Harrington," Susan corrected sharply, bristling. "And can't it wait? Surely you can see she's in shock."

Gracella offered a weak smile. "It's okay, Susan," she murmured. "The deputy is only doing his job."

Martinez led her down into the cellar, which now contained a cocktail of unfamiliar smells – hot metal, oil, burned plastic, and something like tar – overlaying the usual musty scents of old wine bottles and stale air conditioning. No Range Rider beer ever found its way into this rarefied atmosphere. Which was cool with Gracella, because she'd never liked the taste of the stuff anyway.

Halfway down, she hesitated. "Is it safe?"

Martinez almost smiled. "You think I'd be down here if it wasn't?" And she noticed he'd dropped the "ma'am" now they were alone.

At the bottom of the steps he moved aside and indicated the blown safe behind the swing-out door, as if she might miss it.

Gracella hardly had to feign her surprise, but at the damage that had been wrought rather than the safe itself. She took a step closer, gaped convincingly, and turned bewildered, dewing eyes on the deputy. "But... I don't understand. What *is* this?"

"It looks like a hidden strong room," Martinez said. "You didn't know it was here?"

Gracella shook her head. "No, but fine wines are my husband's thing. Clovis is always fussin' around down here. I hardly ever come down." She wrinkled her nose, leaned in conspiratorially. "To be honest with you, I'm a little clumsy, and I guess I'm always kinda afraid of breaking a bottle of somethin' *real* expensive."

The deputy smiled again, a little condescendingly this time, and Gracella finally began to relax. He may not be of the right sexual orientation to want to fuck her, but at least he was beginning to see her as a wide-eyed – and innocent – niña estúpida.

"So you don't know what might have been taken?"

She gave a helpless shrug. "But how could I?"

"Is anything else in the house missing?"

"I don't know. I don't think so. There are other safes I do know about – in my bedroom for my jewelry, of course, and in my husband's study – but nothing like this."

Whatever the deputy might have been about to say next was lost in the sound of commotion from above. Martinez mounted the stairs first, leaving Gracella to admire his tight uniformed butt as she followed.

They emerged into a crowd of ranch hands carrying three injured men into the hallway. The first person Gracella saw through the confusion was her husband. His harsh features were clenched into a scowl that only deepened when he laid eyes on her.

"Clovis! What happened?"

He strode through the men like he was cutting through

cattle, stood over her, looming down. "I was about to ask you that very same question... honey." And from him, the endearment sound like a threat.

"We were robbed! They wore masks and carried guns. Lottie has a busted ankle. It was terrible."

He folded her into his arms, for all the world the loving husband, but his hands on her were hard where they should have been soft, his grip unforgiving.

"I'll get to the bottom of this – you can take that to the bank," he said, his voice rumbling through his chest and into her body. "Nobody fucks with me or my property and gets away with it, y'hear me? *Nobody*."

Gracella knew that as his wife he counted her part of that property. She barely suppressed a shiver.

"Mr. Harrington?"

With a last cruel squeeze, Harrington released her and turned. Gracella recognized a doctor her husband kept on beck and call. Lebermann – a trauma surgeon who favored the roulette wheel a little better than it favored him. He was wearing latex gloves and his hands were bloodied.

"Sir, it's vital the worst of the burns victims is gotten to a hospital. I don't have the equipment here to–"

"Didn't I already tell you no hospitals?" Harrington's tone brooked no argument. "Do what you can. And remember, boy, I'm relyin' on you."

Lebermann swallowed. His shoulders slumped as he scurried away.

Martinez stepped forward. "I appreciate you want to deal with this your own way, Mr. Harrington, but if the man dies..."

Harrington stared him down. "If he does, José, then I'm sure you'll manage to write a real convincing accident report."

Gracella tried to use the distraction to ease out of her husband's reach, but Harrington grabbed her arm with iron fingers.

"Where d'you think you're going, honey?"

"Up to her room." Susan Treacher appeared resolutely by Gracella's shoulder. "The doctor says she's in shock and she needs to rest."

Harrington threw a narrow-eyed glare at Lebermann, hovering in the doorway, and released Gracella with a grunt.

"Okay, but don't think this is over. Later you and I are gonna have a little talk about this here robbery, and you're gonna tell me everything you know..."

A Year Ago

The first punch landed high in the vee under Gracella's ribcage, hard enough to blast the air clean from her lungs. The blow dropped her to her hands and knees on the cowhide rug, roiling from the pain and gasping for breath. Her beaded evening purse was plucked from her arm and tipped out onto the floor in front of her.

The purse held the usual contents – lipstick and powder, pocket book, keys, gum, her compact Smith & Wesson 640, and three condoms. The bare essentials for a night on the town.

She'd been out clubbing downtown and one thing had led to another. It was two a.m. and while she hadn't exactly crept back into the ranch house, she'd hoped her early-rising husband would be asleep in his bed when she did so.

It was a surprise to find him by the lit hearth in the great room, a crystal tumbler of Michter's sour mash whiskey by his elbow, waiting for her. That was nothing to the surprise of when he'd hit her for the first time.

He nudged through the contents of the purse with the caiman-skinned toe of his handmade Tony Lama's. The revolver raised no comment – he'd bought it for her as a wedding gift, after all. But the condoms were something else again.

Something with a purpose that could not be easily excused away.

Gracella had been married to Clovis Harrington for eighteen months at that point, of which only the first three had held any kind of contentment. If it didn't have four legs or dollar signs printed on it, she'd discovered, then her husband tired of it quickly.

But that didn't mean he was prepared to share.

He picked up the three brightly-colored foil packets and fanned them like cards in his leathery hand.

"You had a half dozen of these in here when you went out," he said with a calm that was eerie after his sudden burst of violence. "So, you fuck one guy three times, or three different guys?"

"What do you care?" Gracella threw at him when she had the breath to speak. "And how the hell do you know what was in my purse before I went out? Are you spying on me?"

"With good reason, it seems… *wife*." He grabbed a handful of her hair, twisted her head back to meet his eyes. "I got a dozen classic automobiles in my garage. Just 'cause I don't drive 'em every day don't mean any damn fool can take 'em out for a spin whenever he feels the urge."

"How dare you compare me to a *car*!" Gracella shrieked her outrage.

Harrington gripped harder, discomfort becoming pain. Then his other hand snapped out, striking her across the face hard enough for starbursts to explode behind her eyes. Instant tears blurred her vision.

"Because I *own* you, honey. Body and soul. And because I've got a reputation to maintain." He slapped her again, letting go this time so the weight of it sent her sprawling into the side of the buckskin sofa. "And I won't have nobody laughin' behind my back because my goddamn *wife* will spread her legs for any cockhound comes sniffing."

When he unbuckled his belt, Gracella's first thought was that, finally, he was riled enough to want to fuck her. Then he began to wind the thick leather around his hand and fear pooled in her belly.

She hid it behind a lifted chin and defiant tone, brain working overtime. "Don't you want to know what it was I told that *cockhound* before you accuse me of ruining your fancy reputation?"

"To use your own words, honey, what do I care?" He took a step toward her, intent and merciless.

"Because I made sure the last thing he would do was laugh at you," Gracella said desperately, edging away on her rump.

That made him pause. She grasped the chance offered to her with both hands and appealed to the only thing that really mattered to Clovis Harrington.

His pride.

"I told him you are hung like un toro – a bull – and like to fuck all night until I can barely stand," she tossed at him. "That I am forced to look elsewhere because *you* are too much man for me to handle."

Harrington was utterly still for several seconds, then his arms dropped, allowing the belt to uncoil slowly. He not only cracked a grim smile, but he laughed. A deep belly laugh of genuine amusement.

He picked up the whiskey tumbler and took a sip, savoring

the mingle of flavors that cost over thirty-five hundred dollars a bottle, while Gracella's heart thundered against her breastbone and her swelling face throbbed in suit.

"Honey, if that's the kinda crap you're sellin', you can keep spreading those pretty thighs often as you damn well please," Harrington said. He shook his head. "I never should'a married you, Gracella. I should'a just hired you as my PR."

Twenty-three Hours Earlier

"Fuck. Fuck, fuck, fuckfuckfuck, FUCK!"

Gracella stabbed a thumb on the end call button of her burner phone and redialled yet again. Alone in her private ensuite bathroom, she had been trying to reach Zach Culhane for the past twenty minutes. Ever since she'd escaped her husband's clutches and sought sanctuary upstairs.

Finally, she had to admit the inevitable – that while she'd been aiming to take Culhane for a ride, maybe he'd taken her for one instead.

A part of her even admired him for that. Oh, he would have to suffer, of course, but even so...

Unless something had gone wrong with the getaway. Committing any kind of crime was the easy part, she knew. It was the getting away clean that was the problem. And the bigger the score, the bigger the effort put into making sure that didn't happen.

In this case, it wasn't law enforcement they had to worry about – except the ones who'd sold their soul to Clovis Harrington, or had it stolen and held for ransom by him, like Deputy José Martinez.

No, she knew her husband had other men on call. Men

who frightened her by the lack of pity in their eyes. She had caught glimpses of them coming and going from the ranch in the past, but no more than that. She had not *wanted* to see more.

Gracella bit her lip, indecisive for a moment, weighing up the risk versus the reward.

I have to know.

She hurried to her walk-in closet, dived through the racks of designer gowns right to the back, where disguised in a dry cleaners bag was the same drab black dress, apron, and cap the maids wore. She'd persuaded Cassie Warner to let her "borrow" her spare outfit. In return, Gracella turned a blind eye to the weed the woman smoked when she was supposed to be cleaning.

She stripped and dressed, adding the black hi-tops she wore for her step aerobics classes, and coiling her hair so it was hidden by the cap. She shoved a change of clothes into a bag and took the back stairs to the kitchen, then out to the lot where the staff parked. Harrington liked to keep their compacts, SUVs, and pickups well out of sight of the house. Lord preserve us from any of his high-falutin' guests seeing such inferior stock.

Gracella knew the ranch hand, Traynor, left the keys to his Ford pickup tucked into the sun visor and the doors unlocked, and she reckoned he'd have too much on his plate right now to worry about going anywhere. She took the side road out of the Crystal Q and headed for Fort Worth.

She drove as fast as she dared without getting a ticket, stopping only at a down-at-heels gas station to ask for the key to their restroom. It was unisex and stank, the cracked tile floor sticky with dirt. The faucet ran constantly into the oil-stained sink. For a moment, Gracella stood and stared at her slightly distorted face in the scuffed stainless steel mirror.

If this doesn't work out, I could be wearing these clothes for real. Either that or a shroud...

She changed quickly into jeans and a blouse, and got back on the road. All the way over, she see-sawed between anxiety and anger. It was hard to say which emotion came out on top. By the time she arrived at Zach Culhane's rented house, she was strung so tight she was ready to snap.

There was no response to her hammering on the front door. Peering through the side glass, she saw the living room was now devoid of furniture. Not that Culhane owned much, but even the little he'd had was gone.

Swallowing back the rising nausea, she circled the property, pressing her face to all the windows. The house was completely empty.

As Gracella stepped back onto the front porch, she noticed one of the neighbours – a short black woman who must have weighed in at two hundred fifty pounds – standing by her open screen door, watching her.

"He'p you?" the woman asked in a voice that implied she had no desire whatsoever to do so.

"I was looking for Zach."

"Ain't here no more."

"Yes, so I see. When did he go?"

"First thing. I wuz just turnin' on ma TV for *Jerry Springer* when I heard the U-Haul backin' up to his door."

More in hope than expectation, Gracella asked, "I guess he didn't leave no forwarding address?"

The woman shook her head, looking almost regretful.

"He run out on you, huh?"

"Sure looks that way."

"Ain't it always so. Men! Can't live with 'em, can't kill 'em and bury 'em in the back yard, huh?"

She cackled at her own joke and waddled back inside, letting the screen door bang behind her.

If your back yard is big enough, oh, yes, you can...

Gracella drove back to the Crystal Q on autopilot, her mind revving. By the time she returned Traynor's truck to its space on the rear lot, she was no longer angry, or anxious, but functioning with a coolly logical mind.

Only last month she'd read Sun Tzu's *The Art of War* in eBook form, prepared to tell her husband, if he asked, that it was just some trashy romance. He never asked.

In a battle, she knew the general who managed to follow their original strategy most closely would win, but also that no battle plan survived first contact with the enemy. What mattered was how you adapted to circumstance, used the forces at your disposal, and how decisively you counterattacked.

Well, Zach Culhane was about to find out what kind of a general Gracella would have made.

Back in her bedroom, she changed again into linen pants and blouse, took a last bracing look at the portrait of the multi Marilyn Monroes, then went downstairs. It was too quiet. The injured men were gone from the front room – to where she had no idea and was reluctant to ask – and the house had returned to its stiff normalcy.

But as she crossed the hall, Harrington's voice stopped her in her tracks.

"In here, honey. You didn't think I'd forget about our little chat, now did you?"

The doors to his study were partly open and she could see him slouched behind the huge mahogany desk. Cautiously, she pushed the doors wider and stepped inside.

At once, she saw Harrington was not alone. On the other side of the room sat a guy in his early thirties, pleasant faced and pale eyed. One leg was up on a stool, a bloodied bandage wrapped around his mid-thigh. He was dressed in city clothes, casual but stylish. Gracella did not recognize him.

Not one of our men hurt in the attack. So who is he?

For a moment, the position of his leg reminded her of the maid, Lottie Amaya. Certainly, the guy seemed in as much pain, but it wasn't just physical, she realized. There was a bitter resentment about him too.

Behind the injured man's shoulder stood one of the coldeyed men her husband occasionally had call to use. He was big, wide, muscular, with a military buzz cut. There was a pistol in his right hand, held casually, the way some men might hold a glass or a phone.

A click behind her made Gracella gasp. Another man with the same demeanor had just closed the study doors, and now stood in front of them, blocking her escape. She felt the sweat prickle along her hairline, but managed to turn back to Harrington with one eyebrow raised in calm enquiry.

"I didn't realize we had guests."

"We don't," Harrington said. He indicated the three men with a flick of his fingers. "They were never here."

Gracella said nothing. Harrington regarded her with hooded eyes for a long time, then said abruptly, "What do you know about a thief called O'Conner?"

"Who?"

Her response was automatic. So, it seemed, was that of the man behind her. She never heard him move from his position by the doorway, but the next moment a fist travelling with the size and speed and weight of a small truck hit her in the back, just around her right kidney.

Her legs gave out instantly. The pain was a separate entity, a monster that screeched in her ears and robbed her of sight and breath as it thundered over her in sickening waves.

When she came back to herself, she was slumped on the polished wood floor. Somewhere above her head she heard a tutting sound, realized it came from her husband. She swiveled her eyes – the only part of her body she dared move – and found he'd rounded the desk to crouch in front of her.

"I know you were in on this, honey, and the longer you hold out on telling me what I want to know, the more this man is gonna hurt you. And he can hurt you *real* bad – you can take that to the bank."

Gracella had to moisten her lips before she could whisper a denial.

"Cl-Clovis, please, I don't–"

The man who'd punched her grabbed her arm at the elbow, dug in with cruelly scientific force. Gracella's skin suddenly lit on fire, electric shocks sizzling down the nerve pathways into her hand. She convulsed, screaming.

Harrington continued to watch without emotion. When she subsided again, he said, almost gently, "I know you ain't as stupid as you care to make out, honey. Oh, you play the part well enough, but you think I didn't have you investigated a'fore I married you? Be sensible now, and use that brain I know you got inside that pretty little head."

Wary of saying anything that might induce more agony, Gracella kept silent. It didn't help her. Steel fingers bit into her flesh and she screamed again. Vaguely distant, she heard the man with the bandaged leg protesting, being told to "sit the fuck down."

"Ain't nobody to hear you, honey. I sent the staff home."

Harrington rose, knees creaking, and nodded to the man standing over his wife as she writhed weakly. "Just be sure you don't mark her where it will show," he said. "She'll talk soon enough."

"They all do," the man said without undue conceit – he was simply stating a fact.

And he was right. Gracella held out another couple of minutes, until she prayed for unconsciousness that was never allowed to her, before she caved. She closed her eyes briefly, felt the slide of tears from the corner of her eyes, and gave them what they wanted – Zach Culhane's name.

Six Months Ago

His mistake was thinking he could fuck her, and then fuck her over.

Feigning sleep on the tumbled bed, Gracella watched through slit eyelids as the cowboy stealthily rifled through her purse. She never carried much cash – maybe five hundred for emergencies. If he'd asked, she would have given him what she had in any case. It was chickenfeed, and Lord alone knew the boy had been worth it, but what was his name?

When they got back to her suite, they'd each been in too much of an all-fired rush getting the other naked to bother making introductions, or even closing the drapes. Now, the glittering midnight skyline of Dallas provided enough light for her to admire the cut of his abs as he folded the bills into the pocket of his unbuttoned Levi's.

That same denim molded to his perfectly formed ass when he bent to retrieve the boots and shirt he'd thrown aside. Gracella groaned, managed to turn it into the kind of noise that one satisfied woman might be expected to make in a post-fuck dream. And for once she was only half faking it.

He froze, eyes raking over her. She was still in a face-down sprawl across the king-size bed, head turned toward him, with her right arm under the pillow, her left dangling off the edge of the mattress.

As he came closer, Gracella concentrated on keeping her breathing steady and slow.

But she barely suppressed a flinch when his fingertips touched her hair at the nape of her neck. He let out a sigh as he drew a soft line along bicep and forearm to her exposed wrist. Then those dextrous fingers circled, flicked, and the white gold Cartier Le Dona watch – an anniversary gift from her husband – dropped loose into his waiting paw.

What the fuck? Okay, cowboy, you've had your fun…

Gracella grabbed his hand, twisting her body to yank him off balance and halfway onto the bed. As she did so, her right hand snaked out from under the pillow. In it was her Smith & Wesson revolver, chambered for. 357 Magnum rounds. Right at that moment there were five of the little beauties available at the twitch of her right forefinger.

Since she was eight years old, Gracella had been able to hit a rattlesnake from the back of a moving horse in less than three rounds. Considering she had the front blade sight rammed up hard under his jawbone, she reckoned she'd need just the one.

She'd slipped the gun out of her purse when he'd gone to the bathroom, something about the way he'd gotten out of bed setting her alarm bells ringing.

There was considerate – not wanting to disturb her – and then there was downright sneaky.

Now, he reared back as far as his spine would bend. It

wasn't far enough to escape the prod of the S&W's muzzle. He swallowed, Adam's apple bobbing jerkily in his throat, and spoke past gritted teeth.

"Hey, babe! Ease up, will you?"

"Now why would I wanna go and do a dumb thing like that, huh, cowboy?"

"It's not what it looks like–"

"Oh no, by my guess it's *exactly* what it looks like," she cut in. "Now back off and put the watch on the goddamn table."

He shifted his weight as if to comply, then lunged, knocking her hand away and pinning it to the mattress. She expected he'd either try to wrench the gun from her grasp or make a run for it, but instead he dropped his head and sucked her exposed nipple into his mouth.

The unexpected jolt of pleasure made her breath hitch sharply in her throat. Her back arched of its own accord. When he released her with a last nip of his teeth, he paused a moment, as if expecting her to punch him, or shoot him – or both.

When she did neither, he carefully laid the watch between her breasts like an offering and straightened, reaching into his back pocket for the money.

"Keep it," Gracella said. "You've got some nerve, cowboy, but I like your style."

He grinned and tipped the brim of an imaginary Stetson. "Ma'am."

Raised up on her elbows, she watched him get halfway to the door before she asked, "This how you make your living – rolling bored rich bitches?"

"There are worse ways, babe," he said. "But no, this I do just for fun."

"What else do you do?"

He shrugged. "Whatever will earn me a few bucks."

"Legal? Or 'otherwise'?"

"'Legal' is okay." He grinned again, a flash of white teeth in the gloom. "But 'otherwise' is a whole lot better."

Gracella threw him a sultry look as she threw off the sheets. "Then come back to bed, cowboy. I may just have work for you."

Twelve Hours Earlier

"Gracella, my dear, you look awful. Whatever did those *animals* do to you?"

Gracella lifted her wan cheek for the federal court judge's kiss, aware of the residual pain in her body caused even by so slight a movement. She caught her husband's unyielding gaze from across the great room, holding sway among his political cronies, and gave the judge a fractional smile.

"It was a most unpleasant experience," she said without inflection. "Something you hope will never occur in your own home."

The elderly man followed her sightline and sighed. "Ah. Yes, I'm sure it was," he murmured. He put a gentle hand on her arm. "My dear, I wish there was something I could–"

But Harrington had crossed the distance between them with every appearance of playing the attentive host.

"Judge," he greeted with icy cordiality. "And how's that lovely goddaughter of yours?"

The judge paled and muttered some conventional response. As a warning, Harrington's words came across loud and clear. The girl in question had fallen in with the wrong crowd, hooked into drugs, been tricked into muling for one of the Mexican cartels. Getting her out, and clean, and hushing the whole thing up had taken more money and influence than the judge alone could provide.

He would hardly meet Gracella's eyes as she edged away, trying not to limp. Harrington curved an arm round her ribcage and she went instantly still. He knew where to find every bruise and tender spot under the concealing long gown.

"Goin' somewhere, honey?"

"To my room," she said, voice brittle. "I have a headache – the stress of today's… events, no doubt."

"No doubt," Harrington echoed, his eyes mocking her. "You run along now, and be a good girl."

And those words were a warning too.

She excused herself to their guests and left the great room, with its twenty-four-foot ceiling, flaming fire in the fieldstone hearth, and wagon wheel chandeliers. But as she tottered along the corridors toward the main staircase, Gracella's spine began to stiffen – and not simply from the beating.

With a glance behind her, she slipped off her heels and made her way to the cellar steps. As she descended, noises from the rest of the house faded behind her. Instead, she heard the faint rasp of someone trying to breathe around the pain, a scuffle of cloth against the concrete floor, the clink of metal.

And she became aware of something else too. Something that brought the hairs bolt upright at the back of her neck.

The smell of charred flesh like an outdoor barbecue.

Her mind recoiled even as her feet took her forward. In the far recesses of the cellar, out of reach of her husband's precious wine, slumped a man in bloodied clothing. He didn't move as she approached. Only when she bent to touch his leg did he jerk in reaction, loosing a hoarse cry of protest and drawing his knees up to his chest. Or he tried to. The chain locked around one ankle brought him up short.

"Zach?"

She knelt and tipped his head back, almost wept at what she saw there. Burned into the side of her lover's face was a Q inside a diamond – the same mark branded into every head of cattle on the Crystal Q.

Gracella swore softly and ran her hands down his body. She found numerous other matted, scorched patches where they hadn't even bothered to remove his clothing first before they'd applied the red-hot iron, fusing the fabric into his flesh.

"Zach!" she said again, more urgently this time. "Jesús, cowboy."

His head lifted slowly and he looked at her with glazed eyes. They'd given him something to take the edge off, she realized. Or, more likely, to keep him quiet while the party went on above his head.

"Hey, babe," he slurred. "Sure am a cowboy now, ain't I?"

She sat back, moving slow against the pain stabbing through her own body. Nothing to what he must be enduring, but bad enough, even so.

At last, she said in a small voice, "You were always planning to run out on me, weren't you? I was just another rich bitch to roll."

He hesitated, and that told her all she needed to know.

"Nothing personal, babe."

"S'okay." She shrugged, forgetting, and flinched at the sudden spike through her shoulder. "If I'm honest, I never expected you to do anything different."

Despite the admission, he looked momentarily affronted,

then let out a long, careful breath. "My one chance to make some serious money." He gave a lopsided smile tinged with sadness. "Blow this town and go live like a king down in South America, y'know? Honduras maybe. Shack on the beach. Pretty maid all my own to cook and clean…" His voice drifted away, hazy, then he blinked and dragged his focus back onto her. She could see what the effort cost him. "You know he's gonna kill the both of us, don't you?"

She gave a little nod.

"So run, babe, while you still got the chance." He rolled his head back against the wall, letting his eyes close. "Run fast, and go long."

"Uh-huh. I'm looking at how well that worked out for you."

The same lopsided smile again, the best he could manage. "You're smarter than I ever was, Gracella. If anyone can stay ahead of that old bastard, I'd put my money on you."

She bit back the comment that "his" money had been stolen twice over. Then it was a groan she was biting back as she struggled to her feet and had to grab the nearest wine rack to get her there.

"I've nowhere to run where Clovis wouldn't find me," she said, "so what's the point in running? I'd only die tired."

Three Years Ago

Gracella shoved through the doors to the emergency room at a dead run and skidded to a stop on sequined white cowboy boots. She almost bowled over a junior doctor who was too busy gaping at her sudden appearance to pay attention to his own feet.

"I need help! Please!" she begged, grabbing hold of his

arm with bloodied fingers. He just froze and she glared at him.

The doctor – who must have seen just about everything in his time – was reduced from weary efficiency to tongue-tied stuttering. "B-but you... you're the Range Rider girl!"

Gracella bit back a shriek of frustration, realizing belatedly that she was still in her full promotional outfit. Her attire consisted of the boots, pearl-laden Stetson over wild black curls, a miniscule fringed bikini bra, and suede chaps worn over a diamante G-string that left her ass out in the wind.

"I sure am, honey chil'," she assured him, plastering on the Southern twang her Range Rider contract specified. She was already linking her arm firmly through his and swinging him toward the doors. "Now step right this way."

The sudden chill of the hospital air conditioning had her nipples standing out almost as far as his eyes. As long as she kept her chest thrust out, Gracella knew she could lead him by the cock wherever she needed to.

And right now, she needed him outside.

Out in the windswept night, under the glare of the lights covering the ambulance loading dock, she'd abandoned her car with the driver's door open and the engine still running. The wipers scraped across the now-dry windshield.

And her best friend in the world lay unconscious and broken in the passenger seat, bleeding into the cloth upholstery.

As soon as Gracella yanked the door open and the doctor saw Ashleigh, his big brain finally took over from his little brain. He elbowed Gracella aside and leaned over the girl, checking her vital signs and yelling for assistance.

Everything happened fast after that.

Her part over, Gracella sagged, delayed reaction making

her tremble like a foal in its first thunderstorm. They wrapped a blanket around her shoulders, pushed a vending machine cup of something hot and sweet into her hands.

Later, she recalled only odd images that imprinted almost randomly on her mind. Running figures in ill-fitting surgical scrubs. A gurney with one wheel that skittered on the wet concrete. Sterile wrappings ripped from needles and drips and tubes, and strewn to flutter away into the night. An inflatable bag over Ashleigh's nose and mouth with a nurse squeezing it rhythmically to force air into the girl's unwilling lungs.

One of the hospital staff was asking her questions – Ashleigh's personal details, a number for her parents, whether she had Medicare. Gracella mumbled answers through chattering teeth.

"And can you tell us what happened to your friend? It looks like she's taken quite a fall."

Gracella straightened too quickly and the room lurched around her. "That was no fall! Her bastard of a boyfriend showed up, accusin' Ashleigh of flirtin' when she was only doing the promo work she's paid for, same as me." She jerked a hand dismissively toward her clothing, or lack of it. "Just because the folks at Range Rider dress us up like hookers, that don't mean we behave like 'em. But he kicked her down the damn stairs and kept right on kickin' her."

The woman glanced at her sharply. "Did you call the cops?"

Gracella shook her head. "Didn't have my cell, and if I'd left her there to go get it, the bastard would'a killed her."

The woman hurried away, returning a short while later with two uniformed officers. Gracella repeated her story. They seemed more interested in the event the Range

Rider girls had been attending – and who else might have been there.

One cop moved out of earshot and spoke into his radio. When he returned he murmured something to the other man, who nodded without expression. Then he turned to Gracella again.

"Ma'am, have you been drinking this evening?"

"*What*?" She threw up her hands. "What's that got to do with any damn thing?"

"Just the facts, ma'am. We've gotten reports that your vehicle was seen driving erratically and I smell booze on you. Are you willing to perform a Field Sobriety Test?"

"I work for Range Rider and I just spent the entire evening handing out free beer at some fancy party after the Cowboys game. You think I'm *not* gonna smell of booze?"

But even as she spoke, she recalled the couple of cocktails she'd been persuaded to drink by the vice president of Range Rider as the party wound down, and the glass of champagne. *Or was it two?*

Anxiety manifested as temper. "Of course I was driving *erratically*," she spat. "I'd just watched that bastard Kyle tryin' to kick my best friend to death! How would you expect me to drive after that?"

"Nevertheless, ma'am, if you are *not* willin' to perform the FST, I will be forced to place you under arrest and have the folks here carry out a chemical blood test."

The two cops stepped apart, an automatic move to split her attention. One of them shook loose the cuffs from his belt.

Seriously rattled now, Gracella shot to her feet, the blanket dropping from her shoulders. She *needed* this job to pay her way through school. "Wait a damn minute–"

By the time her immediate boss arrived, with several

other men in tow from the party including the Range Rider VP who'd plied her with drink, she was facedown on the tile floor with her hands cuffed behind her and one cop's knee between her shoulder blades to keep her there. She was cussing long and loud.

They all started arguing over the top of her, indistinguishable harsh voices. She closed her eyes against it all. She knew without being told that bringing the Range Rider brand into disrepute was cause for instant dismissal.

But getting caught on a DUI would mean more stringent penalties. They could even demand she repay everything she'd earned so far this season, and most of it was already long spent...

"Now hold hard," said a loud male voice above her, enough authority in his tone to quell the other men instantly. "Sounds to me like this young lady was on a mission o' mercy, and maybe we should be cuttin' her a little slack."

And before she knew it, she was back on her feet with her hands freed and a silk-soft tuxedo jacket draped around her shivering shoulders.

The voice, and the jacket, belonged to a tall, lean man with the tan of the great outdoors and the watchful eyes of an oldtime lawman. She vaguely remembered him from the party. He was quite a bit older than Gracella, but expensively dressed and still attractive. And clearly, he had power – enough power to hold others to his command – which was his most attractive feature of all.

Within ten minutes she was gliding through night-time Dallas in the back of his stretch Lincoln, all charges dropped. He made calls to the hospital on his cell, bullied his way through the bureaucracy to find out Ashleigh's condition. She was stable, her parents already on their way down from

Tulsa. Alongside him, Gracella sat in what she recognized later was a star struck daze.

When they arrived at her hotel and the driver held open the rear door, Gracella at last remembered her manners. "I'm truly grateful for everything you've done tonight, sir. How can I ever thank you?"

"By havin' dinner with me tomorrow evenin', honey," he said smoothly. "I'll send the limo to pick you up."

He seemed to take her silence as acceptance, and in her naivety she mistook arrogance for sophistication.

She climbed out, paused, and glanced back into the limo. "I don't even know your name."

"My name is Harrington – Clovis Harrington."

Six weeks later he proposed, and Gracella thought she'd reached the end of her troubles.

Instead, they were just beginning.

It wasn't until six months after she married him that she discovered who'd tipped the police to her possible drunk driving that evening. By that time, no act of petty cruelty seemed beyond her husband.

Thirty Minutes Earlier

Clovis Harrington leaned against the rear wheelarch of the Chevy Silverado dually pickup, watching Traynor operate the backhoe. They were way out on one of the more deserted stretches of Crystal Q land, well beyond sight of any habitation.

It was early morning, the sun only just beginning to clear the far hills and chase the chill out of the air. Harrington sipped hot coffee from an insulated travel cup while he watched his foreman work. Traynor was good with the backhoe, manipulating the articulated arm and bucket with a smooth precision that belied the misgivings he'd voiced about the purpose of the exercise.

They'd hauled the excavator on a flatbed trailer towed behind the dually, driving out from the homestead into the predawn darkness to the same GPS coordinates Harrington had cause to use a time or two in the past.

No doubt he would have cause to use 'em again.

Or maybe his wife should take an overdose in her own bedroom? He pondered over this as the hole Traynor was digging grew in size. Being able to show a body might cause fewer questions – especially when he had a tame doc and the local sheriff's department on a short leash.

Anyway, it was high time he traded in his wife for a newer model.

The noise of the backhoe meant the two men didn't hear the approaching Bell 407GX until the downwash from the main rotor began to flatten the shrub around them, gusting grit into Harrington's eyes and threatening to blow the tools and tarp right out of the back of the dually.

The helicopter circled once and set down about fifty yards away. It carried the livery of the sheriff's department. Harrington thought he recognized Deputy José Martinez in the co-pilot's seat and relaxed enough to lift a hand in greeting.

He glanced at Traynor. The damn fool had shut off the backhoe and frozen, halfway out of the cab, a miserable and downright *guilty* look on his face. Harrington glared until the man slumped back into the seat.

Martinez was out of the helo now and striding toward them as the rotor slowly spun down behind him. *So, this ain't no flyin' visit*, Harrington realized, and almost cracked a smile at his own pun.

"Mornin', deputy," he called into the unexpected quiet. "What can I do for you?"

"Mr Harrington," Martinez returned gravely. "Can I ask what it is y'all are doin' here, sir?"

"My land, son. My business." But seeing the set of the other man's jaw, Harrington added, "Matter of fact, we're diggin' a coupla new wells. Cattle gotta have water."

Martinez didn't reply to that, just walked past. Before Harrington could protest, the deputy had put a boot on the dually's outer wheel and hoisted himself up into the pickup bed. He bent and lifted a corner of the tarp with the caution of a man who already knew what he was going to find.

From a ruined face, Zach Culhane's lifeless eyes stared back at him.

Martinez switched his gaze to Harrington, who met it with a cool disregard, and emptied the dregs of his coffee out into the dirt.

"Fuckin' my wife was one thing, but then he had to go fuck with me," he said calmly. "And *that*, son, is never a good idea."

Martinez nodded, like he got the warning for what it was. He dropped the edge of the tarp and climbed out of the pickup bed. Harrington opened his mouth to tell Traynor to get back to work but the deputy forestalled him.

"Sir, I'm afraid I'm gonna have to place you under arrest for the murder of Zachary Elmore Culhane," he said, shaking the cuffs loose from his belt. "You have the right to remain silent."

"What the *fuck* d'you think you're doin' son?"

"Anything you say can and will be used against you in a court of law."

"You gone crazy? I *own* you, boy. You're makin' the biggest mistake of your goddamn life!"

"You have the right to an attorney. If you cannot afford an attorney, one will be appointed for you."

"You're finished! I will fuckin' *finish* you for this!"

"Do you understand these rights, sir?"

"'Course I understand my damn rights. You think I'm some goddamn wetback can't speak English?"

Martinez countered that with a bland stare but his hands were less than gentle as they cinched the steel bracelets tight around Harrington's wrists, his hands in front of him. For the first time, a sense of unease scuttered through Harrington's chest. He swallowed, tamped down his anger, and thought fast.

"Listen, son, the guy was havin' an affair with my wife. I reckon he tried to break it off and she musta killed him in some kinda jealous rage. Maybe it was an accident," he offered in a reasonable, placatory tone. "Anyhow, he was already dead when we found him. I was tryin' to protect my wife. I admit it was the wrong thing to do, but I guess I just wasn't thinkin' straight."

Martinez didn't reply to that either, just turned and waved toward the helicopter.

One of the rear doors swung open and a man jumped down with a bulky bag on a strap over his shoulder. Even though the Bell's rotor was barely moving now, the man jogged forward with his head instinctively ducked, so it wasn't until he got closer that Harrington realized with a jolt it was that little rat, Lebermann. The unease swelled into a sharp pain in the vicinity of Harrington's breastbone. His heart began punching like a fist.

"Doc, if you'd be so kind?" Martinez said.

Lebermann avoided Harrington's eye as he scrambled clumsily into the pickup bed. He pulled on a pair of surgical gloves before making a brief examination of the body. Then the doctor produced a fancy camera from the bag and took photographs from all angles, like some goddamn CSI on the TV. The only noise was the whine of the flashgun recharging between shots.

"This man has been tortured and then shot," he announced when he was done.

Harrington had to force himself not to jeer. He cleared his throat.

"My wife has a gun – a Smith & Wesson. 357. Gave it to her myself."

Martinez asked, "And tell me, sir, does your wife also own a branding iron?"

Harrington did not respond.

Lebermann reached into the bag again, this time for a sheaf of papers with photographs clipped to the pages. The topmost one, Harrington saw, was a close-up of a woman's torso, covered in bruises.

"It's my professional opinion that Mrs. Murieta-Harrington is in no state to have tortured anyone," he said meaningfully. "Indeed, she has been the victim of considerable physical assault herself. It's all right here in my report."

Martinez took the papers with a nod. From the way he didn't even glance at them, Harrington gathered he already knew what they had to say. A cold fear washed down over him.

"What do you want?"

Martinez shook his head. "I ain't the one you need to negotiate with, sir."

The rear door of the helo opened again and two more

people got out. A man and a woman, neither of whom moved easily. This time, Harrington recognized them by their gait alone.

Gracella, leaning on the arm of the federal court judge.

When they neared, he said, "Shoulda known you'd be behind this, honey – you scheming bitch."

"Gracella."

"What the – ?"

"It's *Gracella*. Not honey. Not wife. My *name* is Gracella."

Harrington took a breath to lambast her, until the judge said mildly, "You might want to hold off on expressing any colorful opinions, Mr. Harrington, till you've learned what this lady has in mind."

Harrington grunted.

The judge gave a small smile and withdrew from the inside pocket of his jacket a legal document – Harrington had seen enough to know one instantly. The judge unfolded it and held it up for him to read.

"Divorce papers?" He scanned further down out of ingrained habit, waiting for the catch, but saw nothing outrageous or out of the ordinary.

"Divorce papers," Gracella agreed. "Sign them, and this all goes away."

"You signed a pre-nup," Harrington said, baffled. "You won't get a cent."

"All I want from you is my freedom."

He glanced at Martinez, who offered him a pen without uncuffing his hands. Harrington hesitated a moment, then shrugged and scrawled his signature, letting the pen drop in the dirt when he was done.

He glared at the men surrounding him. "And what do *you* bastards want?"

"From you? Nothing," Martinez said. "Just bear in mind we have all the evidence of what you've done here safely tucked away, and there ain't no statute of limitations on murder."

"As this crime was carried out in retaliation for the robbery at the Crystal Q yesterday, it becomes capital murder," the judge said, "which, as I'm sure you're aware, carries the death penalty here in the great state of Texas."

"And in case you were thinking in terms of a little *more* retaliation, Mrs. Murieta-Harrington has already returned to us certain, um, incriminating evidence," Lebermann said.

Harrington's gaze shot to his soon-to-be ex-wife. She stared right back at him, coolly defiant.

"Looks like you fell real lucky, hon – *Gracella*."

"Luck?" she queried. "Oh, no. Luck had nothing to do with it." She laughed out loud at the consternation in his face, leaned in close enough to kiss – or bite. "You followed the plan I laid out, *honey* – every step of the way."

Harrington's eyes widened and slid involuntarily to the body in the pickup. "But–"

"Yeah, you got it," Gracella said. "If I hadn't thrown you a sacrificial goat, well, we wouldn't be here now, would we?" She glanced at the body, and the trace of sadness in her face was chased away by the fierce note in her voice. "And when it comes to betrayal, well, Zach damn well started it."

Six Hours Earlier

The gathering at the homestead was long over when Susan Treacher showed Deputy Martinez into the living room and closed the doors behind him. He paused uncertainly just inside, his hat in his hands, and nodded cautiously to the three people already present.

"Your Honor. Doc. Mrs. Murieta-Harrington." He focused on Gracella. "What's this about, ma'am?"

Gracella rose, something she achieved only by levering up on the arm of the chair, devoid of her usual grace.

"If I had balls, my husband would have me by them," she said flatly. "Just as he's gotten you all by yours."

She waited for denials. None came.

"I take it, then, that you wouldn't exactly be averse to finding a way out of his... grip?"

Martinez glanced at the others and saw a kind of desperate hope reflected in their eyes. He cleared his throat.

"What did you have in mind?"

Now

As the Bell lifted off, the judge leaned forward in his seat and gave Gracella a worried frown.

"Will you be able to manage, my dear? Under the circumstances, I've no doubt the pre-nup agreement could have been broken."

Gracella shook her head. "I meant what I said – all I want is my freedom."

Martinez twisted in his seat and looked back at her. He was smiling. "Where to, Ms. Gracella?"

"The homestead," she said. She flashed the judge a sheepish look. "Okay, there's one thing I need to pick up there before I leave – of sentimental value."

The portrait of the Marilyn Monroes from her bedroom wall. Oh, she liked the painting well enough, but tucked behind the frame was a memory stick containing a great deal of fascinating information on the members of the North Texas Citizens Improvement League.

She leaned back in her seat and watched the acres of the Crystal Q blur past beneath them. With the sun coming up like this the ranch really did look quite beautiful, but she wouldn't miss it for a moment. She had something far prettier – the dirt on a whole bunch of very influential people.

And the brains to use it.

CHAPTER 5
The Financier
by David Corbett

As the twin-engine Cessna banked toward the Clyde River airstrip, he looked out the weather-scarred window across Davis Strait and saw, looming beyond Baffin Bay over the coast of Greenland, a phenomenon resembling a sky-high wall of rolling smoke.

The pilot – a short-haired, cinnamon-freckled blonde named Rachel, ex-RCAF, proud owner of a malamute named Amos, don't get her started – followed the direction of his gaze and shouted over the engine, "Looks like you could get socked in here for a few days."

He feigned unconcern. "Not a problem. Time's not the issue."

I came all this distance to vanish, he thought. How could a blizzard not help?

With Zach Culhane no doubt dead or nearly so, squeezed of all relevant information concerning the disaster at the Crystal Q – specifically, who else was involved – there was no rush whatsoever in returning to so-called normal life.

Though Culhane didn't know enough to put his finger on a map and say, "You can find him there," and he had no actual name to attach to the moniker "the Financier," the truth remained that no escape plan was perfect, no firewall impregnable, no alias inscrutable.

An arctic snowstorm? Bring it on.

He reached in his pocket for his itinerary, issued to the blandly named Carl Russell. He'd not been foolish enough to try to finagle a phony passport on short notice and wanted to kick himself for not planning ahead with a bit more foresight – or paranoia. That said, in an era of international terror, acquiring false passports that could withstand even routine scrutiny required contacts far above the pay grade of even his most sophisticated criminal associates.

Instead, he'd walked the Rainbow Bridge at Niagara, using his own passport at the checkpoint and telling the customs inspector he was meeting friends for dinner at the Sheraton on the Falls. Then he slipped into a waiting car parked at the casino – courtesy of a hedge fund associate who'd asked no questions – found a counterfeit Ontario driver's license in the glovebox, and, for all intents and purposes, vanished into thin air.

First stop, Ottawa, where the freshly incarnated Carl Russell, using cash, purchased the clothes and other gear he'd need for this excursion, then hopped on a flight for Iqaluit in the territory of Nunavut, where he caught his connection with the malamute-besotted Rachel and headed for the opposite end of Baffin Island.

He'd never been one for bucket lists, but after watching Iditarod coverage on ESPN, he'd developed an itch to hop on a dog sled with a team of huskies and head off into the icy nowhere. Turned out traveling all the way to Anchorage wasn't necessary – the east coast was equally, amenably frigid. And, more to the point, remote.

His destination, lying along the fabled Northwest Passage, lay closer to the Arctic circle than Alaska's North Slope, and even with the onset of spring and the ravages of global warming, snow lay heavy on the ground into May.

And judging from the front he could see moving west from the Cessna's cockpit, more was on the way. A man might very well get lost in it.

An Inuit guide from the trek outfit greeted him on the landing strip, just outside the corrugated Quonset hut that passed for a terminal. He was small, leather-skinned, with a windblown mop of wiry black hair atop a baked apple of a face, creased with a tobacco-stained smile. He wore seal-skin pants, seal-skin boots, and a flimsy wool pullover.

"I am Miki," he said in vaguely accented English, offering a thickly callused hand and nodding eastward toward the oncoming storm. "I am sorry, but I think we will not start out tomorrow. Maybe day after, or day after that."

"That's what I gathered. Not a problem on my end."

"The lodge will charge you for the extra nights."

"Again, not a problem."

"And you will probably have to share a room with one of the hunters."

A sudden pinprick somewhere along his spine. "Beg your pardon?"

"They will head south when we head north. But no one goes out till the storm goes by."

A shared room. With an unknown hunter, which meant a gun of some sort, possibly a knife. Not the plan.

"Is there nowhere else, someplace I could get a room of my own?"

Miki offered a wincing smile and shook his head. "Only one hotel. I am sorry."

Complain too much or too loud, he thought, you'll only draw attention. Make an enemy.

Miki pointed west, suggesting they head off, and once

each man had grabbed a duffel they marched with crunching footsteps toward the scramble of low-slung pre-fab houses that made up the town, each seemingly nailed in place by a twenty-foot TV antenna. Here and there he spotted a wood-plank rack for stretching sealskins, or a husky, beautifully furred with its mask-like face and haunting blue eyes, chained in place on a ten-foot snow drift, its home.

The lodge was a one-story structure of long pinewood hallways and small tan rooms, but a great stone fireplace anchored one end of the lobby, and welcoming flames crackled within the hearth.

A half-dozen men, Americans from the look of them, sat around the fireplace apron, slumped in low leather chairs and sharing a fifth of something brown. The hunters, he supposed.

One of them got up and ambled over, bringing with him the bottle and an empty glass. He had a wind-burned face, rough blond hair, and several days' stubble.

"Welcome to the middle of Bumfuck." He held up the bottle. On closer inspection: bourbon. Wild Turkey. "Dry as a nun's cunt up here. Wanna drink, gotta bring your own. Where y'all call home?"

Neck hairs bristled at the sound of that accent. Texas. Could that really be mere coincidence?

"Ottawa." A brisk handshake. "Ontario, specifically."

"Come up to hunt?"

"No, no. I'll be sledding up the coast toward Eglington Fjord." Inwardly, he chastised himself: Don't talk so much, broadcast your plans. "Just see the sites. Take some pictures."

"Pictures. Huh. Well, we've been out just one day, but already bagged two caribou and tagged a few wolves too, just to scare the others off. Fucking scavengers. But that's not what we came up for. Spring hunt's begun. Polar bear. Then this damn storm."

"Yes. I hear we'll be doubling up. In the rooms, I mean."

Finally, the man poured some of the whiskey, and offered the glass. "Yeah, we all got bunkmates now. Like good little scouts. Pain, ain't it?"

When he reached his room, one of the two narrow beds already lay cluttered with gear. No signs of any weapons, which only begged the question: Were they hidden? Stored elsewhere?

He told himself not to overreact, but there lay the problem, he'd never had to react at all before. The crime had always taken place so far away, the risk an abstraction, so remote as to be negligible. Now? Several men already had died, and they were mere prelude. Clovis Harrington would not stop until every man, woman, and child who'd dared to cross him learned that insolence had a price. And the price would be paid.

But how could that mean he somehow knew about this spot, this trip? Was he really so all-knowing – or capable of near instant phone, internet, personal surveillance?

Maybe that wasn't the issue. What if Culhane let slip information before the heist went south? He was definitely stupid and careless enough. What if inquiries into who else was involved were already being made? If that were the case, it wouldn't take much for a man like Clovis Harrington to assemble a group of killers, kit them out as hunters, and send them at a moment's notice to the frozen edge of the continent.

Or was that just the paranoia talking?

It did seem a bit drastic, even a special kind of madness, to think such a thing, and yet that was exactly what Harrington would do if given the chance. Send men to collect him, truss him up, bring him back like bagged game. Or maybe they'd drag him out onto the snowpack, gut him, field dress him like a buck, then take a snapshot for Harrington's trophy wall.

He studied his absent, nameless roommate's gear, looking for some clear sign of evil or innocent intent. Snow gear, a knapsack, goggles. The fear began to roll in waves, he felt a need to vomit, trembling so bad neither hand could restrain the other. Like the phony you are, he thought. The money man.

A knock came at the door. It creaked open. The baked apple face appeared. "We need to go to the market," Miki said. "To get food. Before, you know, the storm."

The wind had picked up, whipping between the houses and the smoke-blackened snowdrifts. The market lay only three blocks away, but with the ice that had formed beneath the snow the walk felt like climbing a hill of powdered glass.

Once there, he found the shelves stocked with nothing but canned goods – Spam, ravioli, kippers, chili. No liquor, or even beer or wine – alcoholism, he thought, no doubt a plague up here, and he remembered what the Texan had said, they'd brought their own. From wherever.

He bought food enough to last two days, in case the storm lasted. Miki said they'd restock before hitting the sled and heading out. That prospect, a future, if only a day or two ahead, heartened him. There still was a plan.

Back at the lodge, he opened one of the cans of chili and dug in with a spoon borrowed from the pantry, eating it cold, chasing it down with tap water as he switched back and forth between the two TV channels available, both so uninteresting the boredom could have served as a narcotic if not for his banjo nerves.

As he was spooning out the last slithery beans from the can, his bunkmate appeared: one of the hunters – heavyset, almost soft compared to the others, wheezing from lack of breath and eyes in a perpetual, baffled squint. He staggered, clearly drunk, and wordlessly swept his gear to the floor, then collapsed facedown on the bed.

He lay like that, not moving, for hours.

As night progressed, the wind intensified, battering the lodge with howling gusts. Sleep was impossible, so he gathered his coat and went outside.

Three of the hunters stood there in shirtsleeves braving the storm, laughing against the wind, knee-deep in newly drifted snow. They gestured him over, offered some more bourbon, straight from the bottle this time.

How easy, he thought, to die out here – a snapped neck, or pushed facedown into the snow, suffocated. Blame it on exposure. How far were they from the nearest police station, clinic, jail?

Unable to bring himself to accept the bottle, he instead gestured feebly he was going back in. They stared for a moment, as though trying to weigh this lack of grace, then nodded to each other and turned back to the whirling sheets of snow, like drunken sailors on the deck of a pitching icebreaker.

Back in the room, the chubby roommate lay exactly in the same position, like a tuna ready for flailing, still fully dressed, down to the boots, but snoring now. A ruse? Was he simply waiting for this weakling, this tourist, this phony Canadian – the target – to fall asleep, the better to beat him or gut him or strangle him where he lay?

Texas. Christ. Of all the places on earth...

He sat up in bed all night, listening to every rattle and shudder as the wind and snow hammered the roof and outer walls, watching the man across the room, studying his every twitch as he lay there, a shadow in the darkness.

Come noon the next day the storm had yet to lift, but its force was clearly spent. He found himself excruciatingly anxious to leave, his lack of sleep not helping. Walls seemed to sigh as he passed, the floors bucked under his feet as though trying to shake him off.

At one point the stubble-faced, wind-burned Texan sidled up and once again tried to kick-start a conversation. Luckily the door to the room was only a few steps away, and thus easy to back toward, with an agreeable expression in response to whatever it was the man was saying.

Reaching behind, he collected the doorknob, tried to turn it – locked, of course. I'm acting like a coed getting cornered at a party, he thought. He was searching his pocket, trying to dig out his room key, when the door opened suddenly behind him.

He nearly tumbled backward into the room.

It was the roommate. "Thought I heard somebody out here." His voice was a mumble dragged out of his chest. An awkward exchange of nods all around. Then he stepped back, an invitation to enter, and shortly the door closed again, just the two of them. Roomies. Alone.

It took a moment before he noticed the pistol on the bed. Was it too late to turn around and get out? Was the first man, the blond, still outside, guarding the door, making sure no one interrupted whatever was coming next?

The fleshy roommate picked up the weapon, plopped down on the bed, and glanced up sheepishly.

"I wonder if you could do me a favor." He held the pistol like a paperweight. "I wasn't expecting the extra nights up here, the hotel, lodge, whatever the fuck you call this place. I didn't bring enough cash. Don't know why I bought this thing in Montreal, not like I needed it to hunt, but I did, buy it I mean, and now I could use the money back. I know it's a lot to ask – Christ, I don't even know your name – but I was wondering…"

He held the pistol out – a. 38 from the looks of it, revolver.

"Why not sell it to your friends?"

"They're not my friends." The man swallowed. "And I look like enough of an asshole to them already. Seriously, I'll let it go for a hundred. Cost me more than twice that."

The offer felt beyond strange. So now I'd have a gun, he thought, I'd be armed. And all I'd need to do is pull it out, no matter how innocently, maybe even because I was asked – and then someone, anyone could claim I'd drawn on them. I was a threat. Killing me would be self-defense.

"I don't really need it for where I'm going. What I came up here for."

"I'm not asking you to use it. I'm asking you to buy it."

The man's soft face seemed even less forbidding from humiliation, the bloodshot eyes his most noteworthy feature. He really didn't fit with the others. And what to make of that?

"I'll tell you what. Give me the pistol and whatever ammunition you have, I'll pay for your half of the room. Last night and tonight both."

The man tried to smile. "Could you front me a little cash as well? I'm sorry, I sound like a whiny little bitch, I don't mean to beg, but…"

"Sure." He took out his wallet, counted out forty Canadian dollars, the bills colorful and crisp and blazoned with faces that meant nothing to him, handed them over. "That do?"

The man couldn't meet his eyes, just folded the money over quickly, shoved it in his pocket. "Yeah. Thanks. I really appreciate it. I mean that."

By mid-afternoon the snow had stopped, the wind had died. A two-engine Kodiak bearing the RCMP insignia – that distinctive heraldic badge, the crown, the bison head, the garland of maple leaves, Maintiens Le Droit – flew in from the southwest, landing as twilight gathered.

So that was the plan, he thought. Sell me an illegal weapon, God only knows where it came from, how it was used, for what, then snitch me off. How could I be so stupid?

As nonchalantly as possible, he went to the lodge's front desk and inquired of the clerk standing there, "Any idea what the Mounties are coming for?"

The clerk, a tiny, round-faced Inuit woman in an oversized red-and-blue Canadiens hoodie, shrugged. "Just one Mountie. The others are lawyers, a judge. They come once a month. Have court."

He'd heard about this – prosecutors and defense counsel fly in with a bailiff to hear whatever cases are pending, drunk and disorderly beefs mostly, the occasional assault or theft. Once in a while, a murder. If need be, they heard civil cases as well, minor stuff. That can't be all there is to it, he thought, still wondering if or how the gun played into the situation.

On top of which: more bodies. Where would they sleep, he wondered.

The matter resolved itself with the hunters packing up as night fell and heading south in darkness toward their initial campground. So the lumpy roommate won't be around to drop the dime, he thought, tell the Mountie and prosecutor I have a loaded pistol.

He almost relaxed.

For reconnaissance purposes, he chatted them up as they signed in at the desk.

The Mountie was in his sixties, lantern-jawed, taciturn, fit as a lumberjack, his hair close-cropped and white.

The prosecutor, a birdlike, bespectacled man in a long fur coat, coughed nonstop into a phlegm-spattered kerchief.

The other lawyer, an aide juridique, the equivalent of a public defender, was a shambling, middle-aged woman in a fur-collared snow jacket, her hair pushed up clumsily beneath a wool watch cap, the renegade strands giving her an air of mindless distraction.

The last member of the party appeared to be something of a tagalong. Her name was Adelaide Cote, attractive, mid-twenties, barely five feet tall, even in boots, with porcelain skin and opalescent green eyes, her hair a short brown bob.

"I'm here to help out, if need be," she said, nodding toward the distracted defense attorney, her supervisor. "Though it all seems pretty straightforward, and the docket's hardly jam-packed."

Exactly, he thought. There's no real reason for you to

be here, his paranoia still simmering just below the surface despite the departure of the Texans.

The simmer reached a full boil a short time later when Miki, his Inuit guide, knocked on his door.

"Would you mind," he said, his breath smelling of tinned fish, "if someone joined us on the trip to Eglington Fjord?"

Mind? Fucking right I'd mind. "Who, exactly?"

"The young lawyer who came up today. For court."

He felt a trembling sensation in his arms – lack of sleep again. And fear.

"Why isn't she staying behind with the others? Going back once they're done?"

"I didn't ask. She just wondered, is it possible. If she pays, we don't refuse. As easy to take two as one."

Of course. How rude and unfair and thoughtless could this snotty rich American be, forcing Miki and his partner to turn down the money?

"Can I think about it?"

Miki simply stared with a dull, practiced smile, not even bothering to shrug.

Alone in his room, he loaded the pistol, making sure extra bullets were readily at hand in his pocket. Just tell them you've changed your mind, he thought. You'll pay but stay behind, let the lawyer, Adelaide, if that was really her name, go on alone. Feign illness if need be, a sudden bad back from a slip on the ice, arse over tea kettle as they so colorfully say.

Oh, stop your sniveling, he thought. It's simply beyond the realm of possibilities that this woman has any connection to

Harrington. The Texans, yes, fear was at least understandable, if a reach. But how could Harrington identify and locate a lawyer in the French legal assistance program capable of insinuating herself into a team due to come up here at just the right time, not to mention recruit her as an assassin? It was insane. And that just underscored how out of his depth he was, always had been, flirting with crime.

Midlife crisis? Shorthand for juvenile, reckless, and stupid. The idea it would never come back on him, let alone this hard, seemed such a blatant miscalculation he felt his insides boiling with shame. The continuing hangover from his lack of sleep didn't help – a dull current of tension jagged continuously along every nerve in his body. He needed to rest, needed to think, needed to calm down.

God, how I could use a drink.

Again, sleep failed him. Once, as he almost drifted off, his heart began to thrash so erratically inside his ribcage he thought he was having a seizure of some kind, even a coronary, and he couldn't draw a breath for what felt like several minutes. The onset of death. Or simply a panic attack – what if you have one out there, on the ice, middle of nowhere? They'll leave you to die. Harrington's desire for revenge will prove irrelevant. You'll do the job yourself by being such a blubbering coward.

He hadn't felt this helpless against his terror since the very first job, before O'Conner entered his life. A Russian client, one of those extravagantly charismatic wildings with a thundering voice and a crushing handshake and the inescapable whiff of corruption – Murat Nazarov, his name – had suggested fronting a casino scheme. His connections in St. Petersburg had reverse-engineered some of the older machines still in use across the U.S., identifying their algorithms. The operatives would play the slots, hold a cell phone to the tumbler to display the cycle to a scanner in Russia, and once the proper algorithm was identified, a signal would be sent to the phone when it was time to hit the spin button. In a single hour, working several machines in succession, a man could turn a sixty-dollar play into winnings of over twenty thousand dollars. Multiply the number of men to five, extend their play to several hours, you were clearing a million a day, undetected.

Of course, in time, it all fell through. The gang of Russians working the casino floors got rounded up. To their credit, though, they held their mud, lawyered up, ponied up bail, then fled the country. This coincided with six straight weeks of insomnia. He'd never felt so scared.

It should have taught him a lesson, and would have if not for his introduction to O'Conner. The man had a certain kind of power, a reassuring calm and simplicity that let you know it's okay. The bases are covered. I'm thorough and smart and disciplined.

And that's how it had been for the length of their partnership. Until now. For all he knew, O'Conner was dead – how was that for simple and powerful? And if O'Conner could be eliminated...

It took over an hour, but his heart settled down, his breathing went from labored to ragged to fitfully steady. He closed his eyes and waited for the sound of footsteps in the hall, a signal that day had begun, even though darkness would linger for several more hours given the latitude. He would rise from bed and pretend he was ready to go. He would do nothing to arouse suspicion. He would watch everyone with excruciating care.

* * *

Miki's sidekick was a seemingly ancient Inuit named Anik who spoke no English. He laid out the traces for the dogs, ten in all, while Miki loaded gear onto the sled and a snowmobile they called a Skidoo: tents, sleeping bags, fishing rods, waterproof mats, a hotplate with butane tanks, food – human, mostly. The dogs would not get fed every day–"Slow them down," Miki explained – and when they did eat, they'd get strictly protein, seal meat and fish.

For their part, the dogs took in all the activity with languid indifference, looking on while sitting or lying in the freshly drifted snow, blinking against the first real sunlight in days.

Adelaide got kitted out in sealskin – a hooded coat, short-legged britches, knee-high boots, all with the luxurious fur outside, not against the skin. The stiffness of the underlying hide made her arms stick out at doll-like angles. She did a pirouette in the icy air, her breath an immaculate cloud, then danced over, childlike in her happiness.

"I really, really want to thank you for allowing me to come along. I've dreamed of this since I was a little girl in Montreal. We went to the jail last night and found out all but one of the defendants wanted to plead out, which pretty much meant I was free."

She shivered with delight – or so it seemed, hard to know with the biting cold – her smile every bit as radiant as the sun overhead.

"I'm glad to have the company," he told her. And to his surprise, he actually meant it.

In design, the sled seemed hardly different than what it might have been a century before, only the treated wood and stainless steel hardware distinguishing it from traditional predecessors. The dogs accepted their leads like professionals, and once the gear got stacked and strapped into place, it formed a natural backrest, and he took his position, Adelaide seating herself virtually in his lap, with Miki standing behind. No declamatory "Mush!" to launch them off, just a guttural wordless cry – the dogs plunged ahead, the sled jolted forward, Anik kick-started the Skidoo. They were off.

Soon the town vanished in the distance behind them, nothing but endless white all around. The plain gave way to a cliff-bound riverbed, the water frozen over, hard as asphalt, except for a gaping crack dead ahead. Anik and Miki pulled to a stop.

It was decided that Adelaide would remain on the sled, holding on for dear life as Miki, with another bellowing command, sent the dogs racing ahead, straight for the gap. They dove over in loose formation, dragging the sled over the crevasse at top speed, water rushing below. Adelaide screamed with panicky joy as she and the sled went airborne, landing on the gap's far side.

The dogs just kept running, and she would have disappeared from sight, unable to voice a command they would obey, if not for a pick-like anchor she jammed into the snow, which managed at least to slow the dogs down. Anik and Miki took off on the Skiddoo, taking a long route around beyond the gap in the ice and intercepting Adelaide far in the distance. Then Anik returned for the final rider, Mr. Russell from Ottawa, and he held on tight as the Skiddoo sped quickly over the windswept snow toward the sled.

Mid-afternoon, they stopped to ice fish. Using a six-inch hand drill, Miki bored through the ice, then handed out rods and bits of seal meat for bait. Adelaide wandered off toward a distant bluff to relieve herself in private, and as he watched her totter away in the stiff sealskin suit, the hush of the wind the only sound as wisps of snow rippled over the ice, he felt something like fondness, even admiration. She just seemed so relaxed, so unafraid, so small and yet game for anything.

They caught one fish, no more, and Anik cut it up to feed to the dogs. They journeyed on until darkness thickened around them, deep in a long, winding canyon.

Miki and Anik pitched the tents, then laid out the waterproof mats and blankets, unrolled the sleeping bags side by side, a tight fit inside the small tent. The dogs, loosened from their harnesses but chained, would sleep out in the cold. Adelaide petted each one, saying good night, and they lifted their heads to accept her affection.

The butane stove served as heater inside the tent, despite the warning label that it was not to be used indoors. Dinner was served – canned chili again, but hot – and as a treat before bed: cocoa. Only once they were snugly cocooned inside their sleeping bags did Miki turn off the burner.

The air remained close even as the temperature dropped, fouled by the lingering smell of butane fogged by bad breath and flatulence. Anik's snoring sawed through the stark black silence.

He felt Adelaide's body, no larger than a twelve-year-old girl's, stir from time to time beside him. Strangely, he felt himself relaxing, the first time in days. Not that thoughts of death and vengeance never crossed his mind. They were constant companions, like echoes of one's own breath in a cave. If this young woman – or Miki or Anik, for that matter – had plans to take him down, then fine, he thought, let me die – and with that he drifted off into a dreamless sleep.

They rose long before sunrise, ate a breakfast of oatmeal and dried fruit chased with scalding coffee, then packed up their gear and continued heading deeper into the mouth of the river valley, the walls of the bluffs to either side rising up like sentinels packed shoulder-to-shoulder, while off to the east, the first thin rays of dawn cast a bluish sheen along the horizon.

Anik sped off ahead on the Skidoo, searching out possible campsites for that evening, leaving the others alone with the dogs. The silence seemed to descend like a presence, nothing but the sound of the dogs' churning paws and the sled runners skimming over hard-packed snow. He felt Adelaide easing back against him, her body relaxing into his. He resisted the impulse to wrap his arms around her waist.

Come noon, they stopped, pulling up in the shadow of a snow-capped hill that rose from its base like a stovepipe. As Miki tended to the dogs, Adelaide shook off the hooded sealskin coat, wearing only a turtleneck underneath, and wandered off into the sunlight, shading her eyes and scanning the sky.

A lone Arctic tern sailed far overhead. They'd seen precious little wildlife, only the occasional seal sunning itself beside a hole in the ice, ready to dive back into the water at the merest hint of a nearby bear.

She bent over to adjust her boots, tug them back up to her knees. He turned away, playing the gentleman, not wanting to seem too obvious, checking her out, and gazed down the winding path of the frozen river among the low white hills.

A sudden twitch of instinct, prompted from far below the surface of his mind, made him suddenly turn, and that's when he saw it, the buck knife sheathed in leather and pulled from deep inside her boot.

A quick tumble of thoughts – no, not thoughts, impressions – suddenly fit together neat and tight, prompting a response, a near instantaneous decision.

First, thank God for sleep, otherwise he would have seen nothing.

Second, his suspicions hadn't been cowardly, but sound.

Third, a prompt: do what O'Conner would do.

He reached into his pocket, withdrew the .38, stepped quickly toward her, and emptied the cylinder, all six bullets, into her face, her throat, her chest.

The gunshots echoed down the canyon like a giant's handclaps. He stood there, holding his arm out, pulling the trigger over and over as the terrible echoes faded, giving way to the harmless click-click-click. She lay in the snow where, just a moment before, she'd stood crouching over. Blood drained from the face and neck wounds onto the snow. Her sweater darkened around the bullet holes. She stared, wide-eyed, her mouth moving open and closed in silence as her limbs twitched helplessly from shock.

Finally, he turned toward Miki, the pistol still held rigidly out at arm's length. The Inuit guide, standing maybe sixty yards away, stared back in silence, as though waiting to hear the impossible. Then he quickly jumped onto the sled, cried out to the dogs, and the team sped off, heading across the drifting snow toward the mouth of the frozen river, growing smaller, smaller, then disappearing beyond a jagged hill.

He walked over and stood there, watching her die, waiting until she lay there still before reaching inside her boot for the knife. The evidence.

Nothing was there.

He turned to look down the canyon, the shadows of the hills stretching long across the snow in the late-day sun. Soon it would be dark, no way to discern his direction, and viciously cold. Wolves would come out, smelling Adelaide's blood, then him. He was two days from town by dog sled. No telling how long it would take to walk.

CHAPTER 6
Snake Farm
by Manuel Ramos

"It's been almost a week and you still don't have any leads? What the hell you doin', Garza? It was a fuckin' riot in the middle of the Crystal Q. At least a half-dozen assholes shot up the ranch and each other. I can't believe that no one's talkin', no one knows shit."

Antonio "Tony" Garza recognized the red hue creeping up his boss's neck, then along his jaw, nose, finally the forehead. Big Jim Spencer's face looked like a pudgy glob of pink bubblegum. It meant the chief of police was ready to hit something, or someone, and Garza tensed up.

"Believe it, boss. Even Harrington is playing dumb. You know what his statement said. Claimed he didn't know what the hell happened at the house. Says he was busy with details for the party. By the time he got to where the action was, no one was left except the dead and wounded ranch hands. Then, when the feds figured out where they split up the money, the only one around was the dead guy, who no one knows, and he ain't talking."

He moved a few inches further from Spencer and tried to be inconspicuous.

Garza wanted to tell Big Jim that the Crystal Q wasn't in their jurisdiction and that every North Texas agency from the FBI to the county dogcatcher claimed the case as theirs. The Kilroy Police Department wasn't in the mix, official or otherwise. But Big Jim was convinced that some of the thieves scattered into "Kilroy's bailiwick." Big Jim obsessed after a headline, something to grab the attention of the suits in Austin.

"When I hired you, I thought you was an upgrade to the usual inbred mutants that wanna play cops and robbers." Big Jim talked as slow as the tumbleweeds that bounced against the curb of Main Street. "Not by much. You ain't exactly J. Edgar. If I hadn't needed someone immediately, I might've passed you over, just 'cause your history is sketchy. But I hoped with your degree from UT and your experience over in Lubbock that you'd add somethin' to our department. So far, I ain't seen it. Not sure you're all that cut out for police work."

Garza flinched. He took the job in Kilroy because he didn't have much choice. He needed a fresh start more urgently than Spencer needed a replacement. The trouble in Lubbock – that damn Clara Johnson, no way she was only sixteen – had driven him out of Buddy Holly's hometown, but so far it hadn't caught up to him in Kilroy. Clara had cost him a lot of money. Well spent, but expensive.

"We'll get something, boss." The words sounded hollow. "If I could lean on Harrington's wife, Gracella, that'd be a good place to start. But I can't even get on the ranch, much less have a one-on-one with Mrs. Harrington."

"Do whatever you have to do. The shoot-out has stirred up too much negative attention for Texas. The damn Citizens Improvement League is making life miserable for cops. It's bullshit politics but if you can't get results, I'll find somebody who can." He slapped his palm on his desk and Garza took the cue that it was time for him to leave.

Tony drove the dinged-up department Crown Vic straight to his house. Slow but steady. The car had suffered seven years of police abuse and Garza didn't like to test it. He was the least senior cop on the force, which meant he drew the most senior wheels. Fifteen minutes to his rented house on the edge of town and he saw all of Kilroy on the way. The four-room shack was the only place he could afford.

Vivian Dollarhyde stretched on the faded living room carpet. Her lime green workout clothes – skimpy shorts, skimpier top – popped, as she liked to say, against her skin's sweaty glow. She'd been at it since five a.m., two hours before Tony woke up. She'd run her daily five miles in the grayness of the morning moon, safe from prying eyes who might wonder about the dark-haired, obviously not-white stranger. Then for ninety minutes she tormented the used elliptical and a few weights Tony kept for those rare times he thought he should exercise. She finished with yoga twists and Pilate stretches. Tony tried not to think about it but he imagined himself jumping on her prone body and burying himself in the sanctuary of her overheated flesh.

"Hey, baby," he said. "Looks like you could use a drink." It wasn't quite lunchtime.

He opened the refrigerator, extracted two Lone Stars, twisted their caps, and offered her one. She chugged half of the bottle before she looked at him.

"I have to get out of this town. I'm going nuts." She sat at the rickety table and patted her body dry with a gray towel she'd found in a closet.

"You just got here, Vivian. What's the rush? Besides, it's way too hot, and I'm not talking about the weather. Every brand and style of cop is all over this part of Texas. From

Fort Worth to the Oklahoma state line. South to Waco and
west to Abilene. It's like a war zone. Anyone even just a
little bit off is getting rousted by state police, Rangers, you
name it. You and your pals riled up more law enforcement
than we've seen around here since they shot JFK."

"How the hell would you know that? You're older than
me but you ain't that old."

"Whatever. I'm just sayin'."

Vivian wadded the towel into a ball. "That goddamn
pilot."

"Oh, Christ. Here we go again."

"You don't like it, get out."

He thought about reminding her that they were in his
house. He kept quiet.

"I got the right to complain. Ellison tried to kill us and he
almost made off with all the money. O'Conner should've
never let him in on the job. But the old man's getting soft.
I should've told him to fuck off when he said he needed
me. Practically begged. Said I'd get a bigger share since I had
special skills. What bullshit. All the good that share is doing
me now. Can't even buy myself a decent steak. Hell, not
even a hamburger."

She stood up, dropped the towel on the floor and headed
for the shower in the narrow bathroom. She lifted the tank
top over her head and turned to Garza. "None of it would've
happened without me. Seven million. Now look where
I am." She shrugged her shoulders. "Stuck in this pissant
town, as far as I could go after the shit hit the fan, a bag
of money that I can't use, sharing a bed with your horny
ass. Story of my life." She disappeared into the bathroom,
grumbling to herself.

Tony thought about joining her in the shower but decided

the mood wasn't quite right. Vivian liked to play. But she was too wrapped up in her trouble. Too focused on how she was going to get out of the state with her money without confronting the cops or the guy who'd double-crossed the crew at the safe house. Or maybe she wanted to deal her own justice to the pilot.

She's crazy enough to blow it all on revenge, he thought.

He again looked around the shack for any sign of the money but it was a fruitless search. She'd promised him a cut of her take, although she hadn't said where she had it stashed or even how much she had. Tony calculated it was more than a hundred grand, easy. Maybe half a mil, maybe a million? There had to be mountains of money at the Crystal Q.

She'd told him that after it went cockeyed in Fort Worth, O'Conner dropped her off on the edgy outskirts of town. Cops everywhere, no time for long goodbyes. She left the shotgun from the job with O'Conner – too conspicuous to carry around – and she hadn't brought anything else from her own collection of guns since O'Conner provided all the equipment she thought she'd need. She didn't like the way she felt without a weapon but accepted it as part of her situation.

She'd run long and hard to the only person she knew in Texas who would take her in. On the point of exhaustion, she found Garza in Kilroy. Her toned body, strong lungs, parkour training, and iron will carried her across the wind-scarred merciless Texas prairie without much water or food. She described how she hid from police helicopters and curious coyotes and she cursed that she couldn't quit thinking about how it had all gone bad.

Over the years he'd tried to stay in contact. He always had a cell number or email address for her except when she was on the run or sweating out the latest fallout from one of her jobs. She never failed to circle back to him.

Her career, as she called her sins and crimes, didn't bother him. Vivian was the forbidden fruit, the type of girl his mama warned him about.

Good thing he'd let her know he was leaving Lubbock. Here she was, in all her half-naked glory, relying on him to keep her safe and hidden from the heat with more money than he would ever make in Kilroy and all he had to do was bide his time until she made her move.

Then he would get his share.

Or maybe, take it all.

Tony finished his shift at five p.m. but told Big Jim that he would keep on it during the night, "going over the file."

"You have fun with that file," Big Jim said.

"I'm gonna drive over to the Crystal Q in the morning. Try to talk with Gracella, if I can get her away from Clovis Harrington, if I can get past the front gate. I know a guy on the task force who's camped out on the ranch. I'll start with him and see where I end up."

The scheme sounded weak, pointless, but Tony thought he had to propose something.

"Good luck with that. Clovis hangs onto that woman like she was the last remainin' piece of Mexican tail in all of Texas." Big Jim laughed at his own crudeness. "You know it's a good three, four hours to the ranch?"

"Yeah. So I'll be gone all day."

"You'd better come back with somethin'."

Big Jim's response surprised Tony. He expected to be rejected. Big Jim's grasping at straws, he thought.

On the way home, Tony hoped Vivian would go with him to the ranch. Then he shook his head. "Now that is a stupid idea," he mumbled. He again drove slowly through the Kilroy streets until he was back at his house.

"Hey, baby," he hollered from the front door.

"Hey yourself, Tony."

She was in a better mood than when he'd left her earlier. She called him Tony only when she felt at ease, or in bed.

"What've you been up to?" He opened the refrigerator and did not see any beer.

"Well, I finished the Lone Stars, for one thing."

"Yeah, I figured."

"Then I got hungry and grilled that ribeye you said I could have."

"I thought we'd share it."

"It wasn't that big."

"I'll get something at the bar."

She didn't tell him that in the afternoon she'd relaxed on the back porch with homemade lemonade and thoughts about what she would do with the money. She listened to country music on the radio and practiced a few line-dance moves. She'd decided she had to think of this downtime as a vacation. A vacay with eyes out for cops.

"It was good, have to say. Or else I really needed some protein."

"Yeah, don't sweat it. But since I gotta go out to eat, you want to join me, maybe have a little fun?"

She wrinkled her nose. "You trying to get me busted? You think no one will notice me?"

"It's not a big deal. You're my old college amiga in town for a few days on the way to your new job. That's all true. And if one of my co-workers starts asking questions just because you're a stranger, well, too bad. I'll make it clear you're on the straight and narrow. Who'd suspect that you had anything to do with the big shoot-out anyway? You don't look the part, you want to know the truth. No one's after you specifically. Not yet."

"You said it was too hot for me to leave. Now you're saying I got nothing to worry about. Which is it, Tony? Maybe I should just hit the road."

"No, not what I mean. You can't travel out in the open, away from town. It's certain you'll get stopped and questioned. That could go any way but good. But here in Kilroy? No one's thinking about the Crystal Q except for Big Jim and the three stooges he calls officers, and me. And none of us are looking for you. You got nothing to worry about in this town."

She wasn't convinced but she worried that she'd lose it if she stayed one more hour in the pitiful house.

Tony drove the Crown Vic during his shifts or when he ran errands for Big Jim. But at night he cruised in his two-year-old Ford F-150, the only nice thing he owned, or so he bragged. "A work in progress," he'd told Vivian. "I added step bars and the chrome and black wheels to match the Tuxedo Black paint. Gonna trick up the interior next, soon as I have enough saved."

She'd grunted an ambiguous response. Boys and their toys, she thought. Ain't nothing new.

Tony kept up a steady stream of small talk on the drive to the Kilroy Ice House. He went on about his plans for the truck, about how Big Jim was an idiot, and what he thought they could do when it came time to finally leave Kilroy.

Vivian listened with one ear. Her mind was on the money

and how soon she could run. All she had to do was get out of town and across the state line. And dump Garza when some of the dust settled.

Along Main Street, a few yellow lights emphasized the emptiness. He turned onto a cross street in the direction of the pale moon. They drove past old frame houses with thin lawns or gravel front yards. The bushes were permanently bent from the wind. Gray light shone through the blinds or curtains that hung in most of the front windows. Looking at the town made her tired. She'd been in Kilroy one day too long. She couldn't shake the nagging feeling that she had to run. Vacation was already over.

Tony stopped at a squat narrow building lit up with beer signs, Christmas lights, and a blinking billboard that simply announced BEER! The open-air place was surrounded by more cars than Vivian had seen in the entire town since she'd appeared on Tony's porch.

A noisy booze-soaked crowd packed the ice house. Everything and everyone was bathed in orange light that vibrated with the hum of the customers. Tony worked his way through the loud men and women, many wearing cowboy hats. He acknowledged several with a nod of his head or an energetic greeting. Most stared at Vivian. A few smiled at Tony with a look of admiration, a few others didn't hide their hostility.

They stood for several minutes until a pair of underage boys stumbled from a small table in a corner. Another ten minutes and they drank cold beer. In the background, Vivian heard Ray Wylie Hubbard growling – couldn't really call it singing – that the snake farm "just sounds nasty."

"This place ain't happening for me," she said. She almost had to shout to make herself heard. "Maybe we can get something to eat somewhere else? Doesn't look like there's a kitchen in this joint."

Before Tony could answer, a shadow covered their table. Vivian looked up into the bloodshot blue eyes of Big Jim Spencer.

"Well, well. Where you been hidin' this young lady, Tony? Seems like only yesterday you was bitchin' about no action in this town and here you are with what looks like more action than even you can handle. My, my. You're full of surprises. Guess you forgot about that file, eh?" Big Jim straightened up. He extended his hand to Vivian. "I'm Big Jim, sweetie. Chief of police around here. Tony's boss, in case you didn't know."

Vivian took his hand. Big Jim's sweaty, meaty palm surrounded her fingers. She let go as soon as she felt his leathery skin but he hung on until she finally jerked away.

"Yeah, Tony's mentioned you." She stared at her empty beer bottle.

"Uh, boss, this is Vivian," Tony said. "An old friend. From school. She just got into town. I'm showing her the Kilroy sights, such as they are. She's only passing through."

"Too bad. This town could use some prettyin' up. So, where you headed, Miss Vivian?"

"Up to Dallas." She moved her eyes back to Big Jim's and locked him in her gaze until he blinked and looked away. "I got family there. New job. Taking a break before I go back to work."

"Oh yeah? Family, huh? I know a lot of people in Dallas. Maybe I know your kin." He paused, watched Tony for a few seconds. He looked down at Vivian again. "And what kind of work you do? Maybe we could use you here. That way you could stay on. Sure Tony'd like that." Tony smiled at Big Jim. "Where'd you say you're from, sweetie?"

"The coast. Oakland."

"California? Shit, we can't compete with California, right, Tony? Not with the ocean and movie stars and all those fancy houses. Long ways from here. You come by train? I ain't seen any strange cars on the streets and we sure as hell don't have no airport. Trains, we got."

Vivian's fingernail picked at the label on her beer bottle. "You might not believe it but I hitchhiked from Austin. Wanted to see Texas up close. You know what?" She found his eyes again and stared hard at the lawman. "So far, I haven't been impressed. Once you get past Austin, there ain't much to hold your attention. Maybe Dallas will be better."

Big Jim half-laughed, half-coughed. "You right about that. Like someone once told me. He could never live in Texas, that's why he lived in Austin." He faked another laugh. "Anyway, that's mighty dangerous, hitchin'. If you was my daughter, I'd say don't do it. But you ain't, is you?"

"That's funny, boss," Tony said. "I mean, her father and all that." He watched Vivian, unsure about what she might do. He'd seen her in bar fights and it wasn't pretty.

"You know we got some real bad hombres runnin' lose, don't ya?" Big Jim asked. "Tony must've filled you in about the battle at the Crystal Q. Young lady like you could get caught crosswise. Good thing you know a policeman, right? I'm sure Tony is takin' care of you every which way."

She clenched her fists under the table. She smiled at Big Jim. "Yeah, I'm in good hands. I got good old Tony for protection. If I need it. Can't be too careful these days."

Big Jim's face glistened in the orange light. He surveyed

the crowd, patted the gun in the holster on his hip, and tapped his fingers on the brim of his gray stained hat.

"Hate to walk away from such attractive company but I'll leave you two old friends to get reacquainted." He placed his hand on Tony's shoulder. "You takin' off early for the Crystal Q?"

"Yeah, sure. Probably around seven. But I won't be back until day after. Like we talked."

"Sounds good. Hope you dig up somethin'. I got another call from Austin. Somebody has to do somethin'. Might as well be the Kilroy Police Department. Right, Miss Vivian? Think Tony can get his name in the papers and the politicians off my ass? Excuse the French."

"Oh, Jim, I don't know anything about all that. Like Tony said, I'm just passing through. I'll be gone in another day or two."

Big Jim nodded. "You bet." He walked away. The crowd parted to let him through and his tall, bow-legged frame slipped into the artificial haze.

"Goddamn," Vivian cursed. "This was a very bad mistake. He's on to me. I have to leave this town, tonight."

"Hang on," Tony said. "We can't panic." He reached for her hand but she slid away from him. "He doesn't know anything he can prove. He has to get corroboration of his suspicions, especially if he doesn't want to look like a dumbass to all the other cops in North Texas. Or to that damn League." She shook her head. She knew better than to believe Tony. "Just wait," he continued. "Until tomorrow. It's perfect. I'm supposed to drive to the Crystal Q. You'll be with me and we'll run for it. Get the money and take a flight out of Dallas. We can be in another state, hell, another country before Jim figures out I ain't coming back and you're gone."

"He'll watch the house."

"Maybe. But in the morning we'll leave like we're going for breakfast. Nothing wrong with that. He can join us if he's really following. If he is watching, I drop you back at the house after we eat and head west like I'm going to the ranch. But I'll circle back, pick you up at the junction of Burnt Mill Road and the highway as long as you can give him the slip, which I know you can do." He smiled at her but she didn't smile back. "And if he's not on our tail, we hit it, hard, immediately. On the road, if you feel exposed, you can hide in the bed of my truck. It's covered. Only until we get to the city. We'll fly out of Texas and never look back. Or, if we have to, we drive like maniacs through Oklahoma."

Vivian hesitated. "Sounds risky, dangerous. Jim's smarter than you think."

"You saying you can't pull it off? All you have to do is lose him, if it comes down to that. You could do this blindfolded. You ain't afraid, are you?"

"Screw you." She didn't want to go along with Tony but she didn't have another idea to throw back at him. "Let's get home," she said. "Go over this again. I may not have a choice. I don't like that but I guess I can't do anything about it."

Back at the house, Tony babbled for more than an hour about his so-called strategy to escape Kilroy and Big Jim and then live happily ever after on Vivian's stash. To shut him up, she led him to the bed and turned his brain to mush with her usual skill and creativity. When they finished with the sex, she offered him the bottle of Jim Beam. He chugged a shot, curled into a ball, and fell asleep in less than two minutes. Through it all he missed that she was thinking about something else.

She lay in darkness, repeatedly going over every detail of what her next steps had to be. She couldn't wait until tomorrow, she knew that much. When she was satisfied with her vision, she used her training to make her body sleep for one hour. She eased out of bed at three forty-five a.m., threw on fresh clothes, stuffed protein bars, water, gloves, a hat, and other essentials into her backpack. She lifted Tony's gun belt from the coat hook where he kept it. A little after four a.m. she slipped the truck keys out of Tony's jacket and silently left the house.

She'd worried that Tony would hear her start the truck. The diazepam in the bourbon would help keep him in dreamland. Good thing Tony had a pharmacy in his bathroom's medicine cabinet. Same old Tony. As an extra precaution she jabbed the left front and rear tires of the Crown Vic with her knife. She mounted the pickup and began her trek.

She drove without headlights. She expected to confront Big Jim at every corner. Her head moved from side to side and her hands gripped the steering wheel tight, too tight. She stopped at an intersection. Vivian breathed in as much air as her lungs would hold, then slowly let it out through her nostrils. She returned to the lessons she'd learned from hours of grueling practice and training. Focus on the goal; awareness of all obstacles; clarity of action; endurance of mind and body. She took three more deep breaths.

She could handle Big Jim or any other Texas cop.

When she was sure that no one followed her, she flipped on the lights and sped to her money.

* * *

Big Jim grabbed Tony's ankles and dragged him from the bed. Tony woke up when his head bounced on the carpet. He sat up on his haunches, nude and disoriented. Big Jim slapped him.

"You son of a bitch! You let her go. Where the hell she goin', Garza? Where the hell did that bitch run off to? Where's the goddamn money?"

Several slaps and minutes later, Tony Garza realized what had happened and what Big Jim wanted. He struggled to pull on his jeans and then his boots and, finally, a shirt.

He managed a complete sentence. "She's going after her Crystal Q take."

"No shit, Sherlock. And where might that be, you shit-bird?"

"How the hell should I know? She never told me. I was waiting to get it out of her, then I'd arrest her. But you spooked her and now she's–"

Big Jim slugged him, no slap this time. Tony fell back on the bed. Blood leaked at the corner of his mouth.

"Don't give me any of that horseshit," Big Jim said. "You was gonna run off with that black piece of ass and her money. Except she played you like the sucker fish you are and she run off herself with your truck."

"What? My truck? No!" He ran to the window. The empty front yard taunted him. "Goddamn her! I'll kill her, I'll–"

Big Jim raised his fist and Tony shut up.

"Listen to me. We have to find her. If you wanna keep your sorry ass out of prison, you have to help, so you'd better come up with somethin'. I'm not gonna take any heat for letting one of the Crystal Q gang slip through my fingers, 'specially since she was bangin' one of my officers. You're gonna help and we're gonna find her or your next stop is the Walls Unit at Huntsville. That's a whole other existence, Tony. You'll have fun there. Bet on that."

Tony rubbed his eyes. He spat blood on the carpet and shook his head. He clutched the Jim Beam bottle, held it to his lips, stopped, shook his head again. He drank water from the kitchen faucet.

"She can't have been gone long," Spencer said. "I found your door wide open and you still smelling like you had her pussy all over your face. Where she goin'? You spent days with her, you must have some idea. What did she do while she was here?"

Tony needed time. He had to play this right or he would end up in his own private hurt locker. "When did you first suspect her?" he asked. "Last night at the bar? I told her to stay home but she wouldn't listen."

Big Jim laughed. "You sorry... No, not last night. I saw her days ago runnin' out in the boonies along the dry creek bed. In the dark, early, like four or five. I start my rounds before the sun comes up. Insomnia paid off, finally. She was headin' back to town so I watched her. You could've shot me and I wouldn't have felt it when I saw her run into your shack. I thought for sure you'd brag about your girlfriend. But when you didn't say nothin' about her, I figured she was someone I had to know more about. That's quite a young lady you're mixed up with, Tony. Didn't think you had it in ya."

Tony shrugged. "She's a friend from long ago. What else can I say?"

"Oh, no apology necessary. I've seen what that kind of woman can do to a normal, if not too bright, man. You're just human, Tony."

Tony shrugged again.

"A dumb human, no doubt. So dumb you're probably on your way to prison."

Tony slumped against the bedroom wall. He tried to think.

"She's got quite a rep, as far as cops go," Big Jim continued. "Took a couple of days to pin down who she is. There's not much about her in the national database but what there is says she's a pro. I put two and two together and came up with the millions stolen from Harrington. I figured you two would make a run for it tomorrow, do a Bonnie and Clyde when you were supposed to be drivin' up to the Crystal Q. I come by tonight just to double check. That's when I saw your open front door."

"You've had Vivian in your sights all along?"

"I know everythin' that goes on in Kilroy. No way you could've kept that hot cup of chocolate hidden from me." Tony nodded. "But, enough of this. You're gonna help me find her. That is, if you wanna try to salvage the rest of your two-bit life."

"Why didn't you arrest her?" Tony asked. He answered his own question. "The money."

Big Jim grunted.

Tony straightened up. "We should follow the creek bed, look for tire tracks. She ran out there every day, you know that. She must've been checking up on her stash. There's got to be something out there where she hid the money, maybe buried it by a rock formation, or in an empty rattler's nest, or—"

"Or a hole in the dirt," Big Jim interrupted. "Big enough for a box of money but not much else."

"You know something like that?"

"The Cueva Guzman. Guzman's Cave, but it ain't much of a cave. I'd forgotten all about it until now. About four miles up the dry creek. Don't know how she found it. You can't see it until you're almost on top of it and it's mostly a shaft hundreds of feet straight down. But it's the perfect spot to hide somethin'."

"Let's go." Tony reached for his department-issued gun belt with the holstered. 45. The naked coat hook made him curse Vivian again. "I need a gun," he said. The two men glared at each other for a few seconds.

"I need a gun," Tony repeated.

Big Jim nodded. "There's an extra in my car," he said. "Don't try anythin', Garza. I got no qualms about puttin' down a dirty cop, particularly one allegedly workin' for me."

"Yeah, whatever. Don't you get trigger-happy. Remember, we're on the same side."

Big Jim handled his Tahoe PPV with the light touch of a water buffalo. The two men bounced and jerked as Big Jim swerved over, around, and through concrete-hard ruts, massive cactus, and half-buried boulders. As he drove, Big Jim explained that the cave was an opening in a low-lying ridge that allowed for two men to enter, but within ten feet it narrowed so that only one man could fit along the rocky floor. After a few inches, the shaft dropped suddenly and dangerously into blackness.

"You need ropes and lights and other equipment to manage that hole," Big Jim said. "No one's ever been all the way down, not since one of the passages caved in, makin' it more narrow and dangerous. We had a kid trapped in there a few years ago, the Muncy boy, about twelve. His brother was with him when he fell in or no one would've ever known he was down that thing. He got stuck on a ledge, one leg hangin' on by a hair, really. Couldn't move up or down. Took us about eight hours to get him out. It ruined him. He ain't been right in the head since then."

"Jesus," Tony said.

"I put up signs and roped off the hole and even tried to get the town council to allocate money for blastin' the damn thing shut. But kids pay no mind to signs and the town council wouldn't okay anythin' without the city attorney's approval, and that ain't happenin', not from that son of a bitch."

Tony didn't ask why. He didn't really care. He wondered how far down the hole Vivian had crawled to hide the money. She could go deep if she had to. Deeper than either he or Big Jim could manage.

They drove for several more minutes until Big Jim slowed down, almost stopping.

"She's still here." Big Jim pointed to something in the darkness. "Thought we'd missed her. She should be streakin' for Dallas."

He parked about a hundred yards from the ridge. He switched off the interior light and quietly opened his car door. He walked slowly, hunched over.

Tony jumped out of the SUV. He carried a flashlight and hooked Big Jim's extra gun in his belt. His fingers twitched in anticipation.

The long almost flat ridge stretched against the early morning sky. Rays of moonlight bounced off the black silhouette of his truck. A slight breeze caressed the men, who didn't notice.

They inched up to the layer of horizontal rock that marked the opening in the Texas earth. They stared into the darkness and for a few minutes they saw nothing but the darkness.

"Hear that?" Big Jim whispered.

Tony listened. He heard the breeze against his ears. Then, something else. A groan, or a sigh. A soft sound tinged with pain. Tony stared harder into the cave.

She lay on her side, not moving.

Big Jim stood up. He slowly walked into the opening and almost immediately he had to stoop so he would fit. Tony followed.

Vivian lifted her head. "Took you clowns long enough. Feels like I've been laying here for hours."

Tony switched on the flashlight. Vivian stretched along the floor of the opening, crammed against the wall of the cave where it narrowed into the shaft. Her right ankle twisted at a weird angle and Tony could see that it had already begun to swell.

"You fell?" he said.

"Of course she fell," Big Jim said. "You moron. That ankle. Looks broken. Looks ugly."

"Yeah, I fell." Resignation filled her voice. She groaned. "I climbed down that goddamn hole until I got to the ledge where I had the bag. I grabbed it and was shimmying out, up on my knees, when something slithered across my arms. I don't know, I think it was a snake. Something." She stopped talking and let go of the tension in her neck. "I didn't handle it like I should've," she continued. "I jerked away, lost my balance. Did everything I could to not fall backward into that shaft, so I fell forward. Landed funny and my ankle collapsed. I hit my head and must've passed out. Don't know how long. I was coming around when I heard you outside. Of course it had to be you two."

"A snake?" Tony said. He aimed his flashlight away from Vivian. "That thing still here?"

Tony and Big Jim saw the canvas bag of money against the wall at Vivian's back. They both rushed to the bag. Tony lunged for the stash. He dropped the flashlight, pulled the. 45 from his belt, aimed it at Big Jim, and backed against the wall. One hand held the bag, the other his gun.

Vivian snatched the light and pointed it at Big Jim.

Big Jim aimed his gun at Tony.

"Give me that money," Big Jim barked.

"Go to hell," Tony answered.

"Easy, boys," Vivian said through gritted teeth. "You can shoot each other, just let me out of the way."

"Shut up, bitch," Big Jim shouted. "Give me that money, Garza, or you ain't leavin' this hole."

"Then ain't none of us leaving," Tony said.

"I got plans for that cash," Big Jim answered.

"I'm sure you do. And they don't include giving it back to Harrington. Chief of police, my ass."

"You're not one to judge me, boy."

"Aw…" Tony sighed. He pulled the trigger of the. 45 and Big Jim slammed to the ground. Big Jim's gun flew into the blackness of the cave. He rolled in the dirt, clutching his right knee.

"You son of a bitch!" Big Jim screamed.

Tony had to finish off Big Jim, then Vivian. He stepped over Vivian to get closer to Big Jim.

Vivian turned the light into Tony's face, blinding him. She hit his upraised leg with the flashlight and he fell to the side, arms flailing, hands clutching at the air. His eyes flared open. He tried to keep upright but his feet slid out from under him. The gun dropped into the hole. He followed it, hugging the bag.

Tony screamed as he bounced against the walls of the shaft. The screams stopped with a dull thud.

"Oh my God," Big Jim said. "You lost the money. And you killed him Oh my God."

Vivian struggled to her elbows.

"Well, now I got no choice," she said. "You two screwed the pig royally. Have to get out on my own." She looked around the cave. "I'm leaving and you're not stopping me."

"I'm shot, bleedin', in case you hadn't noticed."

"You'll live. As long as you get that bullet hole looked at soon." She caught her breath. "Guess you could bleed out."

Big Jim shuddered. "You have to help me. I can't stand up, can't walk. You can't neither. Together, we can get back to town. The doc'll take care of both of us. Then you can disappear, leave. You're not my problem. I don't care about you."

"You mean now that the money's gone, eh? And Tony?"

"No one will miss him. He's history. Happens all the time around here. People come and go. No one will look for him and for sure no one will look at the bottom of that hell hole."

She painfully maneuvered to her knees, then forced herself to stand on her good leg. Sweat covered her face. She picked up a piece of dried cholla wood and used it to steady herself. Her ragged breathing echoed against the cave walls.

"That's a great offer. But I think I'll pass." She examined her ankle under the beam of the flashlight. "Christ, this could take a while."

"I can help. We can help each other. I'm tellin' ya."

She pointed the flashlight in the direction of the cave opening. "Maybe someone will notice your car and come around. Yeah, that's probably what will happen." Big Jim frantically shook his head. "They're gonna ask where you are sooner or later."

"You can't leave me. I'll bleed to death." His blood-covered fingers hugged his knee. Blood soaked his jeans.

A few hundred dollar bills lay on the ground. She stuffed them in her pockets. Five hundred.

A ray of morning light streaked into the cave.

She leaned against the wall and accepted that the walk to Tony's truck would be the longest walk she had ever taken. She breathed deeply, three times. Her training taught her to envision what she had to do, what the obstacles were and how she would overcome. The first goal was to get out of the cave, then make it to the truck. Retrieve Tony's gun from the glovebox, where she'd left it. Then she would detail the next step. Driving the truck. Staying alert. Avoiding the roadblocks and helicopters. Dealing with the pain. Finding someone to help her. She thought she had a chance. Not much. But a chance.

She limped to the light.

CHAPTER 7
Eel Estevez
by Joe Clifford

Eel Estevez had always hated the heat, since he was a little kid. The way the dry got caught in your throat, the clog of dead things choking passageways, cutting off the esophagus, making it hard to breathe. In the desert, water was scarce, and in the shantytowns of his youth, even more so. He remembered the price his mother paid before she died. Scrubbing rich men's toilets in their air-conditioned mansions, sent back to the swarthy El Paso slums covered in shit, left to bake in a little clay hut. How his father died like a dog in the scorched fields. The heat was like the cancer that killed him. It consumed you, whole. Cooked you alive, from the inside out. What did it say, then, about a man who'd chosen to live his entire life sandwiched below the thirtieth parallel? Even when he got out of El Paso, Eel hadn't escaped the heat. A brief, fruitless stretch in the Army landed him at Fort Huachuca on the Arizona-Mexico border.

Eel stretched, a blast of morning light winning the war against bent motel blinds. He glanced back at the woman. A big gal. Not fat. Full figured. Like that plus-size model they recently put in the swimsuit issue, one of those sports magazines trying to prove that we're progressing

148

as a society; it's okay to love all shapes and sizes. Ashley something. The model. Not the girl. He couldn't remember her fucking name. His head throbbed like it had been back-kicked by an extra stubborn mule with restless leg syndrome. Political correctness had even found a way to weasel its ugly head into soft-core porn.

He didn't care about the girl in his bed, and he didn't bother fishing the name of the sports magazine from the gray matter either. America didn't give a fuck about fútbol, or soccer as they called it here, so Eel didn't give a fuck about American sports. His love of fútbol was the one thread tying him to his homeland. Which wasn't much of a homeland at all. He'd never lived there. The color of his skin meant he'd never be fully embraced here either. He was a man without a country.

This was why Eel didn't go back to Mexico with Carter all those years ago. At least that was the reason he gave. There were other, more significant prejudices, harder to admit, confess aloud, not the least of which was that Eel felt no connection to his heritage. Never had. He was more gringo than most of the gringos he knew. He may not have felt particular allegiance to the States, but he was born in America. What difference did it make what was in his blood? It all spilled the same color.

Carter had had a hard time understanding how Eel, a Mexican, pure bred and blue, could feel no sense of community, no allegiance to what flowed in his veins. Geography, Carter had said, is an address, before pointing at his heart. "But this is who you are."

The only time Eel and he ever got in a fight was that night Carter left, when he called out Eel for his lack of loyalty.

"It's where we belong," he'd said. "Mexico is our home."

By then, Eel's parents were both dead, Carter the closest thing to family he had left. But he didn't feel like learning the ins and outs of a foreign culture, mapping different streets, new customs.

"Our home?" Eel said. "We have lived in Texas our whole lives."

"And what good has that gotten either of us?"

At that point, Eel still wasn't Eel, he was Estaban Estevez. He wouldn't become Eel until later. But Carter was already Carter, having made the switch from Diego Rodriquez long ago. That night, however, what they called one another hardly mattered; they were just two boys who'd run the gamut from boosting to two-bit robbery, at a crossroads, deciding to take different career paths. Carter was going home, enlisting fulltime, signing up for his fate. He had a connection to the drug trade, where the real money was to be made, and wanted Eel to join him. Eel still thought there was good in him.

"I know who I am," Carter said. "What I am."

"You?" Eel had mocked. "You? The one pushing a return to Mexico? You – Diego – who made up your own nickname from an American movie."

They'd grown up on those gangster flicks, *Scarface*, *Carlito's Way*, renegade cowboys, Butch, Sundance, the travels and trials of one-eyed fat men. It was a low blow and a deep cut.

They pushed. They shoved. In the end, no one threw a punch. Soon it was over. This was meant to be a celebration. So the boys forced themselves to laugh, have fun, trading swigs from the bottle, knocking back round after round in a border bar with the hole in the floor that smelled like hot piss and grease splatter. Sealing the sendoff by slitting hands with an all-purpose pocketknife on the curb of an all-night pharmacy. This wasn't goodbye. They'd see each other again. They both knew then some bonds were forever, thicker than blood.

Eel had a lot of rules he lived by, or at least he used to, the first of which had been: no matter how tough you think you are, there is always someone tougher. Maybe it was because it had taken Eel Estevez so long to find that man that he'd forgotten. He'd gotten cocky, arrogant, reckless. As soon as you thought you were on top of the world, you could count on the world coming up behind you to kick you in the ass.

After the shitstorm at the ranch, while Benny and the others were racing off, thinking they'd won some sort of skeet-shooting jackpot, Eel knew better. Too many guns. Too much trouble for a run-of-the-mill smash and grab. Eel spirited toward open roads, all of which headed south, leaving the wreckage in his rearview, with nothing to do but think. Eel wasn't stupid. He knew damn well what he was getting himself into. But that much money? It had been easy to convince himself of untraceable pickings. Plenty of blame to go around. There were countless funnels and monies off the book, the whole state of Texas rife with them, sitting right next to the border, quick access to spin a fresh load, tumble dry cash, spit it out clean. Half a million was pocket change to these men. What did Eel care if a few politicos were greasing palms to pass a zoning ordinance? The price of doing business in a free market economy. But no, that response had been too swift, too efficient and clusterfucked at the same time. Left a bad, bitter taste. It reeked of a set up.

Took a few days and a lot of miles. Phone calls. Inquiries.

Calling in favors. The big one to Carter. It wasn't like the friends ever fell out of touch.

Carter had done well for himself south of the border. Better than well, in fact. Carter's reputation rivaled that of Clovis Harrington, the man Eel and his cohorts had just robbed, the man whom Eel should've known better than to go after. But not because of what Harrington was. It was the men Harrington really worked for. The monsters behind the curtain.

Carter confirmed what Eel already knew. That money they stole? Cartel money. He left Eel to wonder. Juárez? Zeta? Didn't matter. He wasn't walking away from this. He would be hunted down, propped on a post in the Sonora, innards picked clean by vultures and coyotes. His best chance was to broker a deal. Make a trade. Eel was no snitch. But self-preservation trumped all. Carter could be the go-between.

He watched the motel parking lot. No cars other than his, which he'd traded out twice on the road. Untraceable. No motorcycles. No trucks. Nothing but the heat. Vapors rose from the tarmac, gasoline sheens dancing, shimmering in waves. Eel hated waiting almost as much as he hated the heat. But Carter had said to wait. So Eel had no choice but to sit tight. Of course, this extra time meant too much time to think. And not just about the fuckjob on the ranch, his partners who, if they weren't dead yet, were being hunted like game, exterminated one by one. Whether they knew it or not. No, Eel Estevez remembered being a boy, how his life might've turned out differently had he gone with Carter back to Mexico. He sure as shit wouldn't be in this mess. Eel hated dwelling on the past, regrets, alternate futures. It was ridiculous, pointless. It was what it was, would be what it would be.

You know how I knew I was a thief? I knew I was a thief when I stole....

Eel laughed when he thought about those two skinny Mexican peckerwoods living in El Paso. Two boys in love with being outlaws before they even knew what such commitment entailed, glossed-over lessons learned from actors pretending to be the renegades they hoped to be. Some boys wanted to be heroes. Not Eel and Carter. They longed to be the bad guys, rooted for the villains. Eel just fought it longer, tried to take the righteous path, enlisted, did just enough to get honorably discharged. But all roads lead you back to who you really are, eventually. Carter had always been the smarter of the two.

Eel picked up what was left of a bottle, drained the dregs, lit a cigarette, and peered out of the blinds into the sweltering parking lot. Those vapors kept rising from the tarmac, smoking snakes, diablos distorting fields of nothing across the two-lane road. Dry tumbleweeds and tinder brush, snapped coils from the staked posts, whiplashed and now lying flaccid in the dusty culverts. He checked the bedside table. The motel clock either hadn't been plugged in, or had been ripped from the socket in the throes of inebriated, high-octane sex. What was this girl's name? His head swirled. He shouldn't have drunk so much. But goddamn he hadn't wanted to be in his head last night. His dead grandfather's voice crept in once more. The last time Eel snuck south of the border, when the old man was dying. To see him one last time.

"That is why crime pays so well, mijo," the old man said. "Because it's illegal."

His father, on the other hand, Auturo, did not judge his only son for his chosen vocation. A farmer who'd toiled for nothing but fast-acting cancers and an early grave, the senior Estevez all but gave his blessing for the path Eel chose to take. In the movies, American movies, they always showed the honest, hard-working father imparting lessons on their wannabe criminal child, trying to talk sense into them to do the right thing. Drive a bus. Work in a factory. An honest day's wages for an honest day's work meant more than all the riches in the world. Bullshit. Lies. Chupapingas. Money doesn't buy happiness was just what the rich told you so you didn't go after their gold.

Of all the jobs, this one... this one should've been easy. Until that fucking pilot and his buddy had to get greedy. His own men. Whatever happened to honor among thieves? Another bullshit lie Hollywood sold.

The plump girl turned in her sleep woozily, dreamily, mounting her rump in the air, wriggling it, as though it had a mind of its own, begging for another go. The only thing separating her round, luscious ass from the free, open air, that threadbare sheet. Eel could almost hear her moaning, cooing. And he thought about it too. He couldn't remember exactly how they'd met, only that it was at the bar, after he'd arranged to meet Carter this morning, drawing on the bonds of brotherhood to get him out of this jam. Brother or not, this favor was asking a lot. Going behind the back of the cartel wasn't just risky, it was gambling with his life. But Carter, like Eel, had never married, never had kids, was a floating wolf. This made Eel feel better. A man could wager his own life easier when he didn't have to worry about the welfare of others.

Carter said to stay put. Have a drink, relax, get laid. Carter said he was on his way. So Eel drank. And he picked up the girl. A big-boned, beautiful girl. The fucking had been good, and she gave as good as she got. He recalled that much, the way he took her from behind, and she took him right back. At least that was how he chose to remember it. If his raw, aching cock was any indication, his memory wasn't far off. Both drunk, high on the blow she brought with her back from the bar. He felt the claw marks on his back begin to blister, the red, raised lines starting to sting as he sweated, flashes of her thick thighs returning to his mind's eye, the way they bounced off his lap, running through the baker's dozen, before she turned around again, put her head down, ass up, just the way he liked it, just the way it was now. But as tempting as that ass was, Eel turned away, watching for Carter. Now wasn't a time to get distracted. Last night, he'd needed to kill the time. This morning, the focus was more on not getting killed.

He shifted in his jeans, tucked his cock down severely, admonishing the thing with disdain worthy of a Catholic nun, shielding himself from that rump twitching out the corner of his eye. He thought of the horrors, the men who'd wronged the wrong men, the neckties slit across throats to pull tongues through, until nothing stirred below.

Nothing moved in the parking lot either. Now he saw there was one other car in the parking lot besides the one he'd hotwired six counties back. In the far end of the lot, a non-descript, rusted, red sedan lurked in the shadows. He could see it hadn't run in ages, like it had been left in that parking lot so long it had sunk into the melted tar. The bar next door, now closed until probably at least noon, loomed eerily staid, throwing shade. All of it too quiet, too lifeless. He peeked over his shoulder at the broken clock. The big-boned blonde fell back to the mattress, ass returning to slumber.

Eel searched out another bottle, took a pull of mostly backwashed, hot tequila, laughing suddenly for no reason other than he had gotten his nickname for being slippery, slithery. Apparently, "Snake" had been taken. At first, he hated the nickname, but like most nicknames, you didn't get to choose your own, someone made it up for you, you didn't get a say, and those kind always stuck. Carter was smart enough to make his own name. You either named yourself. Or someone else did it for you.

And the slippery part fit the bill. Through all the jobs, all the bad turns and rotten luck, the paydays lost, the backstabs and betrayals, the raids, the DEA and ATF and every other goddamn acronym that closed in – because no matter how good you were they were always closing in – Eel Estevez had never spent as much as a night in jail. It was a source of pride. Being a border Mexican, probably for the best. Especially these days. It was funny. The gringos didn't mind you picking their fucking strawberries for ten cents an hour, but every November, some politico was preaching on the nightly news about the scourge of his kind, stealing the fucking jobs no one else wanted. His kind? No one embraced the capitalistic ethic like the career criminal. You see, you want, you take by power and might. By superiority.

Gennifer. With a G. That was the name of the girl in his bed. It finally came to him. That was how she'd introduced herself when he got off the phone with Carter, having slipped the barkeep a bill to use the houseline and keep his fucking head turned and ears shut, burner tossed long ago. "Hi. I'm Gennifer. With a G. And you look like you want to buy me a drink." He liked that. The sass to go along with that ass. He may've actually said that. He'd already started tying one on by that point. Sure, it was a cheesy, stupid line, but that was why bars serve booze. A drunk man's tongue, a sober man's mind.

Eel let the blinds fall and eye-checked the rucksack handcuffed to the bedpost, patted his pockets, fingering the key like tonguing a loose tooth. A brief, fleeting thought popped in his head. Maybe he shouldn't wait for Carter. Maybe sitting here, he was a sitting duck. It popped out as quick. More than his own hide, he had to help Benny. The others? Fuck 'em. But he liked Benny. He'd brought him in. They'd been tight ever since the Army. Outside of Carter, Benny might've been the only true friend he'd ever had. And Carter was his one shot at making it out of here alive. Once Eel figured out how to do that, he'd call Benny. Not that Benny would listen. By now the poor son of a bitch was probably heading west to make a deposit into his magic piggybank that would one day allow him to retire, fall in love, live a regular life. Men like Benny and Eel didn't get to do that. But Eel owed him that much. If Eel could get himself out of this mess, he'd do his best to get Benny out as well. A two-for-one. Of course, that would involve Benny giving up the money, something he'd naturally resist. Not like he had any choice. All that money would be returned, one way or the other. Poor Benny had always been a dreamer.

Gennifer rolled over, long blonde hair fanning across the pillows as she spread arms and legs, the dark patch between the sheets making it clear she was open for business. The clear, unglazed look in her eyes told Eel she'd been awake the whole time, pretending to be dreaming while shaking that fat ass, teasing him.

"Guess I tired you out last night," she said, reaching for her cigarettes on the scarred end table. When Eel didn't seize the moment, she flicked on the lamp.

"Turn that fucking thing off."

"What's your problem?" She pointed to the bright, sunny window, rays unable to be contained by one-hundred-count curtains and mangled plastic blinds. "It's morning."

"I said turn it off."

Gennifer muttered curses but turned off the lamp, staring at the blank screen of the bedside alarm. "What time is it anyway?"

"I'm guessing eleven." Eel looked at the blank clock, then turned back to the window.

"What's so interesting out there that you don't want another go at this?" Gennifer with a G spread her hands over robust thighs, which she parted wider now, the dark v radiating heat beneath that thin-sheer sheet.

Eel didn't give it a second glance. "I'm waiting on someone."

"Who?"

"None of your fucking business." He let the blinds fall, gathering her jeans and panties, bra off the chair, tossing them on the bed. "I think it's time you go."

"Sure know how to treat a lady."

Eel peeled off a fifty from his wad and tossed that on the bed too. "Go get some breakfast. On me."

"Where you want me to go? There's only the bar next door and it ain't open till three, and they don't serve food anyway."

"Then drive somewhere."

"Don't got no car."

"How'd you get to the bar?"

"A friend."

"Call your friend."

Gennifer with a G nibbled her lip, crawling on all fours,

playfully clawing out for his belt. "I thought you were my friend."

"I'm not." He went back to gazing out the window while she huffed and groaned. He heard her rolling off the bed, slipping on her bra and panties, fumbling for the tight jeans, shoes, parts of a purse he'd spilled in search of prophylactics.

Eel hadn't driven all the way across the state to get blindsided while fucking some piece of ass. Eel computed the hours in his head. It shouldn't be taking Carter this long to get here. Not under the circumstances. Carter wasn't some rookie getting pulled over at a checkpoint. And Carter wasn't pissing away valuable time on anything not one hundred percent necessary. Something was wrong.

A few thoughts hit Eel Estevez at once: What had happened to Carter? Were they on to him that quick? Had they gotten to Carter first? If so, they'd be coming for him next. He had to move. But where to? Why were his feet rooted, refusing to cooperate? The last thought, though, the one that really stung – where the hell had she hidden the gun?

Eel turned slowly, hands up where she could see them before she ordered him to do so. It was a small point of pride but Eel didn't like being told what to do. When she bent and undid the handcuffs around the post, freeing the bag and the money, he resisted feeling for the key in his pockets. He didn't believe in magic, but no one was so good they could pick a pocket ten feet away.

"Duplicate," she said. "Generic."

"What if I'd tried to leave?"

"Honey, I've been awake all night. You wasn't doing anything without me knowing about it. And I'm telling you this for your own good. You make it out of this? Get yourself checked for sleep apnea. You snore like a wild boar."

Eel could only stare.

She titled her head, almost sympathetic, like she really gave a shit. "This isn't personal. It's a job. I got the call. I'm getting paid. I was told to keep you occupied." She let her gaze drift down to his cock. "Worse ways to spend a night." Gennifer stood up like the pro she was, nodded at the door. "Let's go."

She didn't need to tell him not to do anything stupid. She didn't need to warn him not to run. Eel Estevez knew when he'd fallen into a spider's web.

The walk down the motel's baked brick sidewalk and across the arid parking lot with a gun to his back didn't draw any attention. Because there was no one else there to bear witness. But that heat, it sucked what little breath he had left, that diesel ooze cooking in the sun blast, like taking a lungful of broiled oven.

They entered through the back door, the bar wouldn't be open to the public any time soon, and there was a moment before Eel felt the cold rush of air conditioning, where, trapped between the bright heat outside and cold stone indoors, he considered making a move. It was a second, maybe less. She was close enough that if he spun and sprung, he could push her aside and run. But then what? Even if she was a lousy shot, his keys were back in the room. Nothing but fucking desert. Endless miles of scrub brush, dry grass, and sand. How far could he really run? What about Carter? What about Benny?

The cool, dark bar felt different in the day. And not just for the obvious, that light had replaced night, silence snuffing clinking glasses and barroom chatter. This was the moment Eel's fate turned for good, and there would be no turning back. He wasn't eighteen anymore. He wasn't in the Army. He wasn't on Clovis Harrington's ranch either. He could take losing. He could take dying. He'd always known he'd die young. But not like this.

Carter sported more weight than the last time they'd seen one another, that short stretch when Eel returned to Mexico to watch his grandfather die. Two more men were with him. When Eel heard the back door lock, he figured at least one more lurked out of sight.

"Drink?" Carter said.

Eel nodded. Carter pointed, and a set of arms guided Eel to the booth. From the corner of his eye, he saw the woman, Gennifer, hand over the case, taking a thick envelope in exchange. Their eyes never met again.

Carter returned with a bottle of mescal and two shot glasses, nodding back to where the whore just exited. "I remembered you liked them thick."

"How…" It was all Eel could get out.

"Do you know who you fucked with, amigo? Clovis Harrington isn't some hick steer farmer. Soon as you mentioned the name, nothing I could do."

"Nothing, eh?"

"I had to call it in." Carter poured the drinks. "This isn't personal, Eel."

"Feels a little personal."

"I know you don't want to go back to jail."

"Back? I've never been."

"That's not what I meant."

Eel pounded his shot. "So what now, amigo? You take the money? Hand me off to the Juárez, Zeto? Who?"

The other men in the room were far enough away that Eel could break the bottle, get behind Carter. Flush to the door, a hostage came in handy. Then again, there was a reason Carter had them positioned where they were. Eel's short time in the Army taught him about blind spots, turkey shoots, when it was time to surrender.

"That money," Carter said, "goes back to Harrington. Every last cent. I paid Selena out of my own pocket."

"Selena?"

"What name did she give you?"

"Does it matter?"

"No, I guess not."

Carter poured them each another shot.

"How'd she get here so fast?"

"She was here. Harrington owns damn near every border bar in Texas. Or knows who does. He's built his own goddamn wall. And nothing gets in or out without his say-so. He's a loyal employee. He knows better than to cross those boys."

"You didn't have to call him?"

"Me? Call him?" Carter howled. "Eel, the second you and those other dipshits took the money, you were made. Every known associate called. You think the policia can put out an APB? Ain't nothing compared to the men you stole from. You'd've had better luck robbing the U.S. Mint. I don't know who set this up–"

"You think I'm going to tell you now?"

"You don't have to. They'll figure it out. If they haven't already. You were played, holmes."

"Seven million ain't what it used to be."

"Seven million? Is that what you thought you were stealing?" Carter gestured back at the room, where more men gathered, local roughnecks looking for an easy payday. Everyone was for sale, three turning to six, seven, crawling out of the woodwork like cucarachas. "You don't get this kind of greeting for pinching a cow fucker."

So this is what friendship means, thought Eel. But he didn't let himself think it long. Now was not the time for sentimentality.

"Harrington is in deep. Deep, mi amigo. We're talking ops, government, shadow shit. That money was more than slush fund, more than Juárez, Zeta, and it was a fucklot more than seven million dollars. Every gang from here to the Neches uses the Bank of Harrington." Carter shook his head. "What happened to you? How did you lose your way so bad to fall in with this lot?"

"Lose my way?" Eel tried not to laugh. But he didn't try too hard. He gestured under the table. "I was there when you skinned your knee, three inches from that rattlesnake."

"You think I forget?"

"Took its head off with my boot heel and a tug."

Carter looked hurt. "You mean you saved my life?"

"More than once."

"Sorry I can't return the favor. Nothing I can do. You see these men? More are coming. They will make an example of you, Eel. They'll slit your throat, pull your tongue through the hole, stick your head on a pole. Cut off your dick, stuff it in your mouth, before they fuck your corpse."

"You could've just called with the bad news."

Carter didn't look hurt. Carter's feelings *were* hurt.

Blood in, blood out.

Eel, so quick to rush to judgment, assuming everyone had a price, like that whore back in the room. He felt ashamed. He didn't need to be told. Carter hadn't made the trip to deliver the news; Diego had.

"Figured it best if you heard it from me." Carter waited. "In person, like this." He motioned between them, voice quicting. "Me. You. The way it's supposed to be. We kick open the door, eh?"

"I'm sorry," Eel said. He knew now that everyone he cared about, a group that comprised two, was going to pay.

Carter waved him off. "Once you made the call, well, that was that."

"I am sorry."

"Don't be. We swore blood brothers a long time ago."

Carter poured two more shots like it was no big thing. "Could've been either one of us. I mean, I've done some stupid shit too. You wouldn't let me go alone." He caught his eye, sincere. "Would you?"

"No," Eel said, "I wouldn't."

Bringing the shot glass to his lips, Carter's eyes fell to the table, rolling long enough to say, Look what's taped underneath. Soon as they set the shot glasses down, the two men jabbed their hands into the dark depths and pulled the taped guns.

Sure, the odds were against them. Like Butch and Sundance. Eel tried to preserve the frozen moment here. Because before the bullets split the skull, it was the last scene playing that mattered most. The one that would be imprinted, seared for all eternity. And if it stopped there, in a way, that was where the story ended.

CHAPTER 8
I Got You
by Brett Battles

The drone of the highway was just the tonic Benny Parker needed to sooth away the tension of the last few days. The jobs he did with O'Conner and Estevez always took a toll on him, bending him into someone he wasn't, someone who could do terrible things.

He glanced at the duffel bag in the passenger seat. Inside was one hundred seventy-five thousand dollars in untraceable bills. The reason for the hell he put himself through.

If only all their heists were this lucrative, he'd just need to do one more and he could get out. In reality, it would be more like three or four before he could put this temporary life behind him.

Estevez wasn't going to be happy when Benny dropped that bomb, but c'est la vie. Robbing others was Eel's thing. For Benny, the gigs were only a means to an end he could reach no other way.

He stopped at a motel called the Rest Easy an hour before dawn. After a lukewarm shower, he sat on the bed and counted the cash.

It wasn't that he didn't trust O'Conner. The counting was a tradition. One that, on this particular morning, started not at zero, but at one million one hundred thousand. When he finished, he was surprised to find an extra ten grand in the bag, bringing his total count to one million two hundred and eighty-five thousand. Just two hundred and fifteen grand to go.

After repacking the bag, he stretched out on the bed, put an arm through the duffel's straps, and fell into a deep sleep.

"Norris," she said, extending a hand. "Eva."

"Parker, Benny."

He'd just flown in that morning, and Eva had been sent to escort him to their squad.

Attractive? Hell, yes. Five foot five with boots on, and a hundred and twenty pounds of lean muscle. Close-cropped hair, and skin tone and eyes that reminded him a little of Zoe Saldana.

"Well, Parker. Hungry?"

"Very."

They hit it off from the start, sharing the same sense of humor, and a similar view of the world. About their only difference was that Eva had a kid back home from a previous marriage. Benny had neither a kid nor a marriage, previous or not.

There was no denying their mutual attraction, but neither ever acted on it. It was like they had an unspoken agreement that maybe, someday. But for now, the bond of their friendship was more important.

"I got you, Parker," she would say on every mission.

"I got you, Norris," he would fire back.

* * *

By noon the following day, he was in Oregon, off the interstate and driving the backroads toward home in Oregon. The moment the chain blocking the private dirt drive to his grandfather's old cabin came into view he felt the sense of peace he always did upon return.

The driveway wasn't so much a road as a couple of tire ruts the forest kept trying to reclaim. Here and there, the trees encroached so close it almost seemed there was no room to get by, but he knew better.

When Benny inherited the cabin, the place had been but a few winters away from falling apart. He'd been in the Army by that point, and used whatever leave he could get to go up and work on the place. He'd been thinking that after he finally got out, the cabin would be his weekend retreat from city life. Little did he know then that when he actually did leave the service, the cabin's quiet and solitude would be all he wanted, and he'd make it his home.

After parking, he slung the duffel over one shoulder and his travel kit over the other, and walked toward the cabin, road weary and glad to be home.

Nearing the porch steps, he stopped and frowned. The thread he stretched across the middle step before he'd left had been broken. It didn't necessarily mean anything. Of all the traps he'd set around the cabin to let him know if someone had been there, this one was the easiest to trigger. A curious squirrel, a hard wind, a bird wanting the thread for its nest. It could be anything.

A quick check of the dirt in front of the steps revealed a waffle pattern created by a pair of hiking boots. Distinctive. Not his boots.

So not a squirrel or a bird. A person.

The prints didn't necessarily mean trouble either. He'd

had his share of hikers stop by and ask for directions. Likely, that was the source, but it was always better to err on the side of caution.

He set the duffels on the ground, retrieved his pistol from his kit, and followed the prints. They led across the parking area and into the trees where they disappeared in the bed of pine needles and broken branches. A search around revealed another print on a spot of open ground. Not the same waffle pattern as the first, though. Two people? Maybe, or maybe they were made at the same time. He hunted for more prints, but came up empty.

Back at the cabin, he checked his other traps. Nothing else had been tripped, so he picked up his bags and went inside.

Like with the counting, he had a returning home ritual too. An order of how things were to be done.

One: set his kit on dining table.

Two: unlock the padlock and two deadbolts securing the basement door.

Three: carry the money duffel down the stairs.

Four: set it on his grandfather's old desk.

Five: detach the baseboard and remove the false wall.

Six: open the safe.

The safe was large, the interior a good three feet deep by the same wide and another five tall. Even at that size, though, the one point one million it already held took up most of the space.

One by one, he added the new haul to the fund.

"Almost there," he said when he was done. "Almost."

Back upstairs, he warmed a can of stew, ate it standing up, and then dragged himself to bed.

* * *

The wind always drove people crazy.

The undulating howl and the sand in your face and the very air you breathed blowing so hard you had to fight it just to get where you wanted to go.

Benny hated patrolling on nights like this. It felt as if an electric pulse bubbled under the surface of everything, like a buried transformer ready to explode. These were the nights better spent on base in a bunk, praying no one decided to lob a missile your way.

The whole squad was on edge. Conversations stilted. The few jokes told falling flat. And in between, long bouts of tense silence.

A half hour before midnight, the radio crackled through their APC. Gunfire reported. And since Benny and his friends were closest, they won the see-if-it's-a-problem lottery.

"Here we go, here we go, here we go," T-Rod said.

The others checked their equipment and remained silent. Nights like these, you didn't want to temp the gods.

When they arrived at the provided coordinates, Crane, their lieutenant, said, "Norris, take your team and see what you can find out,"

"I got you, Parker," Eva whispered as they piled out of the vehicle with Southside, Dolan, T-Rod, and their translator, Khaleel.

"I got you, Norris."

It took a few minutes before they found a local who pointed them toward where the gunfire had originated.

Eva sent Khaleel back to the APC, and then led the team into a quiet neighborhood of narrow streets. Deep in the maze, they came upon a partially destroyed factory. Bomb damage. Months old at least. No way to know which side was responsible.

"Let's check it out," Eva said.

"Ah, come on," Southside groaned under his breath.

"Thanks for volunteering, Southside. You, me, and Benny on point. T-Rod, Dolan, cover us."

After activating their night vision goggles, Eva nodded to T-Rod and Dolan. Once the two men had the doorless entry covered, Eva, Benny, and Southside swung inside, rifles ready.

Room by room, they worked their way through the building. When Eva spotted the still intact door at the end of a rubble strewn room, she pointed to herself and Benny, and then signaled Southside to remain with Dolan and T-Rod.

It opened with a shove from Benny's shoulder. On the other side, a set of stone stairs led down. Benny went first, rifle butted against his shoulder, Eva following a few steps behind. When he reached the bottom, he swung out and scanned the area.

A small room, its floor littered with toppled furniture and bits of broken building, but otherwise empty. There were two other doorways, one along the wall ahead and another on the one to the left.

He crept over to the opening on the left and peeked through. A small room, empty except for the rubble.

He shook his head as he returned to where Eva waited.

Together, they approached the other doorway. Beyond it was a hall with four additional exits.

Fan-fucking-tastic, Benny thought.

The first two rooms were filled with toppled shelves. Storage space, apparently. The ceiling had collapsed in the third room, making it impossible to get inside. There was similar damage in the last, though not a total cave in. There the ceiling had broken roughly in half, creating a kind of cavern that could be reached through a narrow opening in the wreckage.

They crawled in a few feet and scanned around. There wasn't a damn thing of interest as far as Benny could see. He tapped Eva on the shoulder, and started motioning that they should get out of there when a rifle boomed, and a bullet ripping through the tunnel they were in barely missing Benny's arm.

A second shot when off right on its heels, but the bullet slammed harmlessly into the rubble. A moment later, they heard someone scrambling through the cavern ahead.

"Shots fired! Shots fired!" Southside said over the radio. "Norris, Parker, are you all right?"

Benny had barely replied, "We're okay," when he spotted a person streak across the cavern and pull up into a gap in the half-fallen ceiling. "Shooter coming your way! South of where we came down!"

Benny squeezed through the last of the broken concrete into the cavern, and ran over to where the person had disappeared. As soon as Eva was through the tunnel, she joined him.

"I don't see anything," he said, looking up at the hole.

"Give me a boost," she said.

With his hands he created a step, and lifted her until she had a grip on the broken ceiling.

"Clear," she said after a quick scan. She pulled herself all the way up and held a hand down to Benny, helping him through the opening.

"Dolan, anything?" she said over the radio.

"Can't find the goddamn hole," he said.

"Don't worry about the hole," she said. "The shooter's up already. Just look–"

A sound. Grit scraping the floor under someone's foot.

She motioned for Benny to circle right, and then she headed left.

"I see something!" T-Rod said. "I think it's the shooter!"

"Where?" Dolan asked.

"In the other room. Through that break in the wall."

"What break?"

"Right there!"

The pause that followed lasted no more than two seconds. Then all hell broke loose.

Benny woke before dawn.

Sit ups first. Five hundred, plus an extra hundred because he'd been away. Pull ups next, using the bar in the closet doorway. Two sets of fifty, and the promise of an additional set that evening. Again, as make up.

He took a shower, and started a fire in the fireplace, then poured himself some coffee and headed to the front porch to watch the sun come up. A moment after he opened the door, though, he quickly closed it again. At the far end of the clearing, where the driveway began, moonlight had glistened off the windshield of a pickup truck.

Crouching to stay out of sight through the windows, he crept over to his desk. He retrieved his Glock from the bottom drawer, then reached under the center of the desk and popped loose his Mossberg 930 shotgun from the clips holding it in place.

With the pistol tucked safely into his waistband at the small of his back, he moved into the kitchen and peered through the back window, looking for shadows that shouldn't be there. Seeing nothing unusual, he slipped outside and snuck into the woods behind the house. A wide arc through the forest brought him to within twenty-five feet of the unfamiliar pickup, and gave him his first good look inside the cab.

A bearded man sat in the driver's seat, leaning against the door as if asleep. Benny crept up to the vehicle and checked the license plate. California, with a frame touting a San Diego Ford dealership. A long way from home.

He moved over to the driver's door, and rose up until he could see the man's face.

What the hell?

While the beard was new, there was no mistaking the rest of the man's features. It was Dolan, his old squad mate.

Benny tapped the Mossberg against the glass. Dolan jerked away from the door, blinking in confusion. When he caught sight of Benny, though, he grinned. "Parker!"

"What are you doing here?"

Dolan opened the door, and climbed out, then seemed to notice the shotgun for the first time. "You going hunting?"

"I asked you a question."

"Chill out, man. I'm headed to Idaho to visit my uncle and was in the area, so thought I'd drop by."

"Is that so?"

"Took me longer to find this place than I thought. By then it was pretty late, and I didn't want to wake you." With a shiver, he glanced at the cabin. "Mind if we go inside? I'm freezing my ass off."

"How did you know where I lived?"

"Seriously? You talked about this place all the time, remember?"

"I don't remember telling anyone the address."

"You've heard of the internet, right?" He rubbed his

hands over his arms. "Can we continue the interrogation inside before I start losing circulation?"

Benny wanted nothing more than to tell him to be on his way, but that might make Dolan curious as to why he was so anxious to get rid of him. "I got coffee," he said, and started for the cabin.

Dolan grabbed a bag out of the cab, slammed the door shut, and hurried to catch up.

"You can't stay," Benny told him, glancing at the bag. "I'm not… set up for guests."

"Relax. Not planning on moving in. Just thought I could clean up a little. Change my clothes. I wouldn't say no to a shower, though."

Upon entering the house, Benny hung his jacket on one of the hooks by the door. Dolan followed suit, then looked around.

"So this is the grandpa's cabin. Not bad. Cozy, even." When his gaze landed on the fireplace, he grabbed a chair from the table, planted it in front of the hearth, and plopped down. "You said something about coffee?"

In the kitchen, Benny set the Mossberg on the counter, and put the Glock into the junk drawer by the sink before pouring Dolan his coffee and heading back to the living room.

"Thanks," Dolan said, taking the mug. "This place is nice and all, but man, talk about isolated. You don't live up here full time, do you? I mean, what would you do for work?"

Ignoring the question, Benny said, "How long did they keep you in?"

For the first time, Dolan's smile slipped. "Thirteen months."

His sentence had been almost twice that long.

"And you went back to San Diego?"

"They weren't going to keep me in the Army. Besides, where else would I go? Great weather, no humidity, and the ocean. What's not to love?" He took a drink, and then set the mug down. "You mind if I take off my boots? I can barely feel my toes."

"Go ahead."

Dolan tugged off his boots, and extended his feet toward the fire. "Oh, man, does that feel good." He glanced over at Benny. "You ever run into any of the old gang?"

"Gang?"

"The squad."

"No."

"That was some crazy times, wasn't it?"

Benny grunted noncommittally.

Dolan downed the remaining coffee in a single gulp, then said, "So, any chance I could get that shower?"

"Sure. I'll get you a towel."

After Dolan was set up in the bathroom, Benny carried Dolan's mug into the kitchen and then went back to move his unwanted guest's boots to the door. One of them lay on its side, and as he picked them up, he noticed the distinctive pattern of the tread. It appeared to be an exact match to the print in front of his cabin.

Son of a bitch.

He set the boots by the door and retrieved the Glock from the kitchen, slipping it back into his belt. To cover its presence, he grabbed his Oregon State hoodie from the rack and pulled it on.

He contemplated leaving the Mossberg out where he could easily grab it, but he didn't want to chance Dolan going for it first, so he secured it back under the desk. That way he'd be the only one to know its location.

By the time Dolan strolled out, Benny was sitting at the dining table, ostensibly going through the stack of mail that had been sitting there since before the Harrington job.

"You been gone or something?" Dolan asked.

"I only pick up the mail a couple times a month."

"Really? Huh. Don't think I could ever get used to country life." He walked back over to the fire, but remained standing. "Say, you never answered my question about what you're doing to make ends meet these days."

Benny opened an envelope and pulled out an advertisement for life insurance. "A little bit of this and that," he replied without looking up.

"That's not what I heard."

Trying not to show his surprise, Benny casually glanced at Dolan. "What did you hear?"

"That you hooked up with that Army buddy you used to talk about sometimes. Not from our squad. You called him… what was it? Eel?"

Benny let his arm drop naturally to his side, and began slipping his hand behind his back. "Who did you hear that from?"

"It's true, isn't? I also heard he's into some pretty heavy duty shit."

Benny's fingers closed around the Glock's grip, and began to ease the pistol out.

"Whoa there, Parker," a voice from the hallway said. "You don't want to do that." The floorboards creaked as T-Rod stepped into the light, holding a Smith & Wesson pistol. "Hey, buddy. Long time."

Dolan circled behind Benny, lifted the back of the hoodie, and yanked out the Glock. "Well, look at this."

"The shotgun's under the desk," T-Rod said.

"Is that so?"

T-Rod locked eyes with Benny and grinned. "I've been watching you since you came home. You still snore like a freight train."

Dolan yanked out the shotgun, and then sat down at the table in the chair opposite Benny. He laid the Mossberg in front him. "Word around is that Estevez is in bed with some powerful people, and that he's brought you in on their fun."

"Rumors have a way of not being true."

"I'm talking big scores."

Benny said nothing.

"You remember Billy Carson? We'd see him around the base. I don't remember what squad he was in."

Though Benny's expression didn't change, inside, he cringed.

"I guess he knows your buddy Estevez too. Says Eel hired him for a job, promising a bigger one if things went well. I guess they didn't because Eel never called him again. Carson was telling us the story... when was that? Last month?"

"Yeah," T-Rod said. "Last month."

"The part I found most interesting was that he said you were Eel's partner. Imagine my shock. Mr. Straight and Narrow living a life of crime. I got to thinking if our old buddy Parker's in on this, he should be able to get us in on it too."

Fucking Carson and his big fucking mouth. Eel had paid the guy nicely for subpar work, making it clear that the dumbass was never to speak of the job or Estevez or Benny when it was over.

"So T-Rod and me, we decided we'd pay you a visit, see how we might assist in your operations. I have to say, when we got here a couple of days ago, I was surprised to find you living in this dump. I thought with all the cash you were supposed to have, you'd have fixed it up into some kind of mansion."

"Obviously, your information is shit," Benny said.

"I don't think it is. We go back, you and me. We were tight once."

That was a lie. They were never tight.

"I know you," Dolan went on. "You're a planner, Parker. You'd know that the smart move would be to leave most of the cash untouched. When you'd made enough, you'd skip the country, start a new life somewhere with a new identity. I should have realized that from the start."

Benny couldn't deny daydreaming of doing exactly that. But that's all it had ever been, and while Dolan was right about using only the cash he needed to survive, he couldn't be more wrong about what the remainder was intended for.

"What I want to know is where you are stashing it while you wait for the right moment. The banks report that kind of stuff to the feds, so you'd have to hide it somewhere. Which got my mind whirling around again. Hell, I thought, why ask for work when we can have all your money for doing nothing?" He smiled. "Tell us where it is, and we'll be on our way."

"A nice story. And even if it were true, why would I ever tell you?"

"I'm asking nicely. I won't do that again."

"Go to hell."

Dolan whipped up the Glock and pulled the trigger.

The bullet slammed into Benny's left arm, spinning him sideways out of the chair.

Grimacing, Benny clamped his hand over the wound, then turned toward the kitchen, thinking he could make a run for the back door, but T-Rod was standing in the way.

The chair at the other end of the table scrapped across the floor, and Dolan walked over. "Where's the cash, Parker?"

"Fuck off."

T-Rod kicked Benny in the stomach, knocking the air out of the man's lungs.

"Where?" Dolan asked.

Chest heaving, Benny eked out, "Fuuuck... off."

Whether it was T-Rod's plan or not, his next blow hit Benny in the head, and the world went dark.

Benny hit the floor of the bombed out factory a moment after the barrage of M4 rifle fire started. Bullets and chunks of bricks and mortar flew through the air, some debris smacking down on him, but most sailing over.

"Cease fire! Cease fire," he yelled into the radio.

The pounding continued for another few seconds before stopping. Benny lay there for another beat, just to be sure, and then pushed up and looked around for Eva. He spotted her limp form on the ground a dozen feet away and rushed over.

"Oh, God!"

Her face and the top of her uniform were covered in blood that had come from a wound on the side of her neck, near the base of her skull. The kind of wound you never recovered from.

"Open your eyes!" he yelled, not wanting to believe it. "Eva, open your eyes!" She wasn't supposed to die. Neither of them was ever supposed to die.

Footsteps ran into the room, then slammed to a stop a few feet away.

"Is she... is she...?" Southside couldn't get the last word out.

"Oh shit, oh shit, oh shit," T-Rod said.

"It wasn't me!" Dolan yelled. "I swear. It's wasn't me!"

If the Army investigators ever discovered whose rifle fired the fatal bullet, they never released that information. Dolan and T-Rod received two-year sentences at Leavenworth for some minor charge Benny never bothered to learn. Ultimate blame for the incident was placed at Eva's feet since she had been in charge of the squad. Benny and Southside were cleared of any wrongdoing and transferred back to the States. Though Benny had always planned to reenlist, as soon as his current commitment was up, he opted out.

Three months later, Eel called.

Water hit Benny in the face.

"Snap out of it, Parker."

Benny groaned, his arm and his head throbbing in pain. Slowly, he opened his eyes. He was sitting on one of the dining room chairs, though not at the table. Instead, he was in the kitchen, facing the back of the house, with Dolan and T-Rod standing before him.

"It's about time," Dolan said.

Benny glanced at his arm and saw that there was a blood-soaked dish rag tied around it.

"We took a tour of your place while you were out. Afraid we kind of made a mess of the things, but, to be clear, that's your fault for not telling us where the money is."

Past them, Benny could see the basement door. Though the padlock had been ripped off the wall, the heavy metal door itself was still closed.

Dolan followed his gaze. "Yeah, we already guessed it's through there. How about you tell me where the deadbolt keys are?"

"Water," Benny whispered.

"Keys then water."

"Water… first."

Dolan frowned, but nodded at T-Rod, who reluctantly filled a plastic cup with water and gave it to Benny.

Benny took his time lifting the cup to his lips and taking a drink, allowing the fog time to clear from his head.

If he let them get downstairs, he knew it wouldn't be long before they found the safe. And if he didn't, they'd probably kill him, then spend as long as it took to break the door down themselves.

But when you kept as much money around as he did, you prepared for situations like this.

He lowered the glass and said, "Inside the sugar bowl."

Dolan spotted the white ceramic bowl on the counter and nodded at T-Rod. T-Rod dumped the contents on the counter. Hidden in the sugar were two keys on a ring.

"See," Dolan said, "that wasn't hard."

T-Rod used the keys to unlock the deadbolts. When he swung open the door, cold air drifted into the kitchen.

"Check it out," Dolan said.

T-Rod descended the stairs, quickly dropping out of sight. Benny could hear the thief moving around below.

After about a minute, Dolan yelled down, "You find anything?"

"Just shelves and junk," T-Rod replied

"He wouldn't leave it sitting out in the open, dipshit. Look for hiding places."

"What do you think I'm doing?"

A few bangs and some scrapping sounds.

"It could be anywhere," T-Rod said.

Dolan looked at Benny. "Parker, if you don't want me to kill you right now, you should tell me where it is."

Benny allowed some faux doubt to cloud his eyes.

Dolan smiled. "That's right. No reason to be stupid."

Benny sighed, as if coming to an unavoidable conclusion. "Easier if-if I show you."

Dolan considered it, and nodded. "If you breathe wrong, it'll be your last." He manhandled Benny to his feet.

"We're coming down," he yelled to T-Rod. He pushed Benny toward the doorway and motioned for him to go first.

T-Rod was waiting at the bottom when they arrived. Benny took a step toward him and spit in the son of a bitch's face.

"Fuck!" T-Rod yelled. He wiped a hand over his eyes and snapped a hand out toward Benny's shirt. But Dolan knocked it away before T-Rod could grab anything.

"Rein it in," Dolan said.

Nostrils flaring, T-Rod said, "He just spit at me!"

"Bigger picture, Rodriguez."

"Screw your bigger picture. He spit on me."

"Cool it!"

T-Rod huffed and puffed for a few more seconds before relenting. "There'd better a lot of fucking cash, that's all I gotta say."

"Which way, Parker?" Dolan said.

Benny led them to the secret wall and slid it out of the way, revealing the safe.

"Holy shit."

Dolan grinned ear to ear. "You are a smart man."

"I assume you want me to open it."

"If you wouldn't mind."

Looking appropriately resigned, Benny put one hand on the dial, and the other around the side of the safe for support it seemed. As he worked the combination, his other hand grasped the metal lever that hung against the side.

After clicking the last number into place, he pulled the door open.

"Oh, yeah!" T-Rod shouted, staring at the stacks of cash.

Dolan seemed to have lost his voice, as he, too, stared, wide-eyed, into the safe.

"How much?" T-Rod asked.

"One point two million, give or take," Benny said.

"Are you shitting me?"

The thieves took a step closer. That was what Benny had been waiting for.

Boom went the Mossberg hidden above the safe in the beams, and down went Dolan and T-Rod.

Benny staggering sideways, wincing from the noise.

Turning back, he saw that T-Rod was down for the count, his face taking a direct hit, pulverizing it. Dolan, on the other hand, was on his knees, looking around. He had also been hit in the head, but the blast had caught him on the side, blowing off an ear, unfortunately leaving his skull intact.

Benny saw the gun lying on the floor a moment before Dolan dove for it. He launched himself at the other man, hoping to pin the asshole down, but Dolan was able to grab the gun and begin to turn before Benny reached him. Their collision was underscored by a blast from the pistol. Benny's momentum slammed Dolan's face hard into the concrete.

Benny yanked the gun away, and stuck the barrel against the back of Dolan's head. Delivering the justice that was years delayed, he put a bullet into Dolan's skull. Benny held his position for a moment, wanting to be sure it was truly over, and then slumped against the wall.

As his adrenaline subsided, he began to feel a sharp pain in his torso. He carefully pulled up his shirt.

"Shit," he whispered.

He had thought the blood covering him had all been Dolan's, but apparently not all of it.

The bullet that had been fired when they crashed together had clipped him in the side. Fighting the pain, he reached around and felt his back, and discovered an exit wound. At least the bullet wasn't still inside him.

Leaning against the wall, knowing that if he went to a hospital, the sheriff's office would be informed and a deputy would be sent to check the cabin. And that would be the end of Benny's plan. He couldn't let that happen.

Benny woke to darkness. He reached for his phone to check the time, but stopped moving the instant his side screamed in pain.

Dolan and T-Rod.

The money.

The gunfire.

Shit.

Earlier, he'd patched himself up as best he could, taken a dose of the antibiotics from his med-kit, and then passed out.

How long had he been asleep? Ten hours? A whole day? More?

He carefully swung his legs off the mattress and rose to his feet, squeezing his eyes shut with each spike of pain. Once it was bearable, he picked up his phone.

3:37 a.m.

He'd been asleep for nearly eighteen hours.

He checked his bandages. While there was a large circle of blood in the middle of the one on his torso, it wasn't completely soaked. The bandage on his arm showed even less blood.

He made his way to the kitchen and turned on the coffee. He was going to need it. A lot of it. Before he'd slept, he'd decided on a course of action.

Though he hadn't reached his monetary goal, what he'd already collected would have to be enough. He had a promise he'd made to himself, and he couldn't risk something else happening before he could keep it.

After redressing his wounds, and cleaning up as best he could, he grabbed his three largest duffel bags and headed into the basement.

The smell of blood hit him the moment he opened the door. He did his best to ignore it as he stepped carefully around the carnage in front of the safe.

In his impaired condition, it took him nearly a half hour to evenly distribute the cash among the bags, and another ten minutes to haul the duffels upstairs.

By five thirty, he had Dolan's truck packed and had returned for a final trip down the stairs. While Dolan was the closest to Benny's size, T-Rod wasn't that far off, and with his face already unrecognizable, he would serve Benny's purpose best. Benny first removed all identification from both men, and then slipped his own wallet – in which he always carried one of his dog tags – into T-Rod's pocket. He then doused both men in lighter fluid and set them ablaze. Eventually, investigators would probably figure out the ruse, but by then it wouldn't matter.

He waited by the truck until he was sure the cabin had caught before he drove away.

Ten miles down the road, he stopped at a gas station and used an old pay phone to call 911 and reported seeing flames in the woods. No sense in burning the whole forest down.

With that done, he headed east.

A few hours after he crossed the Mississippi River, the skin around his wound started feeling irritated. He hoped it was part of the healing process, but as he was driving through Ohio the next morning, he knew he had a problem. The redness was spreading. An infection. Maybe even blood poisoning.

Great.

Since stopping to see a doctor still wasn't an option, he upped his intake of antibiotics, hoping that would do the job.

His fever began outside Erie, Pennsylvania. He swallowed half a dozen aspirin and tried to ignore it. He thought about getting a room for the night when he reached Massachusetts, but he was so close now, he wanted to just press on.

In those final hours, the pull of sleep grew stronger and stronger, but instead of winning the battle, the feeling scared him into a determination to keep going at all cost.

By one a.m., he reached the suburbs, east of Boston.

It took him a half hour to locate the house, an old one-story place on three acres that needed a little work.

Though there was a gate at the end of the driveway, it was open. The lights at the house, however, were off. He idled at the side of the road, his face red from his fever, unsure what he should do.

"I got you, Parker," Eva said.

She was suddenly sitting in the seat next to him.

"I… got you, Norris."

She smiled. "You're almost there."

"I know."

"Thank you."

"I… I could have done… better."

It was only after she evaporated that he realized he should have ask her what to do.

Maybe I should walk around and clear my head.

But as he reached for the door handle, his mid-section screamed in pain. He pressed back against the seat, his breaths shallow and rapid. When the pain eased a little, he peeled back his shirt. The infection had nearly spread all the way across his stomach, and the area closest to his wound had turned black.

"No coming back from this," he mumbled.

Taking a page out of Dolan's book, he killed the truck's lights, pulled onto the driveway, and stopped halfway to the house. He turned off the engine.

He stared at the house, thinking of an alternate life, one in which he visited on happier occasions, with Eva at his side. One where everything was –

He sucked in a deep breath.

He'd started to nod off. He knew what would happen if he did, and he still had work to do first.

Fighting the pain, he leaned over and searched through Dolan's glove compartment. As he'd hoped, there were a couple of pens. He grabbed one, and the owner's manual for the truck. Ripping off the back cover, he turned it blank side up, and began to write.

Like most days, Sandra and Larry Norris were in the kitchen by six thirty a.m. While Sandra cooked oatmeal for their breakfast, Larry made lunch for their granddaughter and put it in a well-used paper bag.

It was almost seven by the time they heard Megan coming down the stairs.

"Grandpa, is someone here?" the girl asked from the other room.

"I'm sorry, honey," Larry said. "What did you say?"

Megan appeared in the doorway. "Whose truck is that?"

"Truck?"

"The one parked in the driveway."

Larry and Sandra went to see what she was talking about. Sure enough, there was a black pickup parked halfway down their drive.

"You two wait here," he said. "I'll check."

He pulled on a light sweater and headed outside. The weatherman had said it was going to be a pretty nice day. It was already feeling that way.

The driveway had been graveled once, but years of use and the punishment of winter had exposed more and more dirt. Maybe someday he'd be able to get it done again.

He hadn't expected to see anyone in the truck, so paused for half a second when he realized someone was sitting in the driver's seat. As Larry neared, he gave a friendly wave, but the person didn't respond. The reason soon became clear. The driver, a man, looked to be asleep.

Larry frowned. Why would someone park in his driveway and fall asleep? Well, he sure couldn't stay there. He was blocking half the road, and Larry would have to take Megan to school soon on his way to work.

He walked up to the driver's door, and was surprised to see that the window was open.

"Excuse me," he said. "Hello?"

He rapped against the door, but the guy didn't move.

"I'm sorry, but I need you to move your truck."

Nothing.

He reached in and shook the guy's shoulder, but instead of waking, the man slumped to the side. Larry could now see that the man's shirt was blood stained.

"Are you all right?"

He opened the door and climbed in far enough so that he could check the man's pulse, except there wasn't any. More than that, though, the man's skin was unnaturally cold.

The guy was dead.

As Larry started to retreat from the cab, his sweater caught on a piece of cardboard that had been propped on the steering wheel. He picked it up, thinking it was just a piece of trash, but checked both sides just to make sure first.

Not trash. Not trash at all.

Mr. and Mrs. Norris –

Not sure you remember me. My name is Benny Parker. I served with your daughter, Eva.

Larry did remember him. Benny had made a trip to Boston to bring them some things of Eva's he'd had. It had been obvious to Larry that Benny was nearly as devastated as they were about their daughter's death.

He leaned back into the cab and took another look at the driver's face. It looked like Benny, though older and pale.

I don't have a lot of time, so will keep this brief. I have something for you. I mean, for Eva's daughter. Sorry, I can't remember her name.

It's in the back of the truck. The three duffel bags. They're hers.

Larry read to the end, and then read it again. When he was through, he checked the back of the truck. Three duffels, just like the letter said.

Using the rear bumper, he climbed inside and opened one of the bags. Stacks of cash. More than he'd ever seen in his life.

I want you to know no one will ever come looking for the money. It's all taken from people who didn't deserve to have it, and often earned it by criminal means. You can, of course, turn it in. But I ask you to take some time and think about it first, and how it can give Megan – it's Megan, right? – how it can give Megan a head start in life.

Your choice is simply this, when you call the police, the bags can be in the truck or not.

Sandra would have turned it over to the police right away, no matter how much it might help their granddaughter.

Larry glanced in the direction of the house, and noted that the truck blocked any view from there of the nearby trees along the drive. He then zipped closed the bag he'd opened and grabbed its straps.

"How much is a life worth?"

It was one of those questions. You know the kind. The would-you-rathers and the what-would-you-do-ifs meant to fill time. That's the thing about war, there was always so much damn downtime between bits of action. The sitting, the waiting, the mindless tasks, the boring patrols where nothing happened. Day after day after day after day.

"What kind of life are we talking about?" Southside asked. "I mean, you know, an old man's? A baby's? What?"

"One of ours," Stevens said. He was the one who asked the question, so he set the rules.

"Hell, my life's priceless." T-Rod tapped his chest and then held his hands out wide to the side. "Ain't enough cash in the world to buy this work of art."

"The Army already bought you," Southside said.

"Bullshit. The Army's only renting. No one's buying me."

"A million dollars."

Everyone turned and looked at Eva.

She shrugged. "I say a million dollars."

"A million dollars?" Dolan said. "Man, that's crazy. You can barely buy a decent house in San Diego for a million dollars."

"Then how much do you think?" Stevens asked him.

"Gotta be at least five, right? Minimum."

Southside laughed. "You ain't gonna make five mil in your entire life. No way you can be worth that much."

The conversation devolved from there into a scrum of numbers being tossed about and counter arguments being made. Benny, who was content to listen to the others chatter, thought Eva was a lot closer to right than Dolan. One point five million seemed fair to him. Enough money for those you left behind to get on their feet and maybe do something with their lives, but not so much that they would get lazy.

As questions went, Stevens' was an all-time great, keeping them occupied for a full three quarters of an hour. By the next day, though, when the wind kicked up, making the world crazy, the others had all forgotten about it.

Everyone but Benny.

CHAPTER 9
Racklin
by Gar Anthony Haywood

"Dude, I'm late," the guy in the backseat said, working his way up to a good tantrum. "The fuck."

Racklin didn't feel like offering the little bitch any apologies, but he knew he owed him one. He pulled the Nissan over to the curb, perfectly parallel, and said, "I did what I could do. You saw the traffic."

His passenger yanked his door open, adorable canvas laptop bag in hand, and smirked. "Shit. My grandmother could have gotten me here faster."

And again, because he was right, Racklin just watched him climb out onto the sidewalk, slamming the car door behind him like a jilted lover, and storm off, into this Grand Avenue high rise where he'd be six minutes late for a meeting with, no doubt, some other twenty-something prick or set of pricks, both or all planning to make millions on the backs of people just like Racklin.

Or, not quite like Howard Racklin, because how many fucking Uber drivers had a retirement fund fit for the COO of General Motors?

Racklin didn't need to do this Uber shit for the money, and he damn sure didn't need to do it for love. He just needed the practice behind the wheel. Because it was this or nothing at all, the end of who and what he'd been all his adult life: a driver. A wheelman. The kind of professional you called when you needed vehicular transport between two points, on paved streets or dirt roads, at whatever speed was necessary to outrun all possible forms of pursuit. Racklin wasn't the best, the best never lived as long as Racklin had, but he had always proven close enough, and after the Crystal Q job – botched up shit show that it turned out to be – wheel work had made him a very rich man.

Pity it didn't make him a smarter one, or one with a little more luck. If Charley had taught him anything – and his stepfather had taught him everything about the criminal profession he knew – it was to get out of a game while your pockets were full and there was still an open door through which to make a safe exit. That's how Charley had done it. He'd lost Racklin's mother in the process, and damn near gotten himself killed as well, but in the end he'd walked away – flown away, really, his skills as an old barnstorming pilot playing a key role in his escape – with a small fortune, one he was able to live on comfortably for the rest of his life.

Racklin had been given that same chance and had blown it. The time to walk away from driving for good had been right after the Crystal Q heist, which he'd survived by a thread as thin as the hairs on a horsefly's ass. But he hadn't done it. He'd taken on one more job instead, not so much tempting the devil as spitting in his left eye and pissing in his right, and the cold sweat Racklin broke into today just trying to drive the speed limit in a goddamn Nissan Sentra was a direct result of that decision.

He no longer dreamed about the accident, but for weeks afterward, it haunted his sleep like a ghoul holding a grudge.

The Silverthorne Media heist should have been one of

the easiest and sweetest he'd ever signed up for: a high tech software company out of the Silicon Valley, a week after its first public offering had made instant millionaires of its three college boy owners. Somebody got the bright idea to throw a big party at corporate headquarters in San Jose and share the wealth with the small staff, not by handing out iPods and gift certificates but by tossing cash and prizes around like fucking bridal bouquets. Cash, as in short stacks of C-notes, and prizes in the form of genuine Breitling watches, the kind authorized dealers insured to the tune of eight grand against theft.

Three people were all the job required: the ex-classmate of one of the owners who'd gotten wind of the event; a gunman for muscle; and a driver. Racklin's two partners crashed the party and hustled out with the high five-figure take like kids snatching snacks at the 7-Eleven, and Racklin did the rest. No blood, no drama, and no visible pursuit. All Racklin had to do was get them to the drop in one piece.

But pursuit or no pursuit, Racklin never left a crime scene without haste. The more distance he could put between the crew and the mark before the first 911 call was made, the better he liked it. So from the jump, he had the Silverthorne getaway car, a late model Chevy Malibu with the three hundred horses of a Camaro SS's V6 stuffed into its engine bay, tracing their escape route at an easy fifty, planning to throttle down only when instinct moved him to do so.

Near crashes and pedestrian casualties were part of the job, of course, especially on urban runs like this one. Racklin had seen more than his share of both. But in twenty-seven years as a wheelman, he'd never had a crash bring him to a stop, nor hurt anybody on foot so bad the doctors in the ER couldn't fix them.

When the old guy in the walker stepped off the curb, he knew the odds had finally caught up with him.

There was no place to put the Malibu where it wouldn't up the kill rate or wrap itself around a utility pole; Racklin just ran right through the poor bastard, the two guys in the backseat screaming like bitches as the Chevy launched the old man into space. All witnesses saw after that was a blur of green, Racklin standing on the car's gas as if to pierce the sound barrier. They made it to the secluded drop site in record time, too fast for the cops to locate and give chase, but no one in the car felt like celebrating. They divvied up the take and broke off, Racklin left to trust that his accomplices would keep their mouths shut because their armed robbery had just turned into a murder rap and, like Racklin himself, they'd want to pretend it never happened as soon as their consciences would allow.

He made his way toward Los Angeles in his own ride, prepared for a long stint in hiding, and sensed almost immediately that something was badly amiss. Miles before the grapevine on Interstate 5, his hands on the steering wheel began to shake like a spooked ratter's tail and the road wouldn't stay focused in front of him. He had to pull over twice, to vomit and let his nerves wind down, just to keep himself from plowing into the center divider or another car. Racklin kept seeing the old man climb up the windshield and across the Malibu's roof, making a racket, his aluminum walker vanishing beneath the car's front wheels like so much grass before a lawnmower. Why the fuck had the dumb shit stepped off that curb? Why hadn't somebody stopped him?

Racklin made it to L.A., but he was damn near crawling when he arrived. And every time since then when he'd slip behind the wheel of a car, it was the same: the shakes, blurred vision, nausea. If he hadn't been ready for at least semi-retirement before, he sure as hell had to start considering it now, because fate didn't seem to have any other future in mind for him.

Still, he was a wheelman, and he wasn't going to let go of driving without a fight. So, he traded in his Charger SRT for a new Nissan Sentra four-door, a rolling box painted hospital white with all the horsepower of a goddamned motorized wheelchair, and gave himself a reason to get in it every day and turn the key in the ignition: Uber. Running strangers from one end of Los Angeles to another, listening to their inane stories and whiny complaints, never letting the Sentra's speedometer climb above sixty-five, no matter how much they offered to tip or swore was on the line if they failed to arrive at Point B on time.

In the beginning, he could only take short runs, nothing that would require him to use the freeways. And even then, he'd sometimes have to pull over in a rush to puke at the curb, making some excuse having to do with a rough night out or a change in his meds.

By now, however, he'd worked his way to the point where the cold sweats didn't come until the Sentra was doing the posted limit on the 405, or some impatient jackass in the back was goading him into running yellows on the street. The streets were still the worst, because that was where he had killed a man guilty of no greater offense than being old and slow and careless, and every intersection seemed to hold the promise of a similar disaster. On the street, Racklin's eyes darted from side to side, up to one mirror and over to the next, like a cop on patrol, and he tapped his brakes at any sudden move a pedestrian might make. He felt like a fool.

But it was either this or quit, and he wasn't going to quit. He couldn't. The need for speed was in his blood, and he was going to feel the rush of it again, without his knees buckling and his stomach collapsing into a knot, or die trying. Because Charley had instilled that in him too: persistence. Work with what you've got and turn it to your advantage, no matter how long it takes. Charley had made his own fortune converting what should have been a fatal stroke of bad luck into a million-dollar windfall, so he wasn't just talking out of his ass.

Racklin was an Uber driver, and he was going to go on being an Uber driver until he finally got his chops back and could call himself a wheelman again.

"Hey," the little blonde in the tight yellow skirt said, "you remember me?"

Racklin thought he did, sort of, but he couldn't place her.

"Not really. Help me out."

"You drove me to my mother's place last week. You're an Uber driver, right?"

She snuck a peek at the sticker in the Sentra's rear window. Racklin had been pumping gas near his apartment in Echo Park when the girl walked up, he didn't see from where.

"Yeah, that's right. Your mother's?"

"In South Pas. You picked me up around six thirty at work in Glendale. You really don't remember?"

Racklin really didn't. "Sorry. Maybe it was an off night for me." He figured her to be somewhere in her early twenties; too old to be jailbait and too young to be a good time entirely devoid of guilt.

"Sure. Are you busy?"

"Busy?" Racklin hung the gas nozzle on the pump, screwed the Sentra's filler cap back on.

"I could use another ride. I was just about to call for one when I saw you here. If you're not on, it's no problem. I just thought…"

"Sure, sure," Racklin said, opening the passenger side door for her. "You can make the call on the way."

She wasn't going to South Pasadena today, just a strip mall in Hollywood. Or so she said. When Racklin pulled the Nissan into the cramped little lot and a guy jumped in the backseat with the lady the minute she unlocked the door for him, Racklin figured she had another destination altogether in mind.

"Yo, Rack 'Em Up, how you doin'?"

It was Danny Eaves, the hired muscle from the Silverthorne job. Danny was a pink-nosed, sliver-thin Army vet with dishonorable discharge papers somewhere in a drawer, and he shared his general disposition with a dim-witted hornet trapped in a jar. He was also, Racklin thought, a premonition realized; a loose end that should have been tied up back in San Jose with two bullets behind the ear.

Eaves cheerfully gave the blonde a wet kiss. "Thanks, baby."

"You lunkhead. What the hell are you doing here?" Racklin asked, spinning around in his seat. But, of course, he already had a good idea.

"I need a ride, what else? And I didn't think you'd come if I asked for one, so I had Kelly here ask for me. Worked like a charm."

Kelly smiled like she'd just won a gold star. No wonder Racklin hadn't remembered taking the blonde to her mother's in fucking South Pas last week.

"How did you find me?" Racklin asked.

"Find you? Shit, man, you found me! I came down here for a little R and R, hit the beach and babes for a weekend, and who do I see last Saturday, dropping some old gal off in Venice in this shitbox little Toyota? Ol' Rack 'Em Up himself, baddest wheelman in the business!"

"It's a Nissan," Kelly said.

"What?"

"This is a Nissan, not a Toyota, D."

"Whatever." Eaves looked back at Racklin. "Anyway, I've been followin' you around, off and on, ever since. And I gotta hand it to you, Rack, man. An Uber driver. Gotta be the last thing anybody'd expect a man like you to be doin' with himself."

"Get out, Danny," Racklin said.

"What?"

"I said get the fuck out of my car, asshole. I'm not going anywhere with you today."

"No? You didn't see this piece in my hand when I got in? You don't think I'll use it?"

Racklin had seen it: a blue metal 40-caliber, bound up tight in the wiry man's right fist. Racklin's own gun was in the pocket of the driver side door panel, where he'd have to leave it until Eaves dropped his guard or the forty, one or the other.

"Get this motherfucker started and move. Don't matter which direction, just move."

Racklin did as he was told.

Eaves sat back in his seat and spread his legs, enjoying the ride. "Rack, this is my friend, Kelly. Kelly, say hello to my old partner, Rack 'Em Up."

"Hi," Kelly said.

"Fuck you."

Eaves laughed, tickled as usual by anything that made Racklin see red.

"What do you want, Danny? Spell it out." Racklin had the Sentra up to thirty-five, a crawl he was certain Eaves would take notice of any second now.

"You ever hear the expression, 'some things you can't unsee,' Rack? Well…" He grinned and shook his head. "That's my sitch: I can't unsee you, hidin' out here in Los Angeles. I know you're here. So if somebody were to ask me where you're at…" He let it go at that.

"Somebody like who?"

"I'm not talkin' about the cops. And I don't know their names. I've just heard that some powerful people are lookin' for you. And that they'd pay good money to find you. Real good money."

More loose ends, Racklin thought. This time from the Crystal Q heist, no doubt. O'Conner? Estevez? Or the man Racklin had brought into the job who double-crossed them all, Will Ellison? His bet was O'Conner. O'Conner had shaved Racklin's take from the Crystal Q job by fifty grand as payback for Ellison's act of betrayal, and he might have decided that amount wasn't enough.

"Hey, Rack. Step on it. You're drivin' like an old woman."

Racklin tried to will his right foot to lean harder on the gas, but his foot wouldn't move. Between his flaring vehophobia and Eaves' veiled threat of blackmail, this was the best he could do without causing a six-car pile-up.

"How much?" Racklin asked. Because the sooner they could agree on a price, the sooner he could yank the Sentra to the curb and let Eaves and his little girlfriend out.

"I think a hundred even would be fair. Don't you?"

A hundred grand was almost twice Racklin's take from the Silverthorne job.

"A pointed stick up your ass is what would be fair."

Eaves laughed again, and this time, the girl joined in. "Be that as it may. My price is one-zero-zero, jack. In cash by noon tomorrow. You copy?"

"And I'm just supposed to trust you won't come back for more later. Is that it?"

"I'm not a greedy man, Rack. I can go a long way on a hundred Gs, and so could you while I was spending it. You understand what I'm – Jesus!"

Racklin had suddenly stood on his brakes, pitching them all forward in the Nissan's interior like loose mannequins. The idiot in the mini-van who'd seemed intent on running the red at the upcoming intersection had done nothing of the kind. But for Racklin's money, he may as well have pole-axed the Sentra and killed them all, because Eaves would have to be deaf, dumb, and blind not to know now that something was seriously wrong with his old "partner."

"What happened? Why did you stop?" the blonde asked, dumbfounded. They were sitting in the middle of the intersection, car horns blaring in waves behind them.

Drenched with sweat, Racklin got the car moving again.

"Damn, Rack," Eaves said. "You really have lost it, haven't you? You can't drive no more."

There was no point pretending otherwise, but Racklin felt compelled to try. "What the fuck are you talking about?"

"I told you. I've been watchin' you for days. I thought this granny-behind-the-wheel shit was all an act. But it's not, is it? You've really lost your nerve."

Racklin didn't say anything.

"It's because of that old man you hit, ain't it? The dumb fuck." He chuckled like a kid at a birthday party.

Eaves' laughter was almost enough to make him draw his Smith & Wesson in the door pocket to his left. Take his chances in a close-quarters firefight inside a moving vehicle, if that's what it would take to shut him up.

But Racklin just kept driving instead.

Before Charley and Racklin's mother, Nadine, began robbing banks, Charley flew planes, first in an aerial circus where the pair met, and then as a crop duster. But neither occupation paid worth a damn nor held enough excitement for either of them, so Charley and Nadine turned to a life of crime. Racklin was trapped in boarding school up in Oregon during this time. His father, the circus' abusive and alcoholic PA announcer whom Nadine had left for Charley, had placed him there, terrified of the influence his ex-wife might have on their only child if he didn't wield his court-appointed custody rights to hide the boy away.

And then Nadine died. Technically, she was declared dead after seven years in absentia, but the truth was a lot more nuanced: She took a bullet through the driver side door of the getaway car in the last heist she and Charley would ever pull together and Charley torched her body with the vehicle. The New Mexico bank job had turned sideways on a monstrous scale and covering his tracks became imperative to Charley's survival. But the heist had also made him a rich man, and as soon as he was able to arrange it, he negotiated an unofficial deal with Racklin's father for the boy's custody. Prior to Nadine's disappearance, Racklin used to spend several weeks every summer with his mother and Charley, and Charley had grown rather fond of the kid. Both he and Racklin knew Nadine would want them to be together.

So Racklin had been there, under Charley's wing, ever since, right up until the old man's death in a Vegas convalescent hospital eight years ago. Over the course of their time together, what Charley hadn't taught him about being a thief and a first-class driver like Nadine, no one on earth knew.

Today, Danny Eaves had Racklin by the short-hairs, and Charley was no longer around to offer advice on how to make the asshole disappear. If it was true that ghosts from Racklin's Crystal Q past had a bounty on his head, he had to figure out a way to deal with Eaves, permanently, and within the twenty-four hours Eaves had given him to do it.

Eventually, Racklin came up with a plan he thought Charley would approve of. But the first step would easily be the hardest: he had to pay Eaves off.

"Thanks, Rack 'Em Up. Pleasure doing business with you," Eaves said, zipping up the bag full of cash Racklin had just handed him.

"Go fuck yourself, Danny."

The laugh again. Eaves tossed the bag in the trunk of his car, taking one last look around the parking structure to make sure Racklin had come alone. "Don't guess I have to tell you this is goodbye. You can come lookin' for me if you want, but you ain't gonna find me."

"Famous last words," Racklin said.

But driving off with Racklin's hard-earned money, Eaves sure looked like a man he was never going to see again.

* * *

In fact, Racklin saw Eaves only eight hours later.

The reed-thin gunman entered his apartment in Fresno after his flight up from Los Angeles and Racklin greeted him with a blow to the back of his head, dropping him to the floor in the dark like a tipped cow.

"We meet again," Racklin said, returning custody of the black leather bag Eaves had been carrying to its rightful owner.

Eaves shook his head, trying to clear it. He recognized the voice, but the gun in his assailant's hand was the only thing he could really see with any certainty.

"Rack?"

"I had a guy in the business tell me once, Danny: prepare for all eventualities. I couldn't be sure you or Simmonds would try something like this after I killed the old guy in the walker, but I had to take precautions, just in case."

Simmonds was the setup man for the Silverthorne job.

"Hold on a minute…"

"So I had somebody keep tabs on both of you. I looked upon it as an investment in my future. I've known this was your crib since the day you moved in."

"Hold on, I said! How–"

"How'd I get here so fast? Well, I sure as hell didn't drive." Eaves' eyes had adjusted enough now to the dim light that he could see the small grin on Racklin's face. "We both know that much, don't we?"

He put three bullets in Danny Eaves and left.

The first time Charley ever took Racklin up in his old biplane, Racklin knew he wanted to fly.

Take-offs and landings were hard for him now, of course. The blur out the windows to each side reminded Racklin of nothing so much as driving a car the way he once loved to drive a car, pedal to the metal, balls to the wall. But there was no one to hit on a runway, no sudden movements to jerk your attention from the wheel, so flying just didn't hold the same terror for him.

Still, the two modes of transport held a similar rush. Like driving a car at its limit, flying was the purest form of freedom, lending a pilot the sense of being untethered from the world and all its suffocating hypocrisies.

It was at a private flight school in Indiana that Racklin met Ellison, the pilot he'd recruited just months ago for the Crystal Q heist. An instructor at the school, Ellison was a natural pilot and probably always had been; where Racklin was a sparrow, Ellison was a hawk. Still, they'd made fast friends and had kept in touch. Racklin hadn't seen Ellison's potential for backstabbing until it was too late, and his former flight instructor had made a shambles of the Crystal Q crew so as to try – and fail – to take more than his fair share of the take.

Ten thousand feet above green patches of farmland in northern California, en route from Fresno Yosemite Airport to Bozeman, Montana, Racklin checked his instruments again and patted the leather bag occupying the Cessna 182's passenger seat like man's best friend. And maybe the money Eaves had died for, and all the rest Racklin had socked away, was, in fact, the only friend Racklin had left. It was for damn sure he couldn't count anybody Ellison had left alive back in Fort Worth in that group, most especially Ellison himself.

If so, Racklin could live with being alone. Friends were overrated. Money wasn't. If there was one thing a wheelman knew how to do, it was run and hide.

Even one who couldn't drive a car the way he used to anymore.

CHAPTER 10
Showdown
by Gary Phillips

"He's supposed to be holed up in here," said the one in the passenger seat wearing glasses.

"The cash Harrington spread around says so," Ellison said from the backseat.

"Word is he's panicked and on the run," added the man with the glasses.

The driver looked at this man but didn't say anything.

Harrington's considerable reputation and money, which went further than hands-on beatings, had been used to run down the known associates of the man called the Financier once Zach Culhane had given up his name after the wife had given him up.

Culhane had been tortured and branded mercilessly under the bland stare of Clovis Harrington. He spilled, was chained up, and then disposed of like the slab of meat he'd become. Harington's tactics hadn't produced much else of use because he didn't know much else. Though a bounty was issued for the Financier. As to the career criminal seemingly only called O'Conner, or Connie to his friends, as was alleged, Ellison knew his name and that of Hector from their time on the scouting mission over the Crystal Q. But he knew little else about the two.

But from what the maid had said, Flora whatever her last name was, the one who'd been in the wine cellar, her account confirmed it must have been a masked O'Conner down there breaking into the safe. As he had heavy steps, she guessed the man with him was older but she could see he knew what he was doing. Not that she knew anything about cracking a safe, but while he seemed to be of a certain age, he handled himself efficiently. Ellison concluded that must have been Hector.

When Harrington's money rained, it was learned that one of O'Conner's past crime partners was an old-school box man named Hector Gonzales. Thereafter, a freelance team had been engaged to make inquiries about Gonzales – who it was rumored was out of the country. And when the job had gone down, Ellison had a man called Eel in the cabin with him throwing out the firebombs. His name and description also went out on the underground grapevine.

But all this rigmarole had also produced the one in the passenger seat sitting across from Harrington's other man, who drove. The lean man who'd addressed Ellison was in his forties, a lined face with steel grey hair that looked like it had been cut with him sitting at the kitchen table and a towel around his shoulders. He wore a loose sport shirt and cotton pants, rubber soled work shoes, and dark socks. To top it off, he also sported horn-rimmed glasses with thin lenses. He looked like such a civilian, he could be middle management of a big box store chain. The guy a checker called from out back when the frozen food display started leaking. He even had a square John kind of name, George Collier. Only, he'd been sent in by the board of the North Texas Citizens Improvement League.

Harrington, Ellison had noted, hadn't been happy to see

Collier. He was soft-spoken and observant, not given to talking if not necessary. Collier wasn't about the bluster. His effect on Harrington, given to inflating himself and letting everyone know within earshot he was the fiercest cock of the walk, was subtle. Harrington still barked orders but Ellison could tell the cattleman was conscious of the other's presence, deferential to him even. Like a teacher aware of the principal sitting in the back of their classroom, judging them silently on how well they controlled their classroom. And now he was here with them. It made sense given O'Conner had pulled the string to take down the slush fund.

"How about over there?" Collier said, pointing.

"Okay," the driver complied. Ellison hadn't gotten this man's name. The second one, sitting in back with him, was nicknamed Shim. What that was derived from he had no idea and wasn't interested. But before they'd left the ranch to take a private flight out here to Southern California, it was clear that in the field, Harrington's men would take orders from Collier, no question.

The driver guided the black Lincoln Town Car to a stop atop a low rise. He shut the car off and almost instantly, Ellison was aware of how beguiling the air conditioner had been. The three exited the chilled car into the afternoon heat of Riverside County. Ellison knew there were cities out here, even pristine golf courses that looked like the grass had been spray painted in lush greens, but where they were was sparse and flat, with sandy dirt underneath their shoes. Not exactly the desert proper, but close enough for his tastes, Ellison reflected.

"How do you intend on finding him in this?' Ellison said to Collier.

"Good question." To the driver he said, "Pop the trunk, will ya?"

The driver thumbed the key fob and the trunk unlatched.

Collier retrieved a pair of binoculars from there and, coming back to stand with the other three, scanned the junk yard down below. No, Ellison corrected, it was more of a recycling center on steroids. For what Collier was viewing were several acres of used shipping containers, some of them forty-feet long and others twenty-feet long. Whether the longer or shorter version, the height and width seemed the same.

There were rows of double stacked containers under an overhead metal skeleton of railing and metal lattice work while others were in the open. There seemed to be little to distinguish why there were those under the arrangements and those that weren't.

"Why the hell are these way out here with no ocean around?" the driver said to no one in particular.

"The containers have a second life as portable offices, storage for your business, or even housing." Collier rattled this off like explaining price changes on the tomatoes to the staff as he continued studying the area. Where they had parked was the eastern side of the container compound. There were no gates, as who the hell could steal one, and as far as Ellison could tell, no housing around containing tagging prone teens. There were though a number of heavy duty fork lifts about for moving the shipping containers around.

Collier lowered the binoculars, pointing. "Toward the northern end is an office, several cars littered around this. There's some sort of fabrication set up that way too. There's a two-story L-shaped facility made out of the containers with glass windows installed. That's where I saw some sparking from welding going on. Other than that, there's no personnel about. Certainly not on this end of the facility."

"How could he be inside one of those tin cans and not melt?" Ellison said. He sounded on edge and scolded himself to be cool in the company of these men.

Collier pointed again. "There are power lines snaking around some of those overhead constructions and thick cable crossing the ground thereabouts. He could have fans going, hunkered down in one with windows a couch and flat screen. Who the hell knows. But we have to find out."

He then regarded Ellison. "'Cause it's not like you nor I have much of a choice."

O'Conner had killed his crime partner, who had also been his life partner. He'd made the decision that late afternoon on the gravel parking lot to see to it he ended the thief's life. Why else would he have made his unwise alliance with Harrington. He knew he was a dead man, but he had to end O'Conner's days first – see the light go out of his eyes as he took him out.

From the still partly open trunk the crew took guns out. Ellison hung back. He knew he wasn't going to get a gun. The driver and Shim each acquired a lightweight but deadly efficient Ingram M11. The weapons' stocks were folded in and each had an extended magazine and a suppressor on the end of the barrels. Collier lifted out a handgun and closed the lid. The four then descended. Collier spoke as they did so.

"Like it or not, it makes sense to fan out as we've got plenty of ground to cover. Sweeny," he said to the driver, pointing, "you take that quadrant. I'll take more or less down the middle and you two that way," he said to Shim and the pilot. "Only call if you tag him or have him pinned down."

The four split off into three and began scouring the storage yard. The men walked along hard packed earth amid rows of the stacked cargo containers. Ellison limped slightly from his leg wound. The containers were varied in coloring from several shades of blue, yellows, greens, reds, oranges, and white ones as well. Letter and numbers were marked on the narrower ends of the containers that were designed to be opened for loading or unloading. Cawing crows perched atop the containers, their heads turned as their ink deep eyes watched the interlopers prowl about.

"Why don't you go that way?" Shim said to Ellison. He indicated a side passageway they were almost upon.

Ellison was going to object, but to what end? He'd realized before they left Texas that if a lead to O'Conner developed, he was to be the staked goat, the bait to draw the thief out. Tucked into his sock was a steak knife he'd palmed from Harrington's ranch house. He did as ordered and moved cautiously along the passageway. The efficiency of the containers' design was such that they could be stacked on top of each other and in rows, butting up one against the other. But periodically there would be spaces between these which Ellison concluded must have been done to let the workers walk around the stacks. Width-wise, there were passageways between the rows and he could see these were wide enough for the forklift to access.

The way he'd gone let out onto a clearing of a sort where modified shipping containers were on display. These were not stacked one on the other, but here they sat individually in a semi-circle in this area. Two of the containers been changed over so that the side of the metal box had been retro fit to open on hydraulic pistons as a makeshift awning. Sliding glass doors had also been installed in the thing. The interiors were staged as modest offices. The other two containers had been altered into modular living quarters with built-in beds and cubbies.

Ellison heard a sound behind him and spun around quickly, crouching, hand going toward his hidden knife. A crow now rested at the end of on one of the upraised awnings glaring down at him. "Shit," he muttered, his nerves taut like harp strings. "Get it together." The crow shifted side to side on his clawed feet as Ellison started away.

As discussed with Collier when they were taking their guns from the trunk, Shim was to make it seem that Ellison was off alone. When he'd sent him down the passageway, Shim hadn't gone off in another direction but had crept along a parallel passageway. From his vantage point he could see Ellison in the area with the modified containers. He'd seen when he'd turned around, reaching for his calf. He figured that meant he was carrying a blade. Hey, you couldn't fault a guy for initiative, he concluded. Ellison began moving out of the clearing, and Shim gave him a few beats to get ahead, then he too moved into the space with the display settings. He intended to walk around one of the changed over offices to yet another passageway among so many, but in that way again roughly matched Ellison's steps.

He cleared the corner of the office container and was along the passageway of more double stacked units. This one was narrower than the others, two men abreast couldn't walk along it. The gunman was crossing a gap between dual stacks when he was struck in the temple. He sagged in the knees and O'Conner sprang from the gap onto him.

"Motherfucker," Shim growled, off balance. He tried to

raise his Ingram but was having difficulty. O'Conner had slipped a restraint of a nefarious design past his shoulders. His arms were pinned to his sides. The thing was essentially a large, wide belt that could be adjusted. It was padded and therefore the occupant, apparently a mental patient, Shim guessed, wouldn't cut themselves struggling against the leather.

Shim fell back against a container opposite and was about to curse again but O'Conner raised the collapsible baton he'd first hit him with. Viciously, he whipped the flexible shaft on the man's head several times rapidly and with considerable force. Shim was not able to muster the strength to get out of his leaning position. The hoodlum's eyes went vacant and he collapsed to the ground, blood soaking his short-cropped, sweaty hair. His skull was fractured and if the membrane was torn, he might well develop an infection and die painfully. All this had happened in seconds. A statue-faced O'Conner picked up the hood, draped him over his shoulder, and, noting the head wound didn't drip much, carried him off to deposit him in a shipping container. He returned and retrieved the Ingram, having already searched the unconscious man briefly and relieved him of his smartphone. O'Conner moved off.

Sweeny had a bad feeling about this job. He'd heard about O'Conner second hand before this and it was his understanding this was not an individual given to hasty moves out of uncertainty or fear. The impression he'd been left with was he was a man not to be fucked with. Added to that, all this up and down the aisles in this place gave him the heebie-jeebies. He was getting a crook in his neck from alternately looking up at the tops of the containers and slowing his tread to peek in the gaps between the stacks. That son of a bitch could be anywhere, he reasoned, and if not for the bonus that Harrington had offered, he might just have gone AWOL. They'd passed civilization on the way in and surely there was a meat locker cool tavern back there where a fella could have a beer or two and ruminate on his future. He was pushing fifty and lately had come to the realization that the life of being hired muscle lacked upward mobility.

He neared the end of yet another damn passageway and a body ran past up ahead. Instinctively, he crouched slightly as he let loose a set of rounds that whispered about like ghostly insects. His bullets pinged off the sides of the containers and thumped into the dirt. He knew he didn't hit anybody. He considered doubling back, could be this O'Conner had help. What made them think this dude was alone in this goddamn place? Wide-eyed, Sweeny glanced over his shoulder. Hell of a time to have his mid-life crisis, he groaned inwardly.

Resisting the urge to call Collier, as that would show weakness, he pressed forward. Damn him if the sun hadn't moved in the sky and the shadows at the end of this corridor didn't seem longer, deeper. For good measure, he shot the Ingram again, spraying rounds from right to left in case O'Conner was hidden in the gloom. No body fell out onto the ground. He went ahead and reached the end without incident. He was at an intersection of containers, passageways to either side of him and one up ahead.

"Christ," he gasped. Which way had O'Conner been going? He looked right. He was sure it was that way he'd run. Shit fire, but he'd have to find out for sure or, if Collier didn't shoot him, he'd make sure everyone knew he was a big pussy.

"What a life," he said, shaking his head as he steadied his weapon. Sweeny eased along the walkway between the containers. He had both hands on the Ingram, one on the grip, finger extended across the trigger guard, and the other hand supporting the truncated frame. He wanted to be as accurate as possible. There would be no second chance. Despite being on point, he had the impression the looming metal boxes were closing in on him, constricting the light and cutting off his air. He stopped as he neared another gap between the containers. This one seemed larger than the others and an alarm jangled inside his head. O'Conner was there and would cut him down as soon as he passed by. But he'd get the drop on him, he'd come out on top.

A wry grin on his face, Sweeny rushed forward and peppered the gaps to the left and right ahead of him.

"Yah, yah, yah," he yelled, rounds spitting from the end of the heated suppressor.

He counted on his bullets ricocheting off the ends of the containers, flying everywhere along the length of those gaps. Skip rounds, some called them. In this way, either O'Conner was hit or he had to retreat, the gunman reasoned. As he ran forward, he pulled the empty magazine out and, as it dropped to the dirt, inserted a fresh one. He eyed one of the gaps and, turning, went prone, aiming his gun at the gap opposite. No body, no blood.

"Shit." Pressed to the ground, the breath caught in his throat. He got to a knee, his chest rising and falling rapidly. He closed his mouth, willing his body to slow so he could hear. But he heard nothing, not even the crows. He rose, wary, sweat on his brow and his heart pulsing in his neck.

Where the hell was this bastard? Maybe he'd taken a powder or maybe the whole damn place was rigged to blow. No, that was foolish, wishful thinking, Sweeny knew. He was here. O'Conner wasn't the type to ignore loose ends, and that fuckin' pilot was a loose end who'd tried and failed to kill him and take his money. He could see where that might be a burr in his saddle.

What if, Sweeny wondered, prowling about again, he could make a deal. Give him the pilot on a silver platter and they went their separate ways. Yeah, that could work. But there was Collier to deal with. Still, this was a big yard. He could make the agreement with O'Conner and Collier wouldn't be the wiser. O'Conner could pull the pilot into one of these containers to have at him as he pleased later. Tie and gag him and lay low, how long would Collier want to be here? All fuckin' day? Naw, he could tell by how he acted that Collier was a dollars and sense guy. That's why the League had sent him in. The heist and Harrington leaving dead bodies and fallout in his wake had to be a matter they wanted to get settled.

For instance, far as he could tell, that fine-ass wife of his wasn't among the dearly departed. What was that about, and how come an asshole like Harrington had let her be since, if it was true, she was in on the robbery? Big business was about –

Sweeny stopped again, the hairs at the base of his neck standing on end. He looked up, firing. Two crows fell to the ground. Their small bodies distorted from where his bullets had torn through them. One of the crows had an eye shot out but its remaining orb glared unblinkingly at his killer.

"Dammit," he said, unnerved. Behind him, metal on metal banged.

"Look, O'Conner" he began, trying to turn, trying to show he wasn't a threat, that he wanted to be his ally. He wasn't even a quarter of the way around when the. 380s from the gun O'Conner had confiscated ripped into him. Sweeny was dead before he crumpled to the dirt.

O'Conner had exited a door that had been added to one of the containers post its arrival at the yard. This was common as the various containers were pre-prepared for their after-market uses. He bent down to the body and applied gauze and tape to the fatal wound. He did this so as to not leave a blood trail. Using a fireman's carry again, O'Conner lifted Sweeny off the ground. He strode off with him like he'd done with Shim.

"Shim," Ellison said, louder this time. "He's not going for it." No answer, though he half expected that too. But knowing the man should be shadowing him and realizing he wasn't, he was certain he was dead or at least laid up. They'd been roaming around this place for the better part of an hour and he was now back before the modified containers.

There was the shuffle of footsteps and he glanced over to see Collier on the side of one of the boxy offices. His handgun was down at his side and he stared across the expanse at the pilot. For several moments the two men regarded each other as if strangers at an impasse on a one-lane bridge. Collier came closer.

"I spotted some blood and spent shells scattered about in the section Sweeny was searching," the bespectacled man said evenly. "I would surmise O'Conner has dealt with him and Shim, who doesn't answer his phone. Their Ingrams are missing too."

"Why hide the bodies?"

"Maybe he has help. Clearly, he didn't hole up here in desperation," Collier said, more for his benefit than anything else. "Or maybe he's just fucking with us, keeping us guessing."

Ellison had an odd sense of relief. Possibly, in Collier's estimation, he still had value. Though it could be O'Conner was saving the best for last and Collier was next up to be eliminated. He said, "Now what, send me up and down the aisles and hope he bites?'

Collier looked off at a far point. He looked back. "He's going to pick us off as we head back to the car."

"Then call for backup. You must have people out here."

Collier adjusted his black frames. "By the time I arrange that, we'd be dead. I don't think he's going to wait around and let that happen."

Ellison had a sour look on his face as if he had a hole in his stomach. "We're dead if we stand around. You must have more firepower in the car."

"There is."

"Then like you said, what choice do we have?"

Collier pursed his lips and began walking. Ellison soon fell in step beside him. Collier was about to speak, and that's when Ellison knifed him, jabbing the steak knife in his side and relieving him of his handgun. The knife was dropped to the ground.

"The hell," the League's man wheezed, grimacing.

Ellison pushed him and Collier took a few steps backward, tripping over his own feet and plopping down on the ground on his butt. "This won't help you," he said.

"I'm going to help myself."

When Ellison jogged around the corner of the container,

footfalls receding, Collier took out his smartphone. But before he could dial 911, other footsteps approached. He knew who it was. He looked up to see him backlit against the sun. Even given the distortion of the angle, his impression of O'Conner was his size, big, solid, like he'd been put together with iron slag and tensile wire, and only went into motion when necessary. His hands appeared unusually large to Collier. In one of them was the recognizable outline of the M11.

"Before you gun me, O'Conner, maybe you'll listen to a proposition I have for you."

"What would that be?"

"I'm not one of Harrington's crew."

"Who are you?"

"The League, I represent their interests."

"And their interests are in eliminating me."

Collier winced as he shifted, his hand pressed on his wound. Crimson stained his fingers. "Well, see it from our perspective. Any enterprise will act in the stead of its members. Such is not unusual."

O'Conner raised the weapon. "That's right."

"But," Collier said, holding up the bloodied hand, "there can be certain circumstances that cause a re-evaluation of the normal directives."

"You being wounded and all."

"And you clearly are not going to stop until you've caused considerable disruption to the course of things. There are matters in the works that do not need unnecessary scrutiny. Really, you know, it's not like it's your money."

"It is now," he said flatly. "The League wasn't going to build daycare centers with it."

"Point taken. If Harrington were to back off, if a détente could be reached, how would that be?"

O'Conner recalled that picture of Harrington he'd first seen when he'd begun his research. "He isn't."

"But I would talk to him. I could do that. Like any member of an organization such as ours, he is not immune to the desires of his other board members." He winced again. He would need to make that call soon, he reasoned, pain lancing his abdomen.

"Your board may not see it like you do."

"I can try. I do have some influence."

"Where's the pilot heading?"

"I wouldn't want to guess. You might take umbrage," Collier huffed hollowly.

"But you have some idea. Man like you would have done his research and assembled information on me and him, a wild card. A double-crossing bottom feeder who weaseled his way into you all's grasp as a way to avoid being among the hunted, to try to buy enough time until he could angle an escape. It's not like he's proven he has that much usefulness as a bloodhound."

"He did over sell," Collier allowed. "Though that's understandable given the circumstances."

"Well, it's not like he had a future as a member of Harrington's crew. Think of this as expediting what was already going to happen sooner or later."

"Still, there are lines a professional shouldn't cross."

O'Conner hunched down. "He would."

"I'm not him." Collier said firmly.

O'Conner regarded the man then reached for his smartphone lying next to his leg on the ground. He blew the dust off and wiped off his bloody hand. He then pressed Collier's right thumb on the phone's physical button to activate the device. He then touched and swiped the screen for several seconds and found the app he was looking for. He tapped it alive, his amber eyes intent on the screen. Momentarily, a satisfying grunt rose in O'Conner's throat.

After O'Conner left, Collier used Shim's phone which he'd exchanged with him. His hand shook slightly as he punched in the emergency number and he hoped he wasn't going to pass out from shock before he could tell them his location.

O'Conner had surmised correctly a man like Collier, a detail-oriented sort, would have any car he was in tied to a GPS app. Just in case matters went south. Sure enough, he was able to track Ellison in the Lincoln on the man's phone back to the Los Angeles area and a place called Lawndale. The municipality was on the edge of what was called the South Bay of beach cities. Hawthorne Boulevard, which further north became La Brea Avenue, bifurcated the small city and also intersected the 405 Freeway, which O'Conner had exited. From what he observed through his windshield, this was a majority Latino enclave, though there was a noticeable presence of blacks, whites, and Asians too. The housing stock was modest to creeping gentrification of mid-century models. The Lincoln was parked on a residential street a few blocks east of Hawthorne with single-family homes and low-slung dingbat apartment buildings. Around the corner on one end of the block, not too far from where the Lincoln was parked, was a senior care facility called Golden Gardens. On the opposite end, the way in which he'd come, at the intersection of that street, a numbered one and Hawthorne, was a strip mall with a sheepskin seat covers shop, a beauty supply outlet, and Le Magnifique nail salon. He found a place to park and got out of his car. He placed Collier's phone on the ground and stomped it into pieces.

As he did so, O'Conner wondered if Ellison came to roost here or if he simply dumped the Lincoln and obtained other wheels, maybe even caught the bus or called up one of those driver services to take him elsewhere. A black and white rolled by as O'Conner stood on the end of the block, hand in his pocket. It was a sheriff's car and the female deputy inside didn't seem to pay him any attention, but he knew better than to be complacent. A dispatcher's voice crackled over her radio. It would not do for him to get busted when he was close to solving part of his problem.

He started walking even as the car went away from him. He could feel those cop eyes centered on her rearview mirror, watching his back. O'Conner turned off the block and headed over to the main drag. He loitered in a donut shop slash Chinese food joint over a tepid cup of coffee. Two gardeners were in there discussing boxers and the best flowers to plant for this climate. O'Conner then walked back some fifteen minutes later, figuring the deputy, if she had circled back, would be gone by now.

The Lincoln was still parked when he returned to the street. He frowned, considering what to do next. Walking up and down the block was a sure way to get spotted if Ellison was still around. On the other hand, he needed to be certain of his options. He took a breath and started off. He'd make one circuit of the block and hope the odds were in his favor and Ellison was holed up with a cold one while he too considered his next moves and not camped by a window. O'Conner noted the makes of cars in driveways and discounted the lawns where there was a child's wagon or tricycle. He couldn't see Ellison being chummy with the family type. Then again, nobody could imagine O'Conner living in a subdivision, so who knew? But for the time being, he eliminated those abodes from his calculations.

Around back at one of the apartment buildings, he stood in an empty car slot and listened to the noises from above. A heavyset woman came out of the laundry room pulling a basket of freshly done clothes. He nodded at her as if he belonged there and she didn't give him a second look. Overhead, O'Conner heard a sports talk show on and a vacuum cleaner going. O'Conner didn't hear Ellison's voice. A little further on toward the end of the block, the parking for another apartment building was marked off in front. In the corner of the windshield of a late-model pickup, parked with the back end toward the wall, he noted a parking decal for the Compton-Woodley airport. He knew from Racklin that Ellison had done smuggling jobs. It was a thin lead, but it was worth pulling on. He memorized the truck's license plate number and, back in another public establishment on Hawthorne Boulevard, called on one of his encrypted phones.

"This is O'Conner. I need some additional information," he said to the hacktivist when the line was answered. "Shouldn't take you long, but I'll meet your rate."

"Go ahead," the disguised voice said, a tone of bemusement lurking underneath the words.

Soon, he knew who was the owner of the vehicle and the connection to Ellison was much more solid. Emil Xactos was thirty-seven and had a part-time job handling freight at the Compton-Woodley light aircraft facility less than thirteen miles away. He was a competition surfer and a licensed pilot, and also flew charter flights. What the hacker also uncovered was Xactos had been the person of interest in a drug and cash smuggling operation. But he hadn't been indicted. This could not be a coincidence, O'Conner concluded. It had to be that Ellison was going to get taken over the border by his old compadre. Maybe some airstrip in a small Mexican village they'd used often in the past. To lay low and see if the opposing forces after him would cancel each other out.

He didn't think it would be long before Ellison was in transit again. But he had to be someplace to keep watch yet not be conspicuous. Squinting against the sun's rays, he scanned about.

"Hmm," he sounded. O'Conner walked over to the rest home. There was a parking lot on the side bordered by a low wall. He went through a side door entrance and into bracing, manufactured air. He used the bathroom and wandered around, none of the staff bothering him. Several other adults his age and older were present, some coming out of patients' rooms and others entering to visit a loved one. There was a vending machine and he bought an over-priced turkey sandwich dry as the Sahara.

He left, willing himself to eat the less than desirable food. At the end of the lot was the low wall, shrubbery behind that and a cyclone fence behind the greenery that looked out on an alleyway. He returned to his car then eventually drove it back to the facility and parked it nearer to Golden Gardens. The rear of the building abutted the low wall. Climbing on this, he could make his way along, crouching down below the windows letting into the rooms. From inside one of them a baritone voice hummed various tunes. The paralleled parked cars ended several feet before the end of the building so he didn't think there was much chance of him being seen.

O'Conner had taken a small soft-sided bag with him.

From this he took out gloves and, putting them on, tore away some of the shrubbery. He then climbed the cyclone fence and, getting to the top, was able to lean over and reach the top of the roof. He let his feet go from the fence and the soles of his shoes were now on the building's wall. He was between the windows but he knew from being inside they were high enough up the wall an elder would have to stand on their bed to see him. He clambered up onto the flat roof, and also went flat. He bellycrawled to the right place on the lip and this afforded him a look at the apartment building he assumed Ellison was in. Hours passed.

Past seven, the sun not yet down, Ellison and another man he took to be Xactos came out to the pickup. While O'Conner was vain and hadn't yet admitted to Gwen Gardner he needed glasses for close-up reading, his long vision was still good. He could make out both men. He scrambled from the roof.

"The fuck," Xactos said as he started driving the pickup away.

"A flat?' Ellison said. When the truck had started off, there had been a kind of rendering noise coming from underneath.

"No, that can't be it. But I better see." He put the vehicle in neutral and set the brake. He was about to open the door when Ellison yelled.

"Oh, shit, O'Conner, no, wait…"

The bullets obliterated the side passenger window and entered in a downward angle the body of the pilot who slumped forward, dead. A man in a black hockey type mask and a handgun with a suppressor talked to Xactos from that side of the pickup.

"Keep your hand on the wheel."

"Yes, sir."

"When the police come, tell them everything, except, if I was you, I would not remember my name."

"Yes, sir."

O'Conner had put the child's tricycle underneath the pickup. Collier's checking up on him hadn't disclosed he was a part-owner in the shipping container customizing concern. Hector Gonzales had sent him a message so he had to make a detour. But then he was headed back to Texas to settle matters for good.

CHAPTER 11
Hector
by Richard Brewer

Michael Cochran sat in the Ford Explorer, his breath fogging the air.

"So now we have him," said Morris from the backseat. "Let's take him, find out where the money is, and get the hell back to somewhere warm."

"I second," said Eddie.

"Third," said Dayton.

Cochran wasn't about to give the go ahead. It wasn't his call. That would have to come from Harrington, but he did hope that call would come soon. For one thing, they needed to keep things on the down low, and time mattered. Right now, they were unfamiliar faces in an unfamiliar town, and if they didn't get to business soon, they ran the risk of drawing attention to themselves. Cochran did not want to be one of "those guys" that people remembered once the shit came down.

"What do you think the story is with the woman?" said Eddie.

"Think they're a thing?" said Morris.

"I bet he's boning her," said Eddie. "What do you think, C?"

"Don't know. Don't care," said Cochran.

"Yeah," said Eddie. Continuing like Cochran hadn't spoken. "He's boning her. She's his side thing."

"Dude," said Dayton. "What is she? Twenty-five? Twenty-six? And he's, what? A million years old?"

"Oh," said Eddie. "You telling me that when you're his age you won't be wanting any young pussy? You just gonna sit around and listen to podcasts and shit?"

"She doesn't live there. He's got that big-ass house and she doesn't even live with him. That doesn't make any sense."

"What? You never heard of 'Poon on Wheels?' All the old folks use it. I think it's covered by Medicare. There's something going on there."

"She wears one of those headwrap things."

"So?"

"So doesn't that mean she's religious or somethin'?"

"Yeah, 'cause religion and sex, those two things never hook-up together."

"Both of you, shut the fuck up," said Cochran. "Let's get back to the hotel."

"Good by me, man," said Dayton. "I haven't been able to feel my feet in over an hour."

"Fucking Minnesota," said Eddie.

"Fucking Minnesota in fucking December," said Morris.

It was five days before Christmas. The temperature, according to the readout on the Explorer's dashboard, was four degrees below zero. The four of them had come up from Texas as soon as they had received word on the old man's whereabouts. Thanks to the pilot, Ellison, and a little info from the late and non-lamented Culhane they learned what name the old Mex was using and, more importantly, where he was using it. After that, it was only a matter of showing up, confirming the intel, and doing the job.

Truthfully, Cochran hadn't been sure what Minnesota would be like in December. He was Texas born and raised and had never been out of the state. He knew it would be cold this time of year, but Christ on a pony, not this cold. Sure, it got cold in Texas, but this was enter-the-core-of-your-bones-and-never-leave cold. The weather wasn't what mattered though. What mattered was that Gonzales was here, and if he was here, then the money, or where to find it, was as well. The woman was unexpected, but again, she wasn't what mattered. He would prefer she didn't get in the way, he hoped she wouldn't get in the way, but if she did, well, that would be too bad for everyone.

Cochran and his men had been in town for the past couple of weeks and been following Hector that whole time. It was easy to do. It wasn't like his day to day was complicated. He lived in an old two-story Victorian house. Mornings, he'd take a walk around the neighborhood, giving a wave hello to his neighbors as they left for work. Sometimes he'd stop and shoot the shit with someone before he ended up at the local diner where he'd grab a cup of coffee at the counter and read the newspaper.

"Who the hell reads newspapers anymore?" said Eddie.

Around noon he'd have lunch, then head back to the house where he usually stayed for the rest of the day. Twice he was met by the young woman, once for morning coffee and once for lunch.

Cochran had Morris follow the woman.

"She's a teacher."

"Teacher?"

"Yeah. Over at this elementary school. She walked through the gates and all the kids came running up to her. It was all, 'Oh, Mrs. Samir, this! Mrs. Samir, that!' Then the bell rang, she herded the little shits into a group, and they all went inside."

"Samir? What kind of name is that?" said Eddie.

"How the hell do I know? It's some 'not the fuck from America' shit."

"So what's the connection with the old guy?" said Dayton.

"I'm telling you…" started Eddie.

"There's something going on there!" finished Morris and Dayton with a laugh. Even Cochran had to give up a piece of a smile.

The house was mid-century wood frame, and currently decorated for Christmas. A string of multicolored lights encircled it, and a large handmade wreath, a mixture of pine branches and round bright red holiday ornaments, sat at the center of the front door. The whole thing had a Norman Rockwell feel to it and made Cochran shake his head. If he had half the money Gonzales was supposed to have taken from Harrington, he'd have been living in Acapulco or Hawaii. Someplace warm with sandy beaches and lots of alcohol, that was for sure. Not this freakin' sub-zero, ass numbing place.

Cochran was just about to start the car when his cell phone rang. He picked it up and held it to his ear.

"Hello."

"Is it him?" said the voice of Harrington.

"Yes, sir," he said to his employer. He pulled up a paper copy of an old driver license photo. "Hector Alejandro Gonzales."

"St. Peter, Minnesota," said the voice. "For fuck's sake."

"That the boss?" asked Eddie.

Cochran made a shushing gesture at the man sitting next to him. With a tap of his finger he put the phone on speaker so the rest of the men could hear the conversation.

"It took long enough to find him," said Harrington. "What the hell is an old beaner doing all the way up there?"

"Hiding out from you, sir," said Cochran.

"Any sign of the money?"

"No, sir," said Cochran. "Actually, quite the opposite."

"What do you mean?"

"He lives alone in a house. We took a quick look inside. Gonzales has some clothes, a few books, a bed, TV, the usual household stuff. Nothing special. None of it new. TV isn't even a flat screen. We couldn't find any bank statements. He doesn't live like someone with half a million dollars to draw on."

"What about the people around him? He got friends?"

"He's seems friendly enough with the people in the neighborhood. There's this woman—"

"There ya go," said Harrington. "Who is she? Girlfriend?"

"Not that we can tell," said Cochran. "She's a school teacher. No major connection that we can see. He's met her for coffee, lunch. One night she came to the house and brought him a plate of cookies and one night a casserole or something."

"She stay the night?"

"No, sir. Just brought him some food and left. Didn't even go inside. I think she was being neighborly. It seems like that kind of town. They look to be just friends, nothing more than that. Sir, we can take him right now if you want. We can bag him and have him in front of you in a few days."

There was a silence on the other end of the phone that went on long enough that Cochran began to think he'd lost the connection. He was just about to redial when the voice came from the speaker.

"So no sign of where he's got the money?"

"We get him, we get the money," said Cochran. "It won't take long to make him tell us where it is."

"If he has it," muttered Eddie.

"Who's that?"

"It's Eddie, sir," said Cochran. Giving the man a "shut the fuck up" look. "He's concerned that this Gonzales may not be the Gonzales with the money."

"Why?"

"Like I said, sir, he's not acting like someone who's come into a bunch of stolen cash. Are you sure your intel is correct? I mean, yes, it's the guy you gave us to find. But are you sure it's the guy from the job?"

"Hector Gonzales," said the voice on the other end of the phone. "Hispanic male, sixty-eight years old, did a three year stretch in San Quentin for robbery. And he's a known collaborator with this guy O'Conner. They've known each other for years and pulled a bunch of jobs together. It's him all right. It's him and he has five hundred thousand dollars of my money."

"He's not exactly living like a king here, sir."

"So he's a cheap son of a bitch. Fuck him," said Harrington. "It's him. I'm sure of it, and odds are he'll know where we can find this fucker O'Conner. Do it."

"Sir?"

"Bag him and make him tell you where he's hidden the money."

"You don't want us to bring him to you?"

"I don't need to see his face," said Harrington. "The only faces I want to see are the presidents on the stacks of bills he stole. Get the money. Punch his ticket and get back here."

"Yes, sir," said Cochran. "We'll get it done."

"And find out if he knows where this O'Conner is, or

where any of the other assholes are who were part of the robbery."

"Yes, sir," said Cochran. Then, "Not sure how cooperative he'll be once we're done with him on the money thing."

"Keep at him," said Harrington. "The money's the primary objective, but if you can get him to give up any of the others, that's good too. He can save us some time. Losing an ear or a finger can make people more than willing to give up information."

"Hold in mind, sir. He's an old man. He might not be able to take too much pushing."

"It's not like the outcome is going to be any different one way or the other. As long I get my money, anything else is a bonus. We found Culhane and we'll find the rest of them eventually, with or without this wetback's help."

"Yes, sir," said Cochran. "What if the woman should show up?"

"Is that a real possibility?"

"She's come to the house twice since we've been here."

"I don't like things that can come back and bite me in the ass," said Harrington.

Cochran said nothing.

"Did you hear me?" said Harrington.

"Yes, sir," said Cochran.

"All right then. Call me when it's done and you're on your way back," said Harrington. His tone brightened. "We'll throw a barbecue to celebrate.

"Well, thank you, sir, that sounds–" But Harrington had already cut the connection.

"Okay then," said Cochran to the others. "Let's saddle up and get this over with."

"'Bout fucking time," said Eddie.

The four men exited the Explorer and began to walk down the street toward the house, their shoes crunching in the snow.

Hector Alejandro Gonzales stopped at the doorway to the bedroom, his right hand reaching up to grip the frame for balance as he bent over, the pain in his abdomen making him grimace. He took in a deep breath and let it out with a whoosh as the pain subsided to a more bearable ache. Straightening up, he entered the room. With a sigh he sat on the edge of the bed and surveyed the four walls around him. Until he'd come to stay in this house he'd never spent more than a year in any one residence.

When he first arrived in St. Peter, he'd, not for the first time, been on the run. He and O'Conner had pulled a decent job that had landed him a good bit of swag, fifty thousand in raw, uncut diamonds, but it had been a high profile heist. So he was looking for a place to hold up and sit on the proceeds for a while before attempting to fence the stones.

The sign in the window had read simply "room for rent." The pregnant woman who had answered the door, Maria Delatorre, formerly Maria Fernandez, was friendly and, Hector remembered thinking, beaming in her expectancy. Her husband, Luis, worked construction and doubled as a local handyman around the neighborhood. They had bought the house three years prior. It had been in pretty bad shape at the time of the purchase but the two of them had put a lot of effort and money into renovating it. With four bedrooms and three bathrooms it was more house than a young couple just starting out needed, but there were hopes to fill it with children – the one about to be born being the first of what would hopefully be a happy brood. But despite having done much of the work themselves, the renovations had put a sizable dent in their finances, leading them to rent out the room. The extra income would be helpful in making ends meet. With Luis at work, Maria had shown Hector the room. Set at the back of the house, with its own bathroom just across the hall, he remembered thinking it was the perfect place to hunker down for the next few months. Keep his head low until things had cooled down enough for him to turn the diamonds into cash and move on.

That had been seven years ago.

Three years into his stay and two years after the birth of their son, Joey, Maria was a widow.

It was mid-January and Luis had been working on a construction site in a nearby town. He was on his way home after a long day. He would have been tired. It was later surmised that he had been rounding a corner at a speed incompatible for the winter conditions. He hit a patch of ice, lost control of his truck, careened off the road, and slammed into a tree. He was rushed to the hospital where he lingered for three days before succumbing to his injuries, leaving his grieving wife a single parent and deeply in debt. There hadn't been any life insurance. They had talked of it often, but there never seemed to be enough money. Consequently, there would be no compensation money for Maria and her son.

By that point, Hector, to his surprise, had become a part of the family. With Luis gone, Hector's role grew. He often babysat for Maria when she worked late at one of the two jobs she had to take after her husband's death. He made the boy's lunch each morning, or made sure he had enough money to buy lunch that day at the pre-school he attended.

He also took the boy to school and picked him up afterward. Sometimes he stayed to help the teachers as a volunteer. He'd read stories to the kids and help with the serving of school lunches. Once in a while he'd slip an extra helping or two to some of the kids in line. This particular school served an area of the city that was, to say the least, less fortunate than other sections. An extra apple or slice of bread on a plate could make a world of difference to some of the children he saw. His current situation had forced him to cut back on his work at the school.

After school, he and Joey would play games before Hector made dinner. Along the way he became Tio or Unca Hector to the boy, an honorary moniker that was not discouraged by Maria and brought an unexpected warmth to the old man's heart.

What she did contest was Hector's offer to buy the house from her. He knew she struggled each month with the mortgage and he saw it as way to take some pressure off the single mom. She looked at things differently.

"I can't take your money, Mr. Gonzales," she said. "You need to keep your savings to supplement your Social Security. You need it for your old age."

"Maria," he answered. "Take a good look at me. How much older age do I have? Better you and Joey have my money than the government. This way you won't have to work so hard and I will have a fine house to enjoy what time I have left." He didn't bother to tell her that he wasn't collecting any Social Security and never would. He'd never had a real Social Security card in his life, and as for what time he had left. Well, that was something else.

After much back and forth Maria had finally consented to the sale. Hector had paid her more than market value for the house which led to more back and forth discussion, but in the end she accepted the money. The only condition he placed on the sale was that she keep the ownership of the home in her name.

"But then it is like you don't own it."

"I own it," he said. "I'm paying you for it. It's mine."

"But if something happens to you?"

"Then you do with it as you please."

"But your family."

"Maria, I have no family. You and Joey… I don't want to argue. I can do this. Let me do it."

In the end, there had been tears and, eventually, acceptance. And more tears six months later when Maria and Joey had moved to Florida. Her mother, who had escaped from Cuba in the '60s, lived there along with some aunts and uncles, and she felt it was important for Joey to learn about her side of the family and their history.

Waving goodbye at the loaded to the gills SUV until it turned the corner at the end of the block, Hector walked up the wooden steps to his house and discovered that somehow he'd, without thinking about it, without planning for it, and certainly never expecting it, gone and set down roots.

Hector had come to the U.S.A. from Mexico the old-fashioned way. He crossed the border in the dead of night with nothing but the clothes on his back and a gallon jug of water. He was twelve years old. He was alone. He'd had a mother but she had died when he was seven. There had been a father, but his mother never got around to telling him who it was. In the end, what did it matter?

After her death, Hector had lived the life of a street urchin – begging for change, avoiding predators, selling Chiclets gum to tourists, and thievery. Once he crossed the border into the land of the free, that latter choice proved to be the most lucrative of options available to him.

Oh, he tired the straight and narrow. He took jobs away from plenty of white true Americans. He picked fruit. Painted houses. Washed dishes. Washed cars. But these jobs always found him working for someone else. He needed to work solo, be his own man with no one telling him what to do, and so he fell back on more familiar ways.

He made sure to avoid the gangs. He might have been young, but despite the old saying that proclaimed the virtues of safety in numbers, from what he could see, the incarceration rate as well as the mortality rate in gangs suggested that they offered very little in the way of safety. He also hated tattoos. Eventually, time and circumstances led him to becoming a B&E man. It was less violent and less risky than drugs or armed robbery. He started with cars and then moved on to apartments and homes. An open window or a poorly secured door provided plenty of opportunities to make fast cash. Case a house. Wait for the occupants to go out for the evening or away on vacation and it was all yours for the taking.

His safe cracking skills came more out of necessity than choice. It was easy to grab loose cash or whatever of value was left lying around a house that could be fenced quickly, but the real money was hidden in lockboxes and home safes. The first was simple enough to grab and force open at a later time, but it was the second, the safes, tucked into walls or sunk into floors, that held the cream, and they took an expertise to open that he didn't possess.

At nineteen, Hector was serving his one and only jail term when he met Finny Adaire. Finny was old, older than Hector was now, and was also waiting out his first jolt. He had been cracking safes for over forty years when Hector met him. It was an uncommon relationship, an old Irish criminal at the end of his career and a young Mexican ladrón at the beginning of his. Maybe it was that. The old man was alone and suffering from a variety of ailments. He could see the carrion boat coming his way and, possibly, that made him pay more than a casual interest in an upstart like Hector who kept to himself and didn't associate with any of the undesirable prison elements, or maybe he recognized a bit of himself in the boy. Finny had grown up alone on the streets of Belfast before making his way as a teenager to America, where he learned his trade and became one of the best box men in the business.

Hector once asked him how he'd come to be sent up.

"A man said 'trust me,'" he said.

"And?"

"And I fuckin' did," said Finny. "And you can believe that won't happen again. Fool me once. I should have known better. In this life, trust isn't something you need to proclaim, it's something you earn."

The two men had become friends, and when Finny was finally released from prison, he walked out of the gates to find a classic, coal black, 1968 Cadillac Fleetwood 60 special sedan waiting for him, a grinning Hector sitting behind the wheel. Finny walked along the length of the car, admiring the well-polished exterior, he put his bag in the trunk, and then settled himself into the passenger's side of the car.

"Where to?" said Hector

"Is there a bar close by?"

"More than one."

Finny settled back into the soft, warm leather upholstered seat and shut his eyes.

"Dealer's choice," he said.

Thus began a most profitable partnership. When Finny died seven years later, he had taught Hector everything he knew about the business. There wasn't a lock the young man couldn't pick, a security system he couldn't bypass, or a safe he couldn't crack or blow with an expert use of explosives.

It was sometime later that Hector met O'Conner. The criminal was looking for someone to break into a large walk-in safe, set in a high-rise office building. Hector had been referred to the man by the Financier.

The safe held two hundred and fifty thousand dollars in gold coins. The electronic security system had been complex and had taken Hector nearly an hour to bypass. Once inside, though, the actual opening of the safe only took ten minutes. Hector had walked away from that job with a fifty thousand dollar payday and a working relationship that would last for over a decade.

The Crystal Q job had netted him five hundred thousand dollars. The biggest payout of his career. But then those two assholes, the pilot and his accomplice, had tried to take it away. It was a good thing O'Conner had been prepared. The double cross had failed and left the accomplice dead and the son of a bitch pilot wounded, gone, and penniless. O'Conner had redistributed the take among the remaining crew, then everyone scattered in seven different directions.

That should have been the end of it, but then he'd gotten the call from O'Conner.

"He talked," said O'Conner. "Culhane and the Financier are missing. I'm thinking they're both probably dead."

"The fucking pilot?"

"Yes," said O'Conner.

"And you think they got to Culhane and the Financer?"

"It's a concern."

"So what? They were connected. He doesn't know all of us."

"Someone always knows someone," said O'Conner.

"So what are you doing?"

"Keeping my eyes open. Thinking that something's gotta happen."

Hector was quiet.

"You might want to consider taking a vacation," said O'Conner.

"I don't know," he said. "Maybe."

"You okay?"

"Sure," said Hector. "I'm fine... Just running some things through my head."

"Seriously, you old bastard," said O'Conner. "Take the money. Go somewhere. Lay low until this thing blows over."

"And if it doesn't?"

"It will," said O'Conner.

"You sound pretty confident."

"I'm..."

"You're what?"

"I'm just running some things through my head."

"Hah."

"You watch yourself, Hector," said O'Conner. "I'll let you know when things clear up."

"I will."

"You sure you're okay? You don't sound right."

"Well, I just found out some super rich, pissed off Texan one per-center might be gunning for me. That can change the way a man sounds."

"Fair enough," said O'Conner. "I'll call you."

"Okay," said Hector.

O'Conner disconnected and Hector felt the world around him get a bit colder.

Now, two months later, he knew they had come for him.

Hector opened the drawer of the bedside table and pulled out his vape pen. With a click he sucked in a lung full of heated cannabis oil, the cannabinoids delivering a soft relief from the pain in his gut. The diagnosis had come nine months ago. Well before the Texas job. The doctor, with his most serious face, had sat with him and talked about options, the first of which would be a surgeon gutting him like a fish to get what cancer they could, followed by chemo and radiation. The odds were against him beating the disease. The surgery and treatments would more than likely only buy him a few more months. Months of discomfort and pain with the end result being the same as if he did nothing. At sixty-nine, Hector couldn't really see the point.

He'd first noticed the black Ford Explorer cruising by the house a week ago. He saw it again later in town and again a few hours after that parked down the street from the house. Inside were four men, all looking grim and unhappy in the Minnesota cold.

That's when he began to make his plans.

Cochran and his crew climbed the steps of the house. The windows were dark. They assumed the old man was in his room asleep. Still, they were as quiet as they could be as they approached the front door. From their previous break in they knew that the only thing guarding the house from the evils of the outside world was a standard deadbolt. Pulling out his tools, Dayton had the door opened in just a few minutes.

Once inside, using hand signals to communicate, there had been a quick search of the first floor. As they'd found before, the house was filled with simple, non-expensive furniture. The only extravagance seemed to be a beautiful six-foot Christmas tree with a few brightly wrapped packages sitting around its base. Once they had confirmed there wasn't anyone in the bottom floor, they all gathered at the foot of the stairs leading to the second floor. It was then that the lights came on.

Hector was sitting quietly on a chair at the top of the first landing. Guns quickly came up and pointed at the old man, who continued to sit, his arms crossed in front of him. He had a bemused look on his face.

"Madre de Dios," he said. "How long did it take you to open that lock? Three minutes? Four? And then you clomp all over the place. How much noise were you looking to make? That is just sad."

"Don't move!" said Cochran.

"I will say you did a good job tracking me down," he said.

"But it wasn't just good legwork, was it? That perra of a pilot gave me up."

"Does it really matter how we found you?" said Cochran. He continued to point his gun at Hector. "We're here. You're here. That's the main thing, isn't it? Oh, and the money. There's that too. So, where is it?"

"Money? That's why you are here? You want money? I'm sorry to say, mi amigos, I don't have anything on me. I do have a jar in the kitchen, though, where I keep my spare change. There's at least twenty bucks in there. Maybe more. It is all yours if you want it."

Eddie chuckled but stopped when Cochran gave him a cold stare. The leader then turned his attention back to Hector.

"You really going to fuck with me?" he said.

"Trust me," said Hector, his eyes serious. "I am not fucking with you. There's no money here."

"You went through a half million dollars in two months? Right."

"Well," said Hector, a slight smile coming to his lips, "there was a time in Buenos Aires. I'm thinking I was a little younger than you. It wasn't five hundred thousand dollars, but it was a lot and it was all gone in one glorious week. Oh, now that was… Have you ever been to Buenos Aries? No? You don't know what you are missing. But no, I didn't spend the money. Though who told you it was only half a million?"

That got the men's attention. The guns came down a bit.

"You saying there's more than that?" said Eddie.

"How much more?" said Morris.

"Don't talk to him," said Cochran. "He's full of shit. He's just talking bullshit."

"Where's he gonna go?" said Morris. "Maybe he is talking bullshit. Maybe. But what if he's not? Harrington only wants his share of the money back. Right? He says that's five hundred thousand dollars. If we give him that, he's happy, we get paid, and we're done. But if there's more to be had, we can split that up four ways. Then when we're done, Harrington gets what he expects, we get paid, and we get a little bonus on top of that. Happy all the way around."

He looked back up the stairs. "How much more, old man?"

"At least another three or four hundred thousand," he said. He gave an apologetic shrug. "At my age, I'm bad about keeping track of my money."

"And you'll tell us where all this money is if we let you go," said Cochran. "Is that it?"

"Oh, I'm just answering questions," said Hector. "Did you think this was a negotiation?"

"What the fuck?" said Morris.

"Told you it was bullshit," said Cochran. He raised his weapon again. "Where the fuck is the money?"

"Right now?" said Hector. "It is in a safe place. A good place, I think."

The men were silent.

"The towel head bitch," said Eddie.

"You should watch your mouth," said Hector. "But no, she doesn't have any of what you are looking for."

"What the fuck are you talking about?" said Cochran.

Hector's only answer was a smile.

Corcoran looked around at the house, filled with Christmas decorations. The wreaths, the tree with wrapped packages sitting beneath it. A bitter smile came to his face.

"I get it," he said. "You think we're stupid?"

"That is neither here nor there," said Hector. He rose from the chair. "It doesn't really matter what I think. Does it?"

"Hands, motherfucker," said Cochran.

All four men raised their weapons and pointed them at the old man.

Hector dutifully raised his hands, showing his empty palms.

"We'll see who's stupid. Get your ass down here. We got some talking to do. And trust me, you are not gonna like how the conversation is going to go."

"So," Hector said. "What do you think of my house? Never in my life did I ever think to own a home. With my lifestyle… ay, it never seemed to be in the cards."

"Yeah, it's a great fucking house," said Cochran. "Get down here. You are going to tell us where that money is."

"You guys are determined. I have to give you that. Finding me. That took determination. Coming all the way here? That took determination. But your surveillance skills? I'm sorry to say that they are not worth shit. I clocked you right away. How long you been here? I say a couple of weeks. Am I right?"

"He just keeps talkin' shit," said Eddie.

"I'm only asking once more, old man," said Cochran. "You can walk down or I'll have Eddie here put one in your leg and you can fall down."

"All right," said Hector, his hands still raised. He took the first step down the stairs, his foot landing squarely on a pressure plate hidden under the carpet runner. Immediately a series of pops could be heard coming from outside the building.

"Guys?" said Dayton, speaking up for the first time since they had entered the house. "You hear that?"

"What the hell?" said Cochran.

"Like I said," said Hector. "Your surveillance skills are shit. You know. I really loved this house. Feliz Navidad, gilipollas."

The pops heard inside the house came simultaneously with a series of bright flashes outside the windows. Each of the multicolored Christmas lights encircling the home had been filled with a mixture of plastic polystyrene, hydrocarbon benzene, and gasoline, more commonly known as Napalm. The liquid fire burst from the bulbs and immediately coated the front of the building's old wooden frame. Anyone looking from the street could see the flames ignite and spread their way up the walls.

Inside, Hector took another step down the stairs, tripping another detonator plate that sent an electrical signal to each of the presents under the Christmas tree, causing them to explode, sending a shower of fire across the floor and around the room. In a matter of minutes the building was engulfed in a fire that burned so hot there was no chance of saving the building. It was all the fire department could do, once they arrived, to keep the flames from spreading to the surrounding houses.

Two weeks after the fire, Sarrah Samir was sitting at her dining room table when she heard the loud thump of something being drop on her front porch followed by three short knocks on the door. Rising from the table she walked over to the door and put her eye to the peephole. Through it she could see a man with distinct features dressed in a heavy black coat and a knitted watch cap pulled down to cover his ears. As she observed him he raised a gloved hand and gave another three raps at the door. With the safety chain latched she opened it a crack.

"May I help you?"

"Sarrah Samir?" said the man.

"Yes."

"You knew Hector Gonazles?"

"Hector?" she said.

"Yes," said the man. "You knew him?"

Sarrah smiled. "Yes. Yes, we were friends," she said. "And you?"

"We were friends as well. From work."

"I did not know he still worked. I thought he was retired. What kind of work do you do?"

"Consulting."

"In?"

The man thought for a moment. "Securities," he said. "Hector was very good at helping me in... opening new accounts."

"Hector was a good man," she said. "He used to volunteer at our school. Mostly in the cafeteria, preparing and serving food to the children. We are a poor school and any help is appreciated."

"You're a teacher."

"Third grade. Thomas Paine Elementary. I am also an admistrator, a playground supervisor and sometimes a janitor. It was always a pleasure to have Hector with us. The children loved the days he came to school. Sometimes, he would sit in on the classes. He would tell stories."

"Stories?"

About places he'd lived in his life. Mexico, South America, different parts of the United States. They were usually silly stories, but the children loved them. He used to…"

She paused, an odd look had come over her visitor's face.

"Is something wrong?"

"No. No," he said. "It's just… I guess you never really know someone."

"How did you know about me?"

"Hector," said the man. "He contacted me a week before he… before the fire. He told me about you. About you being friends."

"I'll miss him," she said, then. "Oh, but I am being rude. You should come in. I can make tea."

She undid the chain on the door.

"I appreciate the offer, but I can't stay. I'm only here to pick up…"

He turned and gestured behind him at a black Cadillac parked at the curb.

"Hector's car."

"Yeah. It's a…"

"1968, Fleetwood Cadillac," said Sarrah. "It's a…"

"Classic," he finished for her, and they both smiled.

"Yes," she said. "He has told me many times."

"Well the old bastar... um, the old guy, he went and left it to me."

"See, he was a good man," she said.

"And he left you these," he said reaching down to pick up two heavy looking duffel bags. "May I set them inside?"

"Yes, of course. What's in them?"

"Ms. Samir," the man said pleasantly, "I'm just the delivery guy."

He carried the bags into the house and set them on the living room couch. After refusing another offer of tea he left the house, walked down the porch steps and along the walkway toward the curb.

"And the bags? Don' t you want to know what's in them?" Sarrah called after him.

"Hector left them for you," O'Conner said over his shoulder.

With that, he climbed into the car, brought the engine to life and drove away.

Once he was gone Sarrah shut the door. She turned and studied the two duffels sitting in her living room. Finally she crossed the floor, reached over and slowly unzipped one of the bags. As the contents became visible her eyes widened.

CHAPTER 12
All Debts Paid
by Richard Brewer and Gary Phillips

Déjà vu.

That feeling of having been somewhere before. In this case, though, it was true, he had been here before. In fact, he'd been to the Crystal Q ranch twice before, and one of those times had taken him all the way into the big ranch house and to one of the biggest scores of his career, but he'd never expected to return.

Never say never in this line of work.

Watching the house over the past couple of days had been confusing. He had been surprised to find that security hadn't been beefed up since his last visit. Arrogance or stupidity? O'Conner wasn't sure. His vantage point was comfortable enough. The nights weren't too cold. He had power bars and bottled water, he relieved himself up here, and with a fleece-lined windbreaker he stayed warm enough to nap lightly propped up against a tree, a gun under his splayed hand. During the day there were the usual ranch hands responsible for the cattle going about their business. Texas cowboys on horseback and ATVs making sure that the animals were fed, watered, fattened for slaughter and whatever else needed taking care of in the maintenance of the spread.

That was during the day; nighttime and that personnel wasn't around, gone home or the itinerate ones off into that bunkhouse some acres from the house. Using the wide trunk of one of the old oak trees overlooking Harrington's fancy pool as cover, hunched down or sometimes on his stomach, he'd continually surveyed the terrain. He couldn't see any movement in house. The pool was lit from lights in it but the rest of the grounds were in gloom. The emerald water seemed to float in a sea of dark. The grounds ahead of him were clear. A well-mowed, too green lawn stretched before him, ending at short brick steps leading to a patio area that butted up against the house. Two French doors on this side allowed access to the home. Looking around again through his binoculars, he was struck once again by what appeared to be a lack of security. He had originally come loaded for a battle. A compact Mac10 with an extended magazine was slung across his chest, extra magazines hung from the bandolier. He also had a canvas weekender bag packed with pertinent items. But he was beginning to wonder if such might have been overkill.

Arrogance or stupidity?

Still, he had come with a mission, an action had to be taken. O'Conner could understand vengeance. Maybe more than most people, and maybe now more than ever, but it was time for things to come to an end. This vendetta of Harrington's. The bodies in the ground. Hector one of them. Enough was enough. He refused to spend the rest of his life looking over his shoulder because some shit-kicking Texan yahoo couldn't take a punch and let it go.

As O'Conner contemplated his next move, the backyard was flooded by light. He ducked down behind the tree. He watched as a pair of guards appeared from opposite ends of the house, their bodies having activated the motion sensor lights that covered the back grounds. The two men move toward each other, meeting in the middle of the raised brick patio that marked the center of the house. They scanned the grounds while chatting between themselves. Both carried M-15 rifles, and holstered handguns sat on their hips. One guard pulled out a pack of cigarettes, made an offer to his cohort, and the two grabbed a quick smoke. With one last look around they separated and headed back to their opposite corners. O'Conner stayed where he was, and once the two men rounded their corners, he started counting. Thirty-five seconds later, the lights clicked off.

He watched the cycle two more times. Ten minutes for the guards to make their rounds, thirty-five seconds for the lights. Using his field glasses, he scoured the outside of the house. Again, he didn't see any cameras, but that didn't mean there weren't any around. But his waiting was over.

The next time the guards came around, he readied himself by the tree. As soon as the two men disappeared from view, O'Conner sprinted across the expanse of grass. In twenty-two seconds he made it to the house and flattened to the ground just behind a set of oversized potted plants. Forty-eight seconds later the lights clicked off, leaving O'Conner in darkness. No one seemed to notice the extra seconds it took for the lights to turn off.

Ten minutes later, the lights returned and O'Conner allowed himself to rise into a crouch, like a runner at a starting line. As the two guards met at the center of the patio, both looking out at the backyard, O'Conner charged forward, a taser in one hand and his collapsible baton in the other. At the sound of his approach, the men began to turn. O'Conner raised the taser and fired. Two electronically charged prongs shot out in front of him, their connector wires trailing behind. The darts sunk into the guard to the right in the upper shoulder and neck. The device had been altered to deliver more voltage than a standard taser. The man convulsed and peed himself as he fell to the ground, spasming.

O'Conner immediately dropped the taser to concentrate on the second guard, who was bringing his rifle around toward his attacker. O'Conner, in a smooth, downward motion, slashed the baton across the guard's forearm, forcing him to release his hand on the gun's trigger. He followed up with a brutal palm heel strike under the man's jaw then a punch to the face, smashing his nose and sending him staggering backward. Two quick cracks to the skull with the baton and the guard was out on the patio tiles. O'Conner applied similar cracks to the tasered guard's head. He proceeded to bind them with zip ties and gag them at the base of the house. Still no one else came to check on things.

"This isn't right," O'Conner muttered. Yet it didn't smell like a trap. Being this kind of clever wasn't Harrington's style. He put on his gloves, tugging the supple leather tight on his large hands.

The double glass doors were electronically locked but a quick search of one of the guards produced a key card that let him into the house. Producing a Glock with a suppressor on its end, O'Conner surveyed this part of the house he hadn't been in before. He was in a large room. A pool table sat in the middle of the floor, balls racked and waiting for a break. The walls were adorned with the heads of several exotic and probably endangered animals. He didn't get the supposed sport of hunting four-legged beasts. It was humans who were deadly.

Moving forward, he made his way in the main entry hall. A wide expanse of stone tiles made up the floor and a large curved stairway led up to the second story of the house, the bedrooms, and, O'Conner figured, Harrington. Starting up the stairs, he heard someone coughing from another room. It was a deep, wet cough that built in intensity until it ended with a final hack that seemed to clear things up for the moment.

"Goddamn it," said a voice. "Flora! Flora, you here?"

O'Conner froze, expecting Flora, one of the housekeepers he knew, to respond to the person in the next room. But the only answer was silence.

"Goddamn it," said the voice. "Fuck it."

O'Conner heard the sound of a chair scrapping across the floor, then there was the chuck of a refrigerator door shutting followed by a succession of drawers opening and closing. By now O'Conner was sure the voice belonged to Harrington. With his gun raised in front of him, he moved slowly toward the kitchen door, a sliver of light shining out from under the bottom. With a rush he pushed the swinging door open and stepped into the room, his eyes and gun quickly covering the room in search of any threat.

Harrington sat at a granite kitchen counter, an open carton of ice cream in front of him. He was in his slacks, undershirt, and paisley silk robe. A half-empty bottle of Irish whiskey and glass were nearby as well. He viewed the intruder, a look of surprise on his face. That look morphed into one of weary resignation.

"Sure," he said. "Why not?"

O'Conner leveled his gun on Harrington's chest. Always sight on the center mass.

"Who else is in the house?"

"I'm it."

"Bullshit."

"You're O'Conner."

"I said, who else is in the house?"

"And I said I'm it. You can believe me or not. You want some ice cream?" He looked at the open container then back to O'Conner. "Rocky Road," he said with a bitter smile. "Seems about right, don't you think?"

"How can you be the only one around?" said O'Conner. He lowered his gun but remained alert. "Last time I was here you practically had an army on us."

"Oh, the times they are a changin'," Harrington said. He started reaching into the pocket of his bathrobe.

"Easy," said O'Conner, the gun coming back up.

Harrington raised one hand in innocence, the other slowly pulled a folded sheet of paper out of the robe pocket. He set the paper down on the table and with two fingers slid it across the counter toward the career thief.

O'Conner took a step forward and, gun in one hand, reached inside his shirt pocket and pulled out a pair of reading glasses. Not prescription, the magnifying kind he bought at a Best Value drug store. He then picked up the paper and with a shake of his hand he unfolded it and gave it a quick glance. He looked back at Harrington.

"From your wife."

"Soon-to-be ex. Read it."

Keeping his gun trained on Harrington, he perused the paper. "Huh."

"Keep going."

O'Conner finished reading then set the paper back on the counter. "She really doesn't like you."

"No shit."

"So, she sent this out to all members of the North Texas Citizens Improvement League?"

"Oh, yes," said Harrington. "Each and every mother-lovin' one of them. She has the dates and details of practically every under the table deal we've ever bankrolled and the names of all the participants."

"Including you."

Harrington raised a spoon of ice cream in acknowledgement. "The cherry on top of the shit sundae."

"Leaving you…"

"Abandoned. Cut from the League and any further dealings with it. You read it. I am forever and a day 'persona no bienvenida' to all my former Leaguers. And in addition to my ostracization, they get to contribute a healthy sum of cash each month to support the lifestyle she's so become accustomed to in exchange for her silence, and most of that money is coming from my accounts."

"They can do that?"

"The power of the League is not to be underestimated."

O'Conner figured Collier must have lived. That he'd convinced the board that Harrington was too much of a liability now. He said, "What about the money from the safe?"

"Fuck. That's small potatoes. Teeny, tiny potatoes compared to what's at stake now. They could give a shit."

"What about you?"

Harrington gave a bitter bark of a laugh. "I barely have a shit left to give."

"You came at us hard."

"I did," said Harrington. "It was business. You took from the League. You took from me. Was I just supposed to let that go?"

"People are dead."

"Some of mine too. Like I said, it was business. Now that business is done."

"Not between you and me."

"For fuck's sake. You telling me you never had any collateral damage in your career? Come on, O'Conner, no dead bodies piled up in your past?"

O'Conner's eyes shifted out of focus in remembrance, then he was back in the present.

"Thought so," said Harrington. "I can see the answer in your face. Are my guards dead?"

"No. Damaged."

"But they could have been, yes? I don't think you brought those guns to just wing 'em.

"Correct."

Harrington regarded him.

"What do you want from me, O'Conner? An apology? Well, you aren't going to get it. More money? I don't have it. I'm the victim here. I'm the one who got robbed. I'm the one who's fucked. And not just by you."

"I want the business between us to be over." He'd already fed damning information to his hacktivist contact to leak to the SEC.

"Then it's over. Okay? Done. Finished. Acabado. I couldn't pursue you and your fellow culprits even if I wanted to. I have more to think about. I have to figure out how to get myself back on my feet. I don't have the time, the resources, or the inclination to continue going after you."

Harrington had another helping of ice cream. He put the spoon back into the carton and stirred it around.

"You can do whatever you want," he said. "But I'm out. I've had it. As far as I'm concerned, this whole business between us is over. I really am done."

O'Conner looked at the man sitting alone in a house big enough to have its own zip code eating melting ice cream from a carton. No wife. No money. No power. He looked older than he was. Old and pathetic.

"You are half right," he said.

"Wha–"

O'Conner raised his Glock and put two quick shots into the man's chest. Always go for the center mass.

Harrington fell backward off the stool onto the kitchen floor, the look of surprise having returned to his face.

"Business is never done until all the debts are paid off," said O'Conner.

He turned toward the door. Thoughts of Hector, the Financier in the wind, and the others, from both sides, ran through his head. All dead probably. Well, that was the risk they ran getting into the bull ring. That didn't mean, though, he let certain behavior slide all the damn time. You couldn't call yourself a pro and do that.

"Paid in full, motherfuckah," he said, walking out of the house and away from the Crystal Q.

BIOGRAPHIES

Editors

Richard Brewer, a native Californian, has always loved stories. Following that love he has worked as a writer, editor, actor, director, bookseller, book reviewer, movie development executive, and audiobook narrator. He is co-editor of the critically acclaimed Bruce Springsteen inspired short story anthology *Meeting Across the River*, as well as the speculative fiction collection *Occupied Earth: Stories of Aliens, Resistance and Survival at all Costs*. His most recent short story, *Last to Die*, was included in another anthology inspired by The Boss, *Trouble in the Heartland*, and was noted as one of the Distinguished Mystery Stories of the year in *The Best American Mystery Stories 2015*.

Born under a bad sign, **Gary Phillips** must keep writing to forestall his appointment at the crossroads. He has written various novels, novellas, radio plays, scripts, graphic novels such as *Vigilante: Southland*, and published 60 some short stories. He has had several of his works optioned for film or TV including the graphic novel *The Rinse* about a money launderer, and his short story "The Two Falcons" from *The Highway Kind: Tales of Fast Cars, Desperate Drivers and Dark Roads*. Phillips has edited or co-edited several anthologies including the bestselling *Orange County Noir, Occupied Earth* (with Richard Brewer) and the critically praised *The Obama Inheritance: Fifteen Stories of Conspiracy Noir.* He is the immediate past president of the Private Eye Writers of America.

CONTRIBUTORS

Brett Battles was born and raised in southern California. He is the USA Today bestselling and Barry Award winning author of over thirty novels, including the Jonathan Quinn series, the Project Eden series, and the time bending Rewinder trilogy. Though he still makes California his home, he has traveled extensively to such destinations as Ho Chi Minh City, Berlin, Bangkok, Angkor Wat, Singapore, Jakarta, London, Paris, and Rome, all of which play parts in his current and upcoming novels. Authors who have influenced him over the years include, but aren't limited to: Isaac Asimov, Robert Heinlein, Alistair MacLean, Robert Ludlum, Stephen King, Graham Greene, Haruki Murakami, and Tim Hallinan.

He has three very cool kids – Ronan, Fiona, and Keira – who are all quickly becoming adults, which both excites and unnerves him. As for his neurotic, paranoid, cute Australian Shepherd Maggie, that's more of a… developing relationship. You can learn more about Brett and his books at http:// brettbattles.com

Joe Clifford is the author of several books, including Junkie Love and the Jay Porter Thriller Series, as well as editor of the anthologies Trouble in the Heartland: Crime

Fiction Inspired by the Songs of BruceSpringsteen; Just to Watch Them Die: Crime Fiction Inspired by the Songs of Johnny Cash, and Hard Sentences, which he co-edited with David James Keaton. Joe's writing can be found at www.joeclifford.com.

David Corbett is the award-winning author of six novels, including 2015's The Mercy of the Night and the upcoming The Long-Lost Love Letters of Doc Holliday. Other works include the novella The Devil Prayed and Darkness Fell, the story collection Thirteen Confessions, and the writing guide The Art of Character ("A writer's bible" – Elizabeth Brundage). His short fiction has been selected twice for Best American Mystery Stories, and his non-fiction has appeared in the New York Times, Narrative, Bright Ideas, and Writer's Digest, where he is a contributing editor. For more, visit: www.davidcorbett.com

Gar Anthony Haywood is the Shamus and Anthony award-winning author of twelve crime novels. His short fiction has been included in the Best American Mystery Stories anthologies and Booklist has called him "a writer who has always belonged in the upper echelon of American crime fiction." Haywood has written for network television and both the New York and Los Angeles Times. His most recent novel is Assume Nothing, and the six books in his Aaron Gunner P.I. series are now available as e-books from Open Road/Mysterious Press.

Jessica Kaye is an entertainment and publishing attorney at Kaye & Mills (www.kayemills.com) and a Grammy Award-winning audiobook producer. Jessica owns Big

Happy Family, LLC, an audiobook distributor (www.bighappyfamilyaudio.com.) She created and co-edited Meeting Across the River (anthology, BloomsburyUSA, 2005) and contributed a story to Occupied Earth: Stories of Aliens, Resistance and Survival at all Costs (Polis Books, 2015.) She is the author of the forthcoming How To Produce (and sell) a Great Audiobook (F+W Media Inc./Writers Digest Books, 2019.)

Manuel Ramos is the author of nine published novels and one short story collection. The Edgar® and Shamus nominee lives and writes in Denver. He is a co-founder of and regular contributor to La Bloga, an award-winning Internet magazine devoted to Latino literature, culture, news, and opinion. www.manuelramos.com

Zoë Sharp was brought up on an English dockside and opted out of mainstream education at the age of 12. She wrote her first novel at 15 and created her Special Forces-dropout-turned-bodyguard, Charlotte 'Charlie' Fox after receiving death-threats in the course of her work as a photojournalist. Lee Child famously once said (in writing, with no threats involved): "If Jack Reacher were a woman, he'd be Charlie Fox." When Sharp's not scribbling, undertaking house renovation, or improvising weapons out of everyday objects, she can be found crewing yachts or international pet-sitting. (It's a tough life, but somebody's got to do it, right?) She's been nominated for just about every prize going (always the bridesmaid, never the bride) for both her short and long fiction. For a free ebook download and more info, visit www.ZoeSharp.com